KT-548-832

...... WILLOW WALK

'Tense, atmospheric and gripping from page one. A first-rate psychological thriller.' – Mason Cross, author of *The Samaritan*

'Dark as a smoker's lung, but Good God it's a marvellous read. Perfectly paced and crafted by a writer on a par with any of the big names.' – David Mark, author of *Dead Pretty*

'Feverish and intense, *Willow Walk* is a worthy follow up to S.J.I. Holliday's highly regarded debut, *Black Wood*. A writer who doesn't flinch in the face of twisted impulses and unspeakable desires, few can match her for the creation of truly disturbing characters.' – Eva Dolan, author of *After You Die*

'A hugely compelling, creepy story that ratchets up the tension and delivers moments of perfectly twisted darkness. Beautifully written and a cracking read.' – Amanda Jennings, author of *In Her Wake*

'Drugs, sex and murder are mixed together in another deliciously dark cocktail from S.J.I. Holliday. The effect is intense.' – David Jackson, author of the *Detective Callum Doyle* series

'An addictively creepy exploration of the past coming to call.' – Quentir

'*Willow Walk*: a great, worthy successor to *Black Wood*. It needs to be made into TV!' – Daniel Pembrey, author of the *Harbour Master* series

'Small towns are fertile playgrounds for crime writers, but they're rarely mined with such a feeling for their suffocating nature and invisible ties as practised here.' – Nick Quantrill, author of the *Joe Geraghty* series

'This is a gripping, roller coaster of a novel, which digs deep into the small-town psyche and comes up with a nightmare scenario. I couldn't put it down!' – Helen Cadbury, author of *Bones in the Nest*

'Breathtakingly sinister and darkly compelling Unputdown able.' – Jane Isaac, author of *Before It's Too Late*

'*Willow Walk* is gripping, creepy and tense and covers some highly emotive contemporary issues. It kept me intrigued all the way through.' – Off-the-shelf book reviews

'Close relationships can be the most toxic, and if the thrill of crime fiction is the way it delves into our darkest places, this book truly delivers.' – William Shaw, author of *The Birdwatcher*

'Holliday has that wonderful Hitchcockian knack for making the ordinary seem deeply menacing. You will never see Lego in quite the same way after this.' – James Benmore, author of *Dodger of the Dials*

'A brilliantly dark and twisted tale that expertly builds the tension until you find yourself biting your nails to the quick as the pages fly by.' – Steve Cavanagh, author of *The Defence*

WILLOW WALK

S.J.I. Holliday grew up in Haddington, East Lothian. She spent many years working in her family's newsagent and pub before going off to study microbiology and statistics at university. She has worked as a statistician in the pharmaceutical industry for over sixteen years, but it was on a six-month round-the-world trip that she took with her husband ten years ago that she rediscovered her passion for writing. Her first novel, *Black Wood*, was published in 2015. You can find out more at www. sjiholliday.com.

WILLOW WALK

S.J.I. HOLLIDAY

BLACK & WHITE PUBLISHING

First published 2016
by Black & White Publishing Ltd
29 Ocean Drive, Edinburgh EH6 6JL

1 3 5 7 9 10 8 6 4 2   16 17 18 19

ISBN: 978 1 78530 021 9

ALBA | CHRUTHACHAIL

Typeset by Iolaire, Newtonmore
Printed and bound by Nørhaven, Denmark

To my Dad – the best pub landlord *ever* . . .
Who works a Sunday?

'Invisible threads are the strongest ties.'

Friedrich Nietzsche

Prologue

Four bodies. Vague shapes.

A stale, sticky smell. Spilled beer and vomit. Cigarette smoke. Weed. A sudden flash from the night before: a couple behind the sofa, bangs and thrusts. An audience looking on. The girl riding and bucking. Big grin on her face, eyes closed. Oblivious.

She walks slowly towards the sofa, crouches down. Peers around the back. They're still there, arms wrapped around each other. Totally out of it. A mist of sex lingers. Something else. Something stronger.

That makes six.

Her head spins as she stands up. Her eyes sting. She has a vague memory of waking up in darkness, peeling contact lenses off her parched eyes, tugging at dry eyeballs. She can barely see without them, everything fuzzy-edged and hard to decipher. She squints, stumbles against the sofa. A head lolls against her.

'Shh, sorry,' she says, low, under her breath. No response.

A girl is draped at an awkward angle, long dark hair trailing on the floor. A man sits, head leaning off one side of the sofa; his soft hair tickles her hand. She nudges him gently and his head rolls back onto his chest as she moves carefully away.

Try not to wake them.

On the other side of the room, a skinny figure lies splayed across an armchair, head hanging off one side, legs off the other. Under the window, a girl is curled up and facing the wall. Her fair hair is matted and spread out around her like the head of an old mop.

The room shifts. Tilts.

She feels sick. Brings up bile and swallows it back. The syrupy taste of Red Bull burns the back of her throat. Memories of vodka and cheap fizzy wine whirl around her head and her stomach like an aspirin fizzing in water.

All around, there are shadows. Dark patches and pools. Spilled things. Dirty things. She squints, trying to work out who is who, what is what. But her eyes hurt too much. Her head thrums, and the smell is getting worse. Body odour. Piss. Carnage and decay. Bottles and cans everywhere. Discarded bits of clothing. Upended ashtrays. Her stomach lurches again. She has to get out. Now.

It's too quiet. Too claustrophobic.

She lifts the latch. The door opens with a squeak, and she flinches. Hears a soft thud from somewhere behind her. She turns back. Sees that the girl from the sofa's hand has slid off from where it had been resting on her stomach, and it now flops uselessly on the laminate flooring. But she hasn't woken up.

There's a faint banging sound. *Tap. Tap. Tap.* A draught. Someone has left the back door open. Maybe someone is out there now, having a fag, or a morning sup from one of the cans of warm beer she imagines to be littering the kitchen worktops. She hesitates. Should she go through? Offer to help clear up? Sort out the drunken mess of bodies scattered across the lounge like a pile of coats?

She squeezes her eyes shut and sparks flip and leap across her vision. No. She has to get out. She needs air, water and sleep. She needs a wash too. A long hot bath, to get rid of the stink that seems to be seeping into her pores from the toxic air. She needs to shake off the memories of the night before, threatening and bothering at her like tiny pinpricks jabbing at her skull.

Something happened. Something went wrong.

She walks out into the early morning sun, shielding her eyes. She takes a gulp of fresh air and feels the nausea subside – for now, at least. A chorus of blackbirds twitters in the trees. Will she manage to walk home without bumping into someone, or something . . . or getting knocked down by a car as she stumbles, half-blind, down the road?

She bangs the door shut. Hard. Starts walking. Fast.

Something pings at her. *Get away from here. You need to get away.*

Behind her in the house, no one flinches. No one stirs.

No one breathes.

1

A ribbon of air bubbles trickles upwards, vanishing to nothing as the tiny orbs pop and break the surface of the pale-blue water. She stares at them, eyes wide and stinging. Is the water really blue? Or is the reflection from the tiles causing an optical illusion? Sometimes it's hard to accept what's real, what's fantasy. She closes her eyes. Lets her thoughts drift off. Tries to clear the clutter from her mind.

Forty-seven, forty-six, forty-five . . .

It's been years since she's done it. Wonders if she still can. *Thirty-three, thirty-two . . .* There's fluttering in her chest. She's only halfway there. She blows out through her nose, flaps her palms upwards, gently. Just enough to keep herself anchored to the tiled floor of the swimming pool. *Nineteen, eighteen . . .* She's going to do it. She *has* to do it. Her chest tightens. Pips of pain patter inside her head. *Ten, nine, eight . . .* She lets herself drift up. *Four, three, two . . .* She fixes her feet onto the bottom and thrusts hard.

One.

She bursts out like a champagne cork. Her face burns, her lungs squeal. She grabs for the side of the pool, hugging onto the edge of the drainage channel while sucking in great lumps of air that stick hard in her throat as she tries to gulp them down. Eventually, her breathing slows. Her face begins to cool. She opens her eyes, stares into the drain, watching as the water slips over the lip and gets sucked inside.

A rubber squeaking sound from the poolside stops abruptly

just above her line of vision, and she glances up to see a pair of white trainers. 'Hey, you OK down there? I was about to grab a net and fish you out.'

She tips her head back and looks up. The lifeguard looks about half her age. He must be new, because she comes here every day and she's never seen him before. He smiles down at her, half smirking, probably thinking *we've got a right one here*, and she wonders what he knows about saving anyone's life.

In fact, she's surprised he's even got up out of his chair to come and find out what she's doing. He's definitely new. Give him a week and he'll be nowhere to be seen, like most of the others.

'Sorry, didn't mean to freak you out. Just something we . . . I used to do when I was a kid. I wanted to see if I could still do it.'

'Right. Good on ya,' he says. His Australian accent seems to turn the statement into a question. He nods, gives her another small smile. Continues his ambling circuit of the pool. She swivels herself round, watching him go. Tanned, toned legs in a pair of white shorts. He probably has quite an effect on some. But not her.

A family appears from the changing rooms. A cute blonde girl with pink armbands jammed onto twig-like arms and a father and son in matching blue Bermuda shorts. The mother has her hair tied in a topknot, her expression pulled tight. 'Come *on*,' the young girl screeches. Her voice echoes around the walls. 'Come on!'

Marie turns away, a different pain stabbing at her now.

She slides down the wall, under the surface again, presses her feet against the side, arms straight out in front. Pushes away into a glide, followed by a neat dolphin kick for half a length, before slicing her left arm down, cutting gracefully through the water as she begins a slow front crawl. She tips her head to the left after four strokes, sucks in a breath. When she's about a metre from the end, she flips forwards into a perfect tumble turn, and continues her stroke.

She tries to clear her mind. Tries not to think about the letter.

It's her daily ritual. Sixty lengths – an equal, ordered mixture of front crawl, breaststroke, backstroke and butterfly. She always cools down by taking off her goggles and cap and sculling gently on her back for another four lengths, hands paddling by her sides. She loves the feel of the cool water caressing her scalp, filling her ears. A stir of echoes muffled by water. It makes her feel alive.

She's done.

Sixty-four lengths: sixteen hundred metres. She walks the width of the pool to climb the steps, and that covers the nine-metre shortfall that makes it exactly one mile. She doesn't even know why, but there is something important about it being a mile. Everyone's got their obsessions. She checks the clock. Forty-eight minutes. Three minutes more than usual, but she puts that down to sitting on the bottom of the pool and the recovery afterwards. She hasn't done that since she was twelve. Hearing from him has triggered something.

Memories.

Curiosity.

Fear.

She watches the cute blonde girl in the baby pool nearby as she climbs the steps out of the training pool. The girl is kicking her legs hard, her small pointed chin poking high out of the water. Her mother walks slowly along beside her, trying in vain to avoid being splashed in the face. Marie longs to go into the baby pool. Sit in the warm, shallow water, watching the little ones splash and kick and squeal with delight. Graeme always said it was warm because so many kids pissed in it.

That rumour about the council putting some special dye in there to make it turn bright blue. It never happened.

Graeme.

Marie smiles at the mother as she walks past her towards the changing rooms. The mother smiles back. A 'what can you do?' smile. Marie wouldn't care if she got splashed in the face, if it meant she had a little girl to do the splashing.

She steps into the communal showers and slams the heel of her hand against the 'on' button. One of those ones you have to lean on permanently or it goes off after ten seconds. She tilts her head and lets warm water skitter down over her face. Leans back onto the button, stopping it from popping back out. It digs hard into her back and the pain jolts, wakes her up. She runs a hand down her side, imagines the faint alien feel of the scar tissue through the thin fabric of her swimming costume. Even after all these years, it marks her. It has grown with her. Tortures her. Burns her through her clothes. She wishes she was in a private shower cubicle, so she could peel off the tight, wet Lycra and scrub hard at the scar with cheap pink soap. But all she can do is let the lukewarm trickle rinse her gently, barely removing the scent of chlorine.

Swimming is her quiet time. When you're on your feet all day, it's nice to be weightless for a while. Away from the chatter, the repetitive banality of TV sport, the bells and clatter of the fruit machine, the sounds of the till drawer being slammed shut, of cutlery being scraped on plates and pint glasses being dumped on the bar; the stink of sweat, fish and chips, bleach on lino, old men's farts. The coolness of the water on her skin takes her away. The slow, rhythmic breathing and the gentle movement of gliding through the water is therapy. It's her medication, her *meditation*, her head-time.

But now *he* has invaded it.

Graeme.

2

Sergeant Davie Gray is meticulously scrolling down through the list of results from his recent search on the Police National Computer. He started with 'legal highs' then changed it to 'herbal highs' after getting too many hits on the word 'legal'. Finally he searches on NPS – 'New Psychotropic Substances' – the official name that is supposed to be added to all reports since the government started trying to define them. He normally leaves it to Lorna to check things like this, but she's not in today. Operating the PNC is her job, as well as other admin in the small station. Banktoun only has three members of staff now, including Lorna. Davie is in charge.

For now, anyway.

Inspector Gordon Hamilton was happy to take the retirement package offered to him, albeit under a bit of a cloud, and it's only a matter of time before Davie, Lorna and PC Callum Beattie are offered redundancy or transfer. Despite a recent and unexpected flurry of criminal activity in the town, there is little reason to keep the station open. They've already gone down to part-time hours and, in truth, Davie is bored.

So when his old college buddy, DI Malkie Reid, called him to ask for some assistance with some background searches on a recent spate of drugs overdoses, Davie was glad to help. Who knew where it might lead?

Banktoun has no shortage of drugs. It's the scourge of small towns, and Davie's region in particular is currently going through a bad time of it. Or maybe it's just perception. The latest craze involves various 'herbal' or 'legal' highs, as they're called. Problem is, herbal doesn't mean safe, and when you drill down, some of the components aren't actually legal at all, but, with them being manufactured in places like China and sold under the labels of pet food and bath salts, they are impossible to regulate. The other issue is it's a different type of kid experimenting with them. The type that should know better. The type that can't blame their lack of prospects or a lack of education. The type that can't blame their parents for neglecting them, or knocking them about.

There have been seven overdoses so far in the whole of the Lothians. Two deaths – one on the scene, and one in hospital caused by multiple organ failure. Banktoun hasn't been affected yet, but it's only a matter of time. The biggest issue that CID is facing is trying to find the source, as although toxicology reports have shown that there were some of the same elements in each of the cases they'd analysed, they weren't *exactly* the same. The regional head of toxicology has a theory that this is down to each individual metabolising the drugs differently, which means that people don't know how much their bodies can tolerate. Davie has a feeling that these current cases are only the tip of the iceberg, and he wants to see this stuff stamped out. He has a low tolerance for people who make their money from selling drugs and he finds it hard to sympathise with the idiots who choose to take them.

He highlights the results of the recent search and clicks 'print' just as the phone rings. The noise echoes around the empty office, making him jump.

'Morning, Banktoun Station. Davie Gray speaking, how can I help you?'

'Davie, it's Malkie.' The detective's voice is low, anxious.

'Oh hello. I was going to call you in a bit. I need more to go

10

on. I'm getting hundreds of hits here and I know they're not all relevant, but I don't want to miss anything, so—'

Malkie interrupts: 'I'm not calling about that. It's something else.'

Davie listens while Malkie takes a slurp of something. Coffee probably. Davie glances at the time. It's too early for anything alcoholic. Hopefully.

'A woman's been attacked outside Dalkeith. She was waiting for a bus on the Pencaitland road. We don't know what happened yet, but she managed to crawl to the nearest house before she passed out unconscious. One of the farm cottages out there. Householder was alerted when he thought someone was trying to smash his front door in. He opened it and found her lying there in a pool of blood.' He slurps again.

Davie waits. He feels his heart start to pick up speed. What does this have to do with him? He almost doesn't want to ask.

'Can you come to the hospital, Davie? I'd like you to assist . . .'

'I'm on my own here today, Malkie. Callum and Lorna have gone shopping for engagement rings. Came as a bit of a shock, actually. I didn't even realise they'd been dating. Shows how observant I am . . .'

'You've had a lot on, Davie. I'm sorry to dump more on your plate, but this is important. We've not been able to ID the victim yet. She's still in ICU, but the doctors are confident she's going to pull through. She's got some horrendous injuries, though. Horrendous. I'll explain more when you get here. But listen . . .' He pauses again, draining whatever it is he's been drinking. 'This is going to be distressing for you, but I need you to see her.'

Davie feels dread creep up under his shirt, like poison ivy. Prickling and itching and refusing to let go.

'Why?' Davie says. He doesn't want to hear the answer.

'Because I think you might know who she is.'

He takes the panda car from outside the door. The hospital is fifteen miles away, on the outskirts of Edinburgh. There's little traffic as he races up the city bypass, resisting the urge to stick on the blues and twos. It's not an emergency. Just an enquiry. He's going there to help.

He tries not to think of the possibilities. Of who it might be, and why Malkie thinks he might know her. Maybe she's from Banktoun. Maybe there's something on her that indicates that. A bus ticket from earlier in the day. A receipt from a shop. Unless . . . No. He shakes the thought away.

The hospital is the usual melee of anxious visitors and wandering patients. The obligatory man in a wheelchair attached to a drip-stand, puffing away outside the front entrance, a bored-looking orderly lurking nearby. He tries to stay calm, although he doesn't feel it. The thoughts of who he's going to find in ICU are whirling around inside his head. He stands at the front desk, waiting for the receptionist to hang up the phone. She smiles at him, raises a hand, gesturing she'll be with him in a minute.

'Can you point me in the direction of ICU, please? Detective Inspector Reid is expecting me.'

She nods and gives him a wide, practised smile. She has lipstick on her front teeth. 'Follow the yellow line. It's on this floor. You can't miss it. DI Reid is in the waiting area outside. You're Sergeant Gray, is that right?'

'Yes. Yes.' Davie starts off along the corridor, following the yellow painted line on the grey lino. His shoes squeak. He glances back briefly as he's about to turn the corner, then shouts, 'Thanks.'

Calm down, Davie. You're getting ahead of yourself, he thinks.

Malkie Reid is standing next to a row of orange plastic

chairs, Styrofoam cup in one hand and a measured scowl on his face. Davie remembers that face from their college days. The female recruits were always taking the piss out of him, saying, 'Smile, love, it might never happen.' Malkie's face is set in a perpetual grimace: it's down to his heavy brow and an unfortunate mouth that looks like it's been painted on upside down. He enhances his look by remaining in a constant state of grumpiness. But today Davie sees something different in there. His eyes are wide and wet. His face more solemn than disgruntled.

He nods a greeting.

'Ah good, you're here. Can I get you a coffee? Tea? Have a seat and I'll brief you on the details. DC Jennings is around. She's away powdering her nose, or whatever it is they do in there.'

Davie feels his hackles rise at the forced joviality. 'Cut the crap, Malkie. You didn't bring me up here for tea and cakes. Who's in the unit? Don't mess me about.'

Malkie lays his cup down on the nurses' station, and one of the nurses opens her mouth to complain but shuts it again quickly when she clocks Davie's thunderous stare.

'I don't like being scared half to death, Malkie, as much as it might be the way that you get your kicks. What's going on?'

Malkie gestures for him to walk over to the observation window. 'We can't go in right now, maybe later. But . . . Well, I didn't want to wait. I wanted to rule her out . . .'

Davie takes a deep breath and turns to look through the window. The bed is raised, a white sheet and pale-blue blanket covering the figure underneath. Her face looks peaceful, despite the black and blue markings that someone has seen fit to decorate her with. Her mouth is swollen, her eyes closed. Dark specks of blood dot her hairline where they haven't managed to clean it all off. She has short, dark hair. A few

13

tendrils escape across the pillow underneath. She's barely recognisable, yet Davie can see why Malkie thinks he might know her.

He draws in a breath.

'Here,' Malkie says. He offers up a clear plastic bag. It's full of clothes. A neat white blouse folded on top. Dark-brown stains streaked down the front. 'Black skirt. White blouse with that little black rim on the collar. Black boots. It looks like what she wears to work, doesn't it? You sent me a photo of the two of you—'

'No . . .' he stutters. 'It can't be. I only saw her yesterday. I thought she was working today . . .'

'Davie, I need you to be sure. Are there any identifying features that we can use to verify? Has she got any tattoos?'

Davie nods. 'Aye. A swallow. It's on the inside of her left wrist. It used to be black, but it's going green now. She had it done when she was sixteen, she told me. It was to signify escape.' He pauses. 'I don't know what she was escaping from.'

'There's something else, Davie. The damage to her face is only superficial, although I know it looks worse. It's mainly internal damage. That's what almost caused her to bleed to death. She was lucky to pass out from the pain. Although her hands and knees are scraped to pieces from dragging herself along the gravel path to that farmhouse.'

'What did he do to her, Malkie?' Davie's voice is barely a whisper.

Malkie sighs. 'He sexually assaulted her with a blunt instrument. Some sort of piping, maybe a crowbar. We're not sure. She's already had an emergency hysterectomy. They're trying to patch up the rest.'

Davie clenches his fists. Feels rage boiling beneath the surface.

'And we don't know the significance, but she had something stuck up inside her. A small piece of Lego.'

'Lego? What the fuck?'

'Davie, I'm going to need you to identify that tattoo. Can you do that?'

Davie nods. Silent. He sucks in a breath.

Malkie gestures to the nurse inside the room. Holds up his left wrist, mouths something at her. The nurse nods and pulls back the covers. She picks up the woman's hand and carefully turns it over so they can see.

There is no tattoo. The heel of her hand is criss-crossed with scratches and the remnants of dried blood, but the wrist is pale and clean. No scars, no tattoo.

Davie exhales. His voice is barely a whisper. 'It's not her.'

3

Marie takes her time getting dressed. Pulls on a black pencil skirt and a tight white blouse that sticks to her damp back. She rough dries her short hair, combs it carefully as she stares at herself in the warped glass of the mirror. She doesn't see herself any more. The eyes staring back at her are his.

In the café, she drinks a cappuccino and eats a lemon and poppy seed muffin while listening to two young girls squabbling over who's having the last slice of chocolate cake. Their mum brushes a lock of hair behind her ear and tries to pretend she can't hear them. Marie watches. Smiles, when one of them catches her eye. The usual things. She has just about enough time for a second cup of coffee, so she sits and gazes at the happenings in the pool through the oversized porthole windows that line the edge of the café. The letter is burning a hole through her bag, but it can burn all it likes. She's not taking it out here. This is *her* place. Not his.

The second cup of coffee has made her late, so she decides there's no point in rushing. She'll take the long route to work. The others will manage. It's usually her picking up the slack when someone doesn't turn up. Someone else can do it for a change.

She walks past the old children's home, the once grand building now tired and weather-worn, grey brick blackened from neglect. Ivy is wrapped and tangled around the edges, holding the place together like string round a badly wrapped parcel. Most of the windows are boarded up; the remaining few on the top floor are caked with dirt, smashed and splintered. She stops at the gate, imagining what the place used to be like, years ago. Grounds neatly kept, the grass green and lush. Children playing football and running round the winding paths that snake around the building. She hadn't known it when it was a children's home. It closed down before she moved here, and for some reason it had never been sold.

She stops and glances up at the dark, broken windows. The place has become a haven for junkies and tramps in recent years, but a newly placed sign from a building developer suggests that might change soon. She imagines there are only two options: knock it down or restore it. Either way, it's bound to be turned into posh, overpriced flats. Maybe the ghosts are a selling point. Marie doesn't believe in ghosts. Thinks it's all tricks of the mind played by the subconscious. The only ghosts are the ones inside your own head. She's tried to exorcise her own ghosts. But just like in all good horror movies, some things refuse to stay dead.

She turns to leave and, out of the corner of her eye, a shadow passes behind one of the broken windows. Her skin prickles, and all the little hairs on her arms stand up. *Goose walked over your grave*, her mum used to say. She stares up at the window, hoping it was nothing yet intrigued all the same. Is someone in there? Probably just a bird. Maybe an insomniac bat. Stupid. She starts walking, smiles to herself, thinking *idiot*, but the feeling stays with her until she reaches the end of the road. She realises she is walking quicker. She doesn't look back.

She contemplates phoning in sick, but it's not her style. She'll be fine once she gets there. It'll be busy, and there'll be no time to think. That's a good thing. In fact, maybe she'll ask someone to swap shifts, do a double. Keep her away from home for longer. Might keep her mind off it all. Ever since she

17

moved here when she was sixteen she'd done everything she could to forget about Graeme. Bumping into the postman had put paid to that. Coincidence? Maybe.

She can't keep putting it off. Once she's out of sight of the old house, she sits down on a bench and pulls the letter out of the back pocket of her bag. She turns it over in her hands. The handwriting on the envelope is unmistakeable. Her name and address written with a blue gel pen, smudged at the edges. That familiar calligraphic script, making the '7' look like a '9', the top of the seven overlong and pulled back in on itself. He'd always had problems with those numbers. Just another one of his quirks.

How did he get my address?

She doesn't want to open it.

She'd been on her way out of the main door, heading for the leisure centre, just as the postman was coming in. He handed her the thick pile, and smirked – clearly expecting her to do his job for him and post them into each individual mailbox.

She posted all of the ones that were marked with name and flat number, stuck the ones addressed to 'The Householder' in the junk pile, until she was left with one: *Marie Bloomfield, Flat 7*. She hoped that this was the only one. That the postie hadn't been stuffing them into number nine's mailbox, knowing fine that she lived at number seven. Mind you, the posties seemed to change a lot now. It used to be the same man who came every time. That one this morning didn't look familiar. New lifeguard, new postman – makes her feel old. Like everything around her is changing, moving on – yet here she is, still in the same flat she's lived in since she moved to Banktoun twenty-five years ago. On her own since her parents decided that Spain was where they wanted to be.

She's worried now. How many more of these letters have been delivered to the wrong address? Has he written to her before? No one's lived in Flat 9 for over a year, since a chip-pan fire gutted the place, and the owner – who lives in New Zealand and clearly doesn't need the rental income enough to give a shit – hasn't got round to getting it fixed yet. *Maybe I need to find a way into that mailbox*, she thinks.

She puts the unopened letter back into her bag and goes to work.

4

'Whoooooooo! Whoooooooo!'

Laura punches the boy in the ribs. 'Shut up, Mark. You're not funny. It's the middle of the day. I'm hardly going to be scared by some stupid ghost noises!'

Mark's face falls. 'Aww, come on. I thought you were up for this. Look, if you've changed your mind, you can tell me. It doesn't matter. I just thought . . .'

'Don't be daft.' Laura grabs his arm and pulls him closer. She snakes an arm round his neck, and eventually he stops pouting and turns round. Their mouths are almost touching. Laura feels her cheeks grow hot, and she pulls back, almost stumbling on a small pile of rubble that's been stacked up under the window. 'Sorry, I—'

Mark smirks. Laura wants a giant sinkhole to open up in the car park of the old children's home and suck her right into it. She read something recently about a man in America who'd gone to bed and the whole bedroom had disappeared into a giant pit underground. They never found him. She coughs. 'Right, can you go in first? I know you said it was easy, but I'd rather stay on lookout first, then follow you inside.'

Thankfully, Mark says nothing. He knows that she fancies him. It's not like she's hiding it well. But making the first move? That's a whole other story. Totally no way. She likes to think she can handle herself. She's got a black belt in karate, for God's sake. Apart from that stupid attack a few weeks ago, she knows that she's completely able to deal with her own life without a man. Or even a stupid *boy*, like Mark. He's only a year older than her, and she's not even sure that seventeen officially makes him a man yet. Does it? Saying that though, he does look pretty manly . . . His little bit of stubble and his gruff voice make her feel all fluttery inside. When he asked her if she wanted to sneak into Marchmont Lodge with him, she was hardly going to say no.

Everyone is talking about Marchmont Lodge. It's almost the end of the summer holidays, and there's been no end of stories about who's been in there and the things they've done. Laura is surprised that the place hasn't been sealed off properly. It's been closed down for years, but it's only recently that kids she knows have been going in there. Apparently it's a junkies' hangout – and most kids she knows would run a mile from a junkie. Everyone knows that lot are unstable. They'll do anything for their next fix. But something has happened recently, and she doesn't know what. The junkies have moved on, and the lodge has been taken over by the rampant teens of Banktoun.

It's a small town. It doesn't take much to get people worked up. And since all that business with the bloke up at the Track, the kids who used to hang about up there have started to drift away. They've found themselves a new place to drink beer and smoke and shag. Not that she does any of those things . . . well, not yet. Apart from anything else, her grandmother would kill her if she thought she'd been up to no good. Bridie Goldstone is the local gossip, and she's far scarier than Laura's mum and dad combined.

She planned to ask Davie about the lodge, but karate was off for six weeks during the summer and she hasn't seen him about. She still can't believe that the local police station might be closing down. Something went on with Davie's boss, but, as yet, Laura has no idea what. She misses Davie. Likes being around him. He's a good listener. A good friend. Plus, he's someone else who gives her that little flutter inside. Even if he *is* old enough to be her dad.

'Oi, you coming in here or what?'

Mark is inside the building. His face peers out at her through the broken window. He outstretches a hand. 'Stand on the tyre, then get one foot on the ledge, and I'll pull you in.' An old lorry tyre leans on its side to the right of the window. The idea is to put a foot on the rim, step up onto the top, then stretch across to the window ledge. There's probably an easier way, but this is all part of the *procedure*. This is the way to get in.

Folk like rules and stories and bits to embellish. Once, *apparently*, someone slipped when they hadn't put their foot properly on the window ledge. They fell forward and knocked three teeth out. Laura knows the story is bullshit, because the person it was meant to have happened to was in France all summer on an exchange trip with the music department. Laura knows that because her gran knows everything there is to know. In fact, what Bridie doesn't know isn't worth knowing. She wonders if her gran already knows about Mark.

'Sorry. Coming. I was miles away.' Laura flips herself in through the window in two easy moves. Mark grabs her around the waist as she lands on the floor inside.

'Impressive,' he says. 'You seem very . . . flexible.' He winks at her, and Laura feels herself blush again. This time though, he doesn't smirk. His eyes have gone dark and glassy and huge, and Laura can only stare into them as he pulls her close and brushes his lips over hers.

Her heart starts to thud. Goosebumps run down her neck. *Oh my God*, she thinks. *Oh. My. God.* Mark closes his eyes. She mirrors him.

His lips press harder against hers, and her mouth opens naturally, just a tiny bit . . . then a little more. And then they're

22

kissing. Properly kissing. He tastes of spearmint. His tongue darts into her mouth, making her lips tingle. A tingle that runs all the way from her lips and down . . . across her chest, to her stomach and further until it reaches . . .

THUD.

Mark pulls away. They both open their eyes. Laura's stomach lurches. A beautiful, painful ache. They look up. The floor above them vibrates, slightly. Shuddering with the weight of whatever has fallen on top of it.

'I . . . I think we should get out of here,' Laura manages, trying to catch her breath. Deal with what just happened. That kiss . . . 'I think someone's upstairs,' she says.

Mark seems to have regained his composure, although his cheeks are flushed and his eyes shine bright like wet stones. Laura hopes his reaction is because of her, and not the noise from the room above.

THUD.

Mark spins her around and practically launches her out of the window. 'You go first,' he says, under his breath. Trying to keep the panic from his voice.

Laura scrambles outside. She doesn't need to be told twice.

5

'Nice of you to join us, Marie. Table four have just had their starters. Six are ready to order. I've left the drinks check for two at the end of the bar.'

Damn. She forgot that Wendy was on lunchtime shift today. Wendy is twenty-five and has recently returned from a month's trek to Peru. She's even more of a bossy little cow now than when she left. Bill, the manager, likes her because she runs around like a headless chicken and gives the impression that she's running the show. Marie's worked in the Rowan Tree for ten years, but Wendy treats her like a junior. She holds her tongue. The regulars know what Wendy's like. They know who pours a better pint of Best and knows which channel they like the TV to be left on all day. They also know that 'Bendy Wendy' is more useful for other things than pulling pints, and Marie always has a little smile to herself, wondering if the girl knows her own nickname.

Marie picks up the drinks check. Pint of lime and soda, and a half-pint of Diet Coke. She glances across at the couple at the table. Recognises them as workers from the council offices nearby. She can predict their food order: baked potato and cheese for the slim brunette who thinks cheese is a diet food, because she never puts on weight. Marie knows it'll be the only meal the woman has all day. Anything's a diet food if you only eat one meal. Her companion, an older man with sandy hair, will have fish and chips. She always wonders at people who can eat the same lunch every single day and never get bored. Marie has something different on every shift, but most of the time it gets left half-touched.

She places the drinks at the end of the bar for Wendy to collect, sticks the check on the spike for table two on the corkboard with the sixteen tables laid out in a grid. She's about to start rearranging the glasses that have been shoved onto the wrong shelves by whoever it was that was working late last night when the bar door opens.

Two men that she doesn't recognise walk in. One's early twenties, but with more lines than he should have and dark leathery skin. The other one's older, shaven-headed. They look stern-faced, but there's a confidence in the younger man's eyes as he approaches her at the bar.

'Two pints of Stella, please, love.'

'And a packet of dry roasted,' the older man cuts in.

She takes two glasses from under the bar. Starts pouring the lager. It's the first of the day and it foams up. She lets it settle, tips part of it out, pours again. She can feel them watching her.

'Nice day for it, love.' The younger one again. He has an unusual accent. Scottish, but not local, with an undercurrent of Northern Irish, maybe?

'Pity I'm stuck in here all day,' she says, placing the two pints in front of them both. 'Seven forty, please. Oh, and the peanuts. Sorry. Eight pounds.' She rips a bag of peanuts off a cardboard stand and lays them down between the two men. They've taken the two stools in the centre of the bar, the ones that face through the gap into the lounge.

'We're just taking a break from the setting up,' the younger man says. 'Maybe you'll come over and see us when you finish your shift, eh? I reckon there'll be a few things there to interest you.' He winks, but it's playful.

Marie smiles. 'Oh aye? What're you setting up, then?' She takes in their clothing – dark T-shirts stained with oil and sweat.

'Fairground,' the older one says. 'We're here all week.' He laughs, and Marie notices the dark holes where there should be more teeth.

'I'm Gaz,' the younger one says. 'Speedway and Waltzer. I'll give you the ride of your life.'

'I bet you've said that line a few times.' Marie leans in close, lays an arm on the bar and whispers, 'Tell me, then. Does it work?'

Gaz picks up his pint and drains half of it, looking into her eyes. He's trying to read her, but he can't. 'Feisty one, you, I bet,' he says.

Marie returns his stare. She can do this all day, if she has to. She likes them to think they've got the measure of her, but none of them have and none of them ever will.

'Marie, drinks check for you.' Wendy's shrill voice breaks the spell and Gaz turns away.

'See you later, boys,' Marie says. She leaves them, disappears through to the other side of the bar. There's a satisfaction in flirting with men who think they've got the upper hand. She's got no interest in them at all, but she likes to knock them off their guard. Let them know that she can handle herself. She's spent years perfecting that stance. But it's all smoke and mirrors.

She picks up the new drinks order. A table of four have come in since she was through in the public bar. The door to the lounge bar has been propped open with a stool and she didn't hear them come in. More council workers. This group only come in on Thursdays. They don't even look at the menu. Always have the specials off the blackboard. Marie realises she hasn't even checked the specials board yet. Most days, she's in early enough that she goes through to the kitchen and gets the list herself, writes on the blackboard and props it back up on the ledge next to the bandit. But today she was late, and today she's distracted. She takes the drinks over to the table, and there's a murmur of hellos, but they are deep in conversation, like they always are. Talking about the weekend plans. She checks the blackboard and recognises Wendy's familiar badly spaced capital letters, each line slanting down to the right. She has an urge to grab a cloth and wipe it all off, write it again in her neat, looping style. Cottage Pie, Macaroni Cheese, Vegetable Korma ... Sticky Toffee Pudding, Chocolate Fudge Sundae. The soup of the day is Tomato and Basil. She hates basil. Something a bit too floral about it.

She leaves the board and walks back to the bar. A figure is disappearing out of sight, heading outside from the lounge. Someone's been in, changed their mind and left again all while she had her back turned. The carpet has been replaced recently and its thick pile completely muffles the sound of footsteps. A strange feeling pricks at her again, just like at the old children's home. A feeling of someone being nearby: in her space yet out of sight.

Through the gap between the two bars, she sees the pair of empty pint glasses and the crumpled peanut packet from where the fairground guys have been. The glasses still look cold, their drink break lasting only a few minutes. As she walks through to collect the glasses for the dishwasher, something crunches beneath her foot. Broken glass? She looks down and sees a small piece of clear plastic. Picks it up and examines it in the palm of her hand. A piece of Lego. One of the flat pieces that never seem to be much use. She throws it into the bin under the sink. Runs a cloth over the section of bar where the cold pints sat. Feels disjointed, out of sorts. Wishes she'd phoned in sick after all.

* * *

When the lunchtime rush is over, Wendy announces that she's done for the day. 'I was only covering for Bill. I've no time to hang about. I'll leave you to clear the last of the dessert plates and the mats, if that's OK? I doubt you'll have much else to do before the five o'clock club come in.'

Marie waves her away. 'Fine. See you later.'

Wendy takes off with a flounce, pissed off at Marie's apathy. Marie walks round to the tables near the door, collects the salt and pepper pots. Typical Wendy. She's no idea what happens in the pub in the afternoon. Assumes that the two hours between lunch and the post-work drinking crowd are boring and uneventful. It's quiet, giving Marie time to think, without the constant chatter and action of what's happening around her. But that's the only time she has to stock the shelves and clean all the nooks and crannies behind the bar. The quiet gap seems to shrink more and more every day. Most of the tradesmen knock off at four, even though they're paid till half past. Their foremen turn a blind eye in exchange for drinks. They come in, stinking of plaster dust, ready to kill a couple of hours with a couple of pints before going home to the long-suffering wives. Thankfully, she's only working until seven. Part of Bill's new shift pattern, where he's trialling some younger staff on the late nights – Thursday to Saturday – which suits Marie just fine. She hates those late shifts when the workmen who take it easy during the week keep going to the end, five, six, seven pints . . . Ordering bowls of chips for their dinner and buying Marie endless drinks that she ends up giving away to the other staff. She tries not to drink too much. Alcohol has never really agreed with her. She drinks to be polite, more than any real enjoyment. Anyway, she's glad to be finishing early because there's a possibility of a date tonight. If he turns up.

Marie has been on three dates in two weeks, which is more than she's been on in about six months. Longer, maybe.

Things have a habit of fizzling out quickly, after the initial spark of lust. She often wishes that her primal instincts would become dulled altogether, saving her from the inevitable disappointment that going out with a man usually brings. This one is different though, she hopes. This one might be a keeper.

She sees off the last of the lunchtime crowd, clears away the final plates and mats. Orders a tuna sandwich from the kitchen and wonders if she'll actually eat it. Food's a struggle at the moment. When she starts to worry about things, it seems to lose its appeal.

When the place is empty, at last, she takes her bag out from the shelf at the end of the bar and retrieves the letter. She turns it over. Hesitates. Takes the sharp blade she uses to slice lemons and runs it across the top, opening it like a pouch. The piece of paper inside has been folded into four. It's cheap A4 printer paper. The handwriting is only on one side, but the pen's been pressed so hard the ink has gone through to the back, leaving small blobs and smudges. She takes a deep breath. *Ten . . . nine . . .* Unfolds it.

It's a few lines from the Bob Dylan song 'Absolutely Sweet Marie', asking where she is tonight. She hears his voice, singing that song to her. So long ago. Her hands shake. She closes her eyes. The door to the bar opens and three men file in. Laughing at something she hasn't heard. She folds the letter back up and shoves it under the bar next to her bag.

'Ah, there she is – a sight for sore eyes. How's it going, sweet Marie?'

She wants to be sick. *Don't call me that. Don't ever call me that.* Maybe she misheard them? They usually call her 'the lovely Marie' or just 'doll' or 'hen' or 'darling'. She can handle these. But not the other one. Not 'sweet Marie'. She takes a deep breath. Turns and smiles at them. 'Usual, is it, lads?'

'Just a soda and lime for me, Marie. I'm working at six tomorrow. Need a clear head.'

Laughter.

The banality of it all refreshes her. She sweeps the memories away. Joins in with the banter. 'You? Working? I thought you just liked wearing those jeans to show us your builder's arse, Sam.'

The second man cuts in: 'When he says *working*, he means he'll get on the bus and fall asleep, and when we get there he'll say he's got a dodgy gut and he'll sit in the gaffer's office drinking tea all day, pretending to do *admin*.' He holds his hands up and makes air quotes around the last word.

'Aye right, Paul. We're not all the gaffer's wee pet.'

The third man rolls his eyes at Marie. 'Pint for me and Paul then, hen.'

'Sam's been skiving, then, has he, John?' Marie says. She plucks two glasses from under the bar and fills them with lager. She does Sam's drink last. She catches his eye when she lays it on the bar and he looks away. His eyes are red-rimmed, and she can tell he's been overdoing it. Someone's had a quiet word. She's glad about that. She doesn't want to be the one to have to take the van keys off him again. They're hardened drinkers, most of the builders who frequent the Rowan Tree, but some of them can handle it better than others.

Paul and John take their pints and go off to sit in the corner, where they can get a better view of the television. Sam pulls out a stool and sits at the bar.

'All right?' he says.

Marie picks up a cloth and a glass and starts to dry it. 'Always better for seeing you,' she says. Winks.

Sam gives her a half smile and looks down sadly at his drink for a moment, before picking it up and draining half of it. 'Actually, that's quite nice. Maybe I'll get used to it.' He stares at Marie until she turns away. 'You going to that party tomorrow?'

'What party's that?' Marie puts the glass on the shelf and picks up another one to dry. She's sick of asking Bill to buy them a dishwasher. *No one likes hot glasses*, he always says. Drying glasses is quite therapeutic, though. It's always a good excuse not to be running around too, if you need a break.

'Jack Henderson's. Just his usual Friday-night thing. You know.'

'Sending out invites now, is he?' Marie has been to Jack Henderson's a couple of times. It always ends up in a mess. Too many druggies and pissheads for her liking. 'Besides, won't be much fun for you if you're not drinking.'

Sam gives her a look. 'Aye. Maybe.'

The bar door swings open and a tall skinny blonde in a too-tight white T-shirt totters in. 'Evening, lads,' she says. Winks. Grins. She slaps Sam's arse as she walks past his stool. 'All right, Marie?' Helen is all heels, tits and gob. She's the quintessential clichéd barmaid. The lads love her.

Marie couldn't be happier to see her. Now that Helen is here, she can get back home and decide what she's going to do about this letter.

6

Once Mark is safely out of the old house, he grabs hold of Laura's hand and they run across the tarmac and out onto the street. The fence was knocked down long before, and a broken strip of safety tape flutters in the wind. They keep running until they're round the corner and the building is no longer in sight. They stop, and Mark lets go of her hand. He bends forward and leans on his knees, panting. Laura isn't breathless at all, but her heart is thumping – from fear, more than the run.

'I thought you said no one was in there any more?' she says.

'There's not meant to be. I heard the user crew had moved on. Something spooked them. I dunno what. There's a thing everyone's trying at the moment, it's—'

'I'm not really interested in the latest headfuck of choice. That shit's for losers.'

Mark grins. 'Maybe you should live a little, Laura. You're too straight for your own good.' He doesn't let her react. He's trying to wind her up, and it's working. 'Actually, tell you what – I know the perfect place to go right now, if you're up for a bit of fun. What time is it?'

'Nearly three, why? What you thinking?' Laura hopes he's going to suggest going back to his place. She knows that both of his parents are out all day at work. There's no point going back to hers, with her mum doing her stupid stuffing-envelopes-for-cash job, and her dad doddering about in the garden, waiting for his next project to come in. He works freelance in IT, and it's always a case of him sitting about bored for weeks on end, or never seeing him for months while he jets off to work twelve-hour shifts in Dubai or somewhere. He's on a home stint at the moment, and he's doing her head in.

Mark grabs her hand and starts walking fast down the road towards town. 'When was the last time you went to the shows, Laura?'

Laura frowns. 'Not since I was about ten and I got scared by the midget in the seven dwarves exhibit. There was a Shetland pony in there too, for rides. I don't know what I was more scared of.'

Mark laughs. 'I remember that! They don't do stuff like that any more, though. Not politically correct or something. Shame. My sister loved the Shetland pony. Come on. I think it opens at three.'

'I don't know. I'm not really great on those rides and, Christ, the food from the vans there is *awful*.'

'Come on. I'll try and win you a goldfish. You can call it after me.'

They don't give out goldfish any more . . . too many people complaining about it being cruel, Laura thinks, but she doesn't correct him. She lets herself be dragged, just happy that she's holding his hand. She wonders if he'll drop it when they're out on the main road, where people might see them. She hopes not.

She decides not to tell him that the last goldfish she had died after three days . . . and her dad flushed it down the toilet.

★ ★ ★

The shows are already in full swing, despite it being early in the day. Everyone's still off school, so there'll no doubt be a load of people from her year hanging around. Younger kids, too – with parents more than happy to spend too much cash on the hook-a-duck if it keeps the bairns occupied for a while.

Laura doesn't have any younger siblings, and her older brother moved out three months ago, the minute he turned eighteen. He lives in a shared flat in Edinburgh now, and she's hoping she might get an invite to one of his many parties before long. He's still playing the protective big brother with her, though – which is nice but doesn't really help her in her quest to become more worldly-wise. Was that not the whole point of big brothers? Mark has an older brother and sister, and some of the things she's heard about them make Laura ache with jealousy, mixed with shock . . . and awe. Maybe Mark's right – she needs to live a bit. It's not like she's going to do something stupid like get mixed up in drugs and end up pregnant before she's old enough to go to university, is it?

The fairground – or the shows, as they call them locally – are set up on a piece of empty grassland on the edge of town, opposite an old cemetery, not far from the local golf course. It's a huge expanse of land, but she can't remember seeing much happening on there apart from the annual visits from the shows and the circus. It's the kind of land that's too big and too plain to have much use for playing on. It's not level enough for football, and it's too exposed to play host to any more interesting games. Most people still hang about in Garlie Park across the other side of town, where there's an adventure playground, tennis courts and loads of space for games – as well as loads of dark, wooded areas for people to get lost in while they drink or snog or whatever else they do in shady corners. For a small town, Banktoun has its share of places for kids to hang about – she doesn't know how anyone could ever be bored. She loves the leisure centre, too – the only one in the county to still have a full-length slide into the deep end, although it seems to be out-of-order more often than not. Too

34

many half-drowned kids getting fished out can be a bit of a health and safety nightmare.

From the outside, you can't see much – there's the backs of the rides – the Waltzer, the Octopus . . . then the backs of the food stalls, already spewing out their temptingly disgusting aromas of cheap greasy burgers and sticky candyfloss. Tooth decay on a stick, her mum used to call it. Laura has never been keen, being more of a savoury girl. Burgers from a van, though – they're a special thing – you get dragged towards them by the smell, and they taste so good, in a totally wrong sort of way, but they always give her a sore stomach afterwards. It's not going to stop her today, though. Or maybe she might have a poke of chips, sitting up high on the Speed Wheel with Mark, swinging her legs and tasting salt in his kisses. She wonders if he'll take her back to his after this. She gets a flutter in her stomach again, imagining it.

The music is pumping hard out of several sets of speakers as they walk hand in hand through the gap between two food stalls. Directly opposite, a dad is helping a five-year-old boy hold a rifle on his shoulder, prepping him to shoot some skittles to win a giant SpongeBob SquarePants toy. Laura pauses to watch, seeing the look of concentration on the small boy's face.

'Three goes for two quid,' the man behind the counter says, looking straight at her. 'Up for it, love, or want to get your boyfriend to try?'

'Come on,' Mark says, 'we'll come back later.'

Laura hangs back, waiting for the boy's first shot. It hits the foam wall behind the skittles, wildly off target. The boy holds tight to the gun but turns to his dad. Laura can't see his face, but she can imagine his look of bewildered disappointment. 'Here,' the dad says, 'let me try, then you can take the last one, OK?'

Mark pulls at her hand again, and this time she follows.

35

'Fancy a go on the Dodgems?' he says. 'I haven't been on those in years.'

'OK. But after that, I want to go there.' She points over at a small tent draped with a purple cover. A gold-painted sign sits outside, where a black velvet curtain has been dropped down and kept shut by a gold rope. A sign says: 'Reading in progress. Please wait.'

'A clairvoyant? Are you mad? They'll tell you all sorts of shit, they will. You know they just make it all up, right? My sister went to one on Brighton pier, she told me all about it – said it was one of those ones that's meant to be world renowned, endorsed by celebrities and all that. They told her she was pregnant, but that she would lose the baby . . . and they said that her boyfriend was seriously ill. They told her she would take a job in the legal profession and she would move to another country by the end of the year. That was five years ago. She lives round the corner from us, with a guy she met a year after that – they've got three kids and she's pregnant again now. At the time of the reading, she'd just qualified as a make-up artist. She was single. She's never been outside Europe. She gets scared if the menu doesn't have sausage and chips on it.' He laughs and shakes his head.

'OK, maybe not so accurate then.'

'Right, which is fair enough. But saying stuff about losing a baby – that's pretty hard-core shit. She was really upset by it. Said she'd never go near one again.'

Laura sighs. 'Well, I can't say I blame her. From what I've heard, they ask you questions and use them to guide what they say to you. I suppose a lot of it's guesswork and instinct, based on people's mannerisms and their age and stuff. They can't get it all right – it's more like a psychology experiment than anything.'

Mark rolls his eyes. 'Ah, right. That's what you want to do at university, isn't it? Psychology?'

'Yeah, I was thinking psychology and biology so I could get into behavioural-type stuff – why people do what they do – I think it sounds fascinating . . . I'm thinking of asking Jo Barker if I can use her as a case study.'

'Jo Barker? She's fucking mad, doesn't take a psychologist to work that one out. Just ask your pal Davie. Plod the Mod. He's practically her guardian now, isn't he? After she tried to fillet that bloke up at Black Wood . . .'

'That *bloke* tried to rape her, Mark. Twice. She didn't have a choice. I'm more interested in her relationships with other people. What led her to act like she did. Oh, I dunno. I just think it would be good. I want university to be useful, you know?'

'Well, yeah, that's kind of the point – as well as the non-stop partying, of course . . . but then I need to get used to that anyway, if I'm going to work in the City.'

'You still think that's what you'll do? Go and be a broker or a funds manager or whatever it is they do there.'

'Yep – and travel the world, go work in Singapore and New York, and anywhere I want, actually . . . you could always come with me, if you like. You don't even need to work. I'll look after you.' He grabs her and spins her round so they're face to face, then he kisses her again – no hesitation this time, right in full view of anyone who might be watching. The tingle hits her hard, shoots down her body. Her cheeks burn. He runs a hand up and down her spine, and there's a moment: dance music blaring out all around them, shrieks and laughter, the pops of rifles, the ringing of bells, the mingling scents of hot dogs and candyfloss, the thick smell of engine oil from the ancient rides, the thump of the Dodgems bumping off each other . . . it all swirls around them both, and they're lost in each other, in a daze, and Laura thinks that she could never, ever – if she lived for a hundred years – be as happy as she feels right now . . .

37

'Oi, you two – get a room!'

Someone slaps her on the back. Her teeth rattle against Mark's, and Laura bites her lip. She can taste blood. They pull apart. She catches Mark's eye, and it's like slow motion . . . they're still gazing at each other, as if they've been drugged. Laura knows right at that minute that she will sleep with him as soon as he asks. She's sixteen. There's nothing to stop her, and everything inside her body is telling her she wants it.

The person who slapped her on the back is standing with an arm around each of them. Laura turns to meet his gaze and realises she has no idea who he is. She shrugs herself out from under his clammy grip. He's about their age, maybe a couple of years older, but he has a hard, weatherworn face, and dirty blond hair. He smells strongly of grease, sweat and fags. He grins at her, showing cigarette-stained teeth. He has no top on and, despite his repulsiveness, she can't help but notice the defined muscles on his chest. He's one of the fairground boys. He makes her skin crawl. She moves away from him.

'Your missus isn't very friendly, is she, mate?'

'All right, Gaz. Give it a rest, eh?' Mark moves away from the other boy, and Laura watches as a cloud seems to darken his face. 'Listen, Laura – why don't you wait here, pop in and see that mystic what's-her-name, if you want? I just need to talk to Gaz about a few things, then I'll be right back.'

Laura stares at Gaz, trying to read his expression. He is still grinning at her, but his eyes are hard, cold. 'Off you pop, love. Come back and see me after and I'll give you the ride of your life.' He tips his head towards the Waltzer, then plucks a half-smoked cigarette from behind his ear, using the other hand to guide Mark away by the elbow.

'I'll come and find you . . .' Mark's voice carries on the wind and the two of them disappear into the crowd. She sees them huddled together in between the Dodgems and the Helter Skelter, and then they're gone.

Laura feels a little shiver. The charged, happy mood from earlier has vanished into the thick, greasy air. She glances around, taking in the hoards of excited children, hands and faces covered in candyfloss, cellophane bags of cheap sprinkle-coated chocolate buttons wedged under their arms. She turns back towards the clairvoyant's tent and sees that the black curtain has been lifted, tied at the side by the gold rope. A flame-haired woman in a long emerald dress is standing next to the entrance, smiling placidly. *How predictable*, Laura thinks. She can't help but be drawn to the woman. Catches her eye. The woman raises a hand, curls a finger towards her, beckoning her.

Laura walks towards the tent.

7

Marie walks home quickly. She'd checked her phone as she'd left the pub and noticed a couple of missed calls and a text, all from Davie. 'Am I still seeing you later? Call me' the text says. Maybe later. She's in no mood for a date now.

She opens the front door to her building and hesitates in front of the row of mailboxes. Number 9 . . . she takes a chance, pulls at the flap on the front, but it doesn't open. Of course it doesn't. They're all locked, and there's only one key per flat. You can't even get a copy made. There's a phone number on the inside of the mailbox with a code on it, and that's the only place you can get a replacement.

She slides her hand into the narrow flap, but the space is too small. Her fingertips brush against paper. There's mail in there. Probably just junk. She doesn't want to imagine that there's anything in there that's meant for her.

Forget it.

She pushes open the door of her flat and is almost assaulted by a large brown ball of fur.

'Oh shit.' She drops her bag on the floor and picks up the cat. It's miaowing, but not in a 'pleased to see you' sort of way. 'I'm sorry, Cads. Did I leave you shut in there all day?'

Despite the fatness and furriness, Cadbury has never been much of a house cat. She likes to roam the streets, only coming back occasionally for treats and, if she was feeling particularly loving, a tummy tickle. Cadbury is one of those cats that make you feel like they're doing you a favour just by hanging around.

Marie can't remember shutting the cat inside that morning, but she obviously had. 'I'm starting to think I'm going a bit mad,' she says to the cat, dropping it on the floor and watching it shoot off into the hall. There's a cat flap on the main door to the building, but not on her internal door. She usually leaves the kitchen window open so it can come and go as it pleases, but the sky had been threatening rain when she'd left that morning. She must've closed it.

She watches as the cat hesitates, turns to look at her, then coughs up a hairball, before disappearing through the flap. She wonders if other pet owners have cats that are capable of such disdain.

Marie takes a tissue out of her bag and picks up the hairball. Tries not to grimace, thinking of the crap that might be packed in there with the hair. She closes the door behind her, balls up the tissue and throws it in the bin. Sighs. She's in. She's about to flick the kettle on, when her phone buzzes. Another text.

Davie again: 'Where are you?'

She replies: 'Home. Talk tomorrow. Sorry.'

Switches the phone off.

It's starting already. Pushing him away. She thought that maybe he was the one. The one to help her open up, move on. God knows she'd spent a long enough time trying. But she has that same feeling every time – as soon as someone tries to get close, she clams up. Pulls back. So far they've only been out a few times. Kissed. He'll be expecting more soon, but Marie's not sure she has more to give. Yes, she could have sex with him. But she knows she'll feel nothing when they do; and there's not a damn thing that either of them can do about it.

She makes herself a tea, takes a Twix out of the cupboard. Pulls the letter out of her bag. She takes a bite of the Twix and lays it back down – it's tasteless. Like sawdust. Her mouth is dry. She takes a drink of tea, but it tastes stale. Bitter. She picks up the letter and tries to stop her hands from shaking. She skims past the lyrics. *Sweet Marie* . . . Tries to push the voice out of her head. It's dated 31 July. Over a week ago.

31st July 2015

Marie,

We were ten, I think. You were playing in my room, I was playing in yours. It was that little game we used to love. You'd pretend to be me, and I'd pretend to be you . . . I know you loved my toys more than I loved yours. Yours were pretty fucking lame, actually. For someone of your obvious intelligence: Sindy dolls, Girl's World, those books full of cardboard outfits with the little tabs on the sides to hang them on the stupid cardboard dolls? I suppose Mum and Dad were just giving us what they thought they were supposed to.

Pink for girls, blue for boys.

Little did they know that we played our own games, though . . . I remember the first time. Do you? Anyway . . . I was talking about my toys: G.I. Joe (who was pretty much as useless as Sindy, although I did like the idea of the two of them fucking — if they hadn't had such useless non-genitals), Meccano . . . that chemistry set? We had chemistry, didn't we, Marie?

I know what you liked best, though.

You were good at it too — much better than me. Smaller hands. More patience. I watched you through the keyhole as you built the final turret on that castle. The smallest of bricks at the top to make it seem as if it was curved. Quite clever.

42

Did you hear me breathing that day, Marie? Did you feel me watching you? I always loved watching you …

Anyway … that's it, I think. I'm done now. I started on our birthday and I stopped today. Do you know why I stopped today? I guess you'll work it out soon. I'm not going to write again. But I hope you think of me, Marie. I hope you remember. What we did. All the things we did.

You loved it, once. You loved me.

With all my love, always.

Graeme xxx

Marie lays the letter down on the table. She rubs at her eyes as if trying to erase what she'd just seen. How can this be happening? He's not allowed to contact her. How did he get her address? Even with the wrong flat number, it still got to her.

Graeme would always be able to get to her.

Why was he talking about the toys? The … oh God. She remembers what happened in the pub earlier – how she'd thought it was nothing, dismissed it. Someone had been in the pub and left before she'd seen him. She'd felt his presence. He'd left an imprint. He'd left something else, too.

A piece of Lego.

That was the thing of Graeme's that she'd loved playing with so much. She remembered the castle. Remembered adding the final touch – two little blue plastic flags. She'd stood back and admired it. Was about to run downstairs and tell her mum to come and have a look. But then the door had burst open, and Graeme had come in.

'Ooh, nice work,' he'd said, smirking. Marie turned and smiled, but felt her smile drop when she saw what he was carrying.

'What have you done?'

Graeme offered his hands to her. Prom Queen Sindy's dress had been ripped up the middle. Her hair was hacked off. One of her arms had been pulled from its socket.

Marie felt her lip start to quiver. 'Why? You didn't have to play with them if you didn't want to . . . you could've come in here. We could've built the castle together.'

'You're the queen of the castle, Marie. I'm the dirty wee rascal.'

He'd walked further into the room, and Marie felt herself backing away. She'd never seen him like this before. Sometimes he had rages. Sometimes he smashed stuff up in the garden, and their dad always pretended he hadn't seen. But she'd never been scared of him before. His eyes seemed to have turned a different shade of blue, so dark that she could barely see if he was still inside.

He lurched forward at her, laughing, and she stumbled back. She hit the edge of the table and couldn't stop herself. Her arms windmilled uselessly as she fell back, knocking the castle off the table and hearing it split into pieces as she landed on top of it with a painful thud – bits of plastic dug into her back and her bare arms, and she had to bite her lip to stop herself from crying.

Graeme stared at her for a moment. Then he blinked. Smiled. As if he'd been somewhere else. In a trance and just snapped out of it.

'Oh Marie,' he said, heading towards her. 'Oh Marie, are you OK? Look what you've done to that lovely castle . . . Here.' He leant down and offered her an outstretched hand. 'Let me help you build it back up again, all right? I love you, Marie.'

In shock, she took his hand and let him pull her up. Her pain was forgotten when he hugged her tight, stroked her hair.

'I love you, too, Graeme,' she'd said.

Marie blinks back tears and tries to shake the memory out of her head. She folds the letter up and puts it back in the envelope. This isn't the first one. It can't be. She pours the remains of her tea down the sink and reaches up to the top cupboard. A half bottle of dark rum. Two bottles of wine. Some dodgy-looking blue cocktail mix that someone gave her for Christmas.

She takes down the bottle of rum, picks up a small tumbler from the draining board. Walks through to her bedroom, knowing that this is the only way to keep the nightmares at bay.

8

Inside the small purple tent the heat and the cloying incense-heavy air is suffocating. The effect is meant to remove her from reality. The red-haired woman peers down at Laura's palms, resting on a velvet cushion. She shuffles the cards. Laura hadn't expected her to do tarot.

'I'm not sure I want the cards,' she says, quietly. She turns her palms face down and the velvet feels slightly rough and worn under her fingers.

'Don't worry, dear. I like to do a combination of things here. I have to do what feels strongest for the person who comes in here, and with you – I knew I had to read your cards. I'll do your palms, too . . . but glancing at them there, I think you need to know more. Only the cards can tell us more . . .'

Laura feels stupid, but it comes out before she can stop herself. 'But . . . what if I get death? Doesn't that mean I'm going to die? I'd really rather not know about that, actually.' She tries to laugh, but it comes out as a small whimper. The woman lays the cards down, turns Laura's palms over again. Presses down on them to show that she wants Laura to keep them there.

'OK, in crude terms, dear. Don't worry about the death card. For one, it doesn't actually mean death at all. It usually signifies a big change – and the meaning of that change is all down to the other cards that are paired with it.' She strokes Laura's palms with soft fingers. 'Besides, I can see the basics from your hands, my love. You're not going anywhere unworldly any time soon.'

Laura looks into her eyes. The woman's eyes shine bright in the muted light of the tent. What is it lit with anyway? Oil lamps? Laura has a sudden fear that the place is going to burn down. The woman goes back to the cards, shuffling them once more.

'I need you to think of a question while I cut the cards. Anything you like. Don't be scared. It can be something big, something small. But make it something that you really want to know the answer to. Just nod when you're done.'

Laura takes a deep breath and closes her eyes. She thinks of a question – the first one that pops into her mind. She opens her eyes. Nods. 'I'm ready.'

'This is the Celtic cross. It's the one that gives you the most information,' the woman says. She places the first card face down, then another on top, making a small cross. Then she lays the other cards out in the correct order, until all ten are on the table. Laura feels her heart start to beat faster. The woman is humming a tune, softly, under her breath. The smell of incense seems to grow stronger, catching in her throat. The sounds from outside the tent have all but disappeared. Laura feels herself drift, like she is half-asleep, half-dreaming . . . on the verge of waking up. Panic slides up her throat.

'I can sense that you're scared, dear. Tell me – what are you so scared of?'

Laura tries to calm her breathing. 'Could I have a glass of water? Sorry, I think it's the air.'

The woman bends down beneath the small table. She reappears holding a bottle of water. 'Sorry, I don't think it'll be cold.'

Laura snaps back to reality. She lifts the plastic bottle to her lips and smells the faint hint of burgers. The bottle has come from one of the food vans. The woman in front of her is just a normal woman, who eats and drinks like everyone else. She lives in a caravan and probably has to put up with the leering gropiness of boys like Gaz. All the time. Suddenly she feels sorry for her, for her situation – and realises the ridiculousness of her own.

What on earth is she so scared of?

She has a sexy new boyfriend, still has two weeks before she has to go back for her final year of school – and then after that she'll be off to university, away from this place. Away to new things and a new life. She gulps down half the water, then places the bottle on the table. She smiles. 'I'm fine now. Sorry.'

The woman smiles back. 'OK, let's get started.' She turns the first two cards. 'Firstly, we have the Papess, crossed with the Queen of Swords. What this means is that you're at a stable point in your learned or professional life. For you, I think this means at school, and possibly your plans for the future. You're happy with what you're doing, and you're achieving good grades. Does that sound right?'

Laura nods, smiling now. Her psychology head is kicking in. The woman has looked at her – at the way she's dressed, how she's conducted herself, picked up on her nerves – she's concluded that Laura has her head screwed on. She isn't a fuck-up. *Nicely done, Red*, Laura thinks, warming to it now, excited by what she's going to say next. This is excellent research.

She turns over the next set of cards, slowly, one by one. Then hovers her hands over them all, as if trying to absorb them. 'Then we have the Four of Cups and the Star – you see the way the cards are placed? It's not just the faces of the cards that matter, it's the way they're drawn. I think you have a couple of very significant people in your life right now. One of them is becoming more and more important to you. I think the Fool is a boyfriend, although he doesn't yet have strong links with you, but he is trying hard. This can mean new discovery, new beginnings – but it can mean the opposite too. Recklessness.' She pauses and looks into Laura's eyes. 'Be careful. However, you have Justice looking on as your protector. He's older. Not a parent. Not a sibling. Is there someone like that in your life?'

Laura nods. Thinks, *Davie*.

The woman carries on. She turns the final pair of cards. The Tower and the Moon. She pauses, sucking in a small breath. She keeps her eyes on the cards, doesn't look up. Laura feels a small flicker of fear. 'What is it? What do you see?' She's been drawn into this mysterious woman's world of the cards. Her rational brain is refusing to kick in.

There's something bad here, she can sense it.

'These are your hopes and fears and the outcome of your question. There's someone else involved . . . someone you don't know.' She leans across and picks up the bottle of water. 'Do you mind?' Laura shakes her head and watches as the woman drains the rest of the water. 'I might've got it wrong. I think I dealt them slightly wrong.' She's stammering, falling over her words. She frowns, staring at the cards. Places a hand over them, as if she's planning to rub them all together, removing the pattern and the story that they've told.

'What is it?' Laura says. Her voice shakes. 'Just tell me.'

The woman looks into her eyes. 'Someone is going to cause you all great pain, my dear. I'm so sorry. This kind of vision doesn't come very often. In fact, I think I'm going to have to take a break. Please . . .' She stands and gestures towards the door of the tent. 'I have a migraine coming on. I need to get out of here, and go and lie down. No charge, dear . . . and please – just be careful.'

Laura stands, feels her legs wobble. She backs away towards the door, a natural reflex. 'Please, can't you tell me what it is?

What do you mean "you all"? Who? Who else?'

The woman shakes her head, a genuine expression of sadness across it. 'I always find, in these situations, that it really is better not to know.'

Laura stumbles outside. Feels like she's about to faint.

'Hey you, you've been in there for ages – I was starting to wonder if you'd gone home and left me here.'

'I—'

Mark senses her distress. He steps forwards and grabs her just as her legs buckle beneath her. He scoops her up, carries her across to a small area where people are sitting on benches eating their food. They look at her, briefly, before going back to their burgers. He sits her down. 'Wait here,' he says.

Laura lifts her head, sucks in deep breaths. Watches him retreating away from her as the crowd swallows him up once more. Notices he has a plastic bag stuffed into the back pocket of his jeans, and wonders, vaguely, what's in it.

Dear Marie,

I'm not even sure where to start. Hello, maybe? Happy birthday? I'm trying to imagine you reading this, and I realise: I don't even know what you look like. What colour is your hair? Is it still so long that you can sit on it? You used to tuck it into the back of your trousers and put your sweatshirt over the top and pretend you'd cut it off. You used to tie it up in a twist and stick a chopstick through it to keep it in place. You used to let me brush it for hours and hours, with that little red brush with the pink pony on the side. God, I loved brushing your hair. I loved the smell of it, like apples and peaches, strawberries and cream. Rapunzel, you used to say. You wanted to lock yourself in your bedroom and only throw your hair out of the window when a handsome prince came along. Was I not handsome enough for you? Did you really think someone else was going to come along? Someone who could love you more than I did? Than I do?

I'm sorry. That's not what I set out to write here. Not at all.

I just wanted to write . . . to tell you that it's OK. You should never feel bad about what happened. I've learned to live with it, over the years. I still miss you, of course. I think about you every day.

Do you think about me?

I hope you read this, Marie. My sweet Marie.

I hope you haven't cut your hair.

All my love,

Graeme

9

Marie wakes up and tries to remember the last time she called in sick. It's not something she does. She's the type of person who would rather hobble in to work on crutches and be sent home than call in to say she'd broken her leg. It's the way she's always been. Trying hard not to draw attention to herself, not wanting to elicit sympathy . . . and there's plenty for people to be sympathetic about, although her mind always tries to tell her that there is no such thing as sympathy – only nosiness and smugness and one-upmanship.

She knows she is damaged.

She remembers arriving in Banktoun all those years ago. Her wrist still stinging from the small tattoo she'd got in that place in Gorgie. She remembers sitting there, her and two others. One of them a biker, with arms the size of her legs and whole sleeves filled with nude women and Celtic symbols. The other a neat-looking businessman who, when he removed his jacket, unbuttoned his shirt to reveal a series of cartoon characters across his bony chest. He'd smiled at Marie, displaying two rows of yellow teeth, and she'd looked away. Disgusted. You never knew what people had hidden beneath the surface.

She knew what tattoo she wanted. She explained it as the tattooist rubbed a small alcohol-soaked pad across her wrist.

'How old are you?' he said, not looking her in the eye.

'Old enough.'

'You know, I don't normally do these on the wrist. Not

unless you've had a bit of ink before. Are you sure you don't want it somewhere you can hide it more easily?'

'I don't want to hide it. I want people to know.'

He laid down the tattoo gun and looked up. 'Know what?'

She looked at him, and she knew that underneath his craggy face and tattooed forehead he was a kind man. Marie had an instinct for people now. She'd learned the hard way.

'I need them to know that I've escaped.'

The man looked at her pityingly and switched on the gun. The noise reminded her of a shaver. She blinked away a memory. Took a deep breath. He'd already outlined the design on her wrist. It was small, but it was clear. A tiny outline of a swallow. Freedom. She'd done her time.

'This will feel like a small scratch. Tell me if you need me to stop.'

'Don't stop,' Marie whispered. She closed her eyes and felt herself go numb.

That pain was nothing.

Marie rolls over in bed, rubs at her wrist. The bird is more green than black now, fading away like everything it was put there to signify. But today it seems to hurt, a phantom itch.

She feels sick. Picks up the phone and texts her boss: 'I can't come in this morning. Got a migraine. Sorry.'

She scrolls through her other messages. Knows that she needs to contact Davie or he's going to start wondering what the hell is going on – asking too many questions. She can't deal with questions, not yet. Not until she knows what's going on.

She sends a text to Davie: 'Having a quiet day. Call you later.' Then she gets out of bed and realises that she's about to be sick.

After some time spent hugging the porcelain toilet bowl, she splashes her face with cold water. Drinks a pint of orange squash. Tries to stop shaking.

Graeme's letter is on the kitchen table. It emanates some sort of aura, and she knows she can't read it again. She picks it up and stuffs it into the kitchen cupboard, where she has a tray of junk mail and other things that she hasn't got round to sorting out yet. On the floor, a small trail of round biscuits tells her that Cadbury has managed to find her own breakfast again. She scoops them up and throws them in the bin, remembering the hairball from yesterday – thinking it was odd, as the cat was generally quite well trained and tended not to spit stuff out like that in the hallway. She wonders if maybe the cat had eaten something bad, berries or something it had found out in the garden. She knows that checking the small lump she'd picked up in the tissue would definitely make her sick again, so she closes the door of the cupboard that houses the bin and decides to deal with it later.

This is becoming a pattern. Why can't she face up to things head on?

She picks up her swimming costume and towel that are hanging on the radiator from the day before. There's a chance that someone might see her at the pool, but as no one really knows which shifts she does every week, it's hardly an issue. Besides, Bill isn't going to sack her for taking one morning off.

Making sure the kitchen window is open just enough so the cat can get back inside, she picks up her swimming bag and leaves the flat.

In the hallway, she pauses by the mailboxes again. Opens her own. Nothing. She sticks her hand into Number 9 but can't tell if anything new has been put in there or not.

Forget it, Marie.

As she walks out of the main entrance, she senses a movement to the right of the building, at the part where the alley disappears around the back to the small piece of garden that is shared between her and the other ground-floor flats. There's a gate there, but it's never locked. Her skin prickles.

'Cadbury? Is that you?' She doesn't expect the cat to answer, but if it has been lurking around in the alley, there's always the small chance it might appear at the sound of her voice. She hasn't seen her much in the last couple of days and she's probably sulking. There's a faint rustling, but it might just be the leaves on the trees that are overhanging from the house next door. She's about to walk round and have a look, but something stops her. She shakes her head and walks down the path towards the street. *Stupid.*

The swimming pool is heaving. School kids on holiday fill the main pool as well as the kiddie pool, and Marie realises she's not going to get much of a peaceful swim.

She finds a space against the far side, swims ten lengths while hugging so close to the pool wall that she can only do front crawl to avoid smacking her fingers against the side. She stops in the deep end for a breath. This is pathetic. Drinking the rum has affected her stamina. The upside is that the cool water is soothing her fuzzy head, even if the echoing shrieks of the children are trying hard to counterbalance it.

She leans one arm in the drainage channel and gazes out across the pool, towards the café, where a few people sit drinking coffee and watching the swimmers. Without her contact lenses, she can't make out any of the faces, but some of the shapes of people look familiar. At the table at the end, a man stands up from his seat and steps closer to the window. Marie peers. He's probably trying to find one of his kids. You see them sometimes, the anxious parents. They bang on the glass and a child in the pool starts waving. Then the parent sits back down, pleased that they've shown their vigilance.

But the man doesn't bang on the glass. He just stares out

at the pool. Marie scans the bodies in the water, waiting for someone to suddenly spot him and wave. No one does.

She turns back towards the café. He's gone.

Marie slides down the wall to the bottom of the pool, holds her breath for a few seconds, then pushes off the wall and into her final length. She tries not to think about who the man might have been.

Who he was watching.

Why there was something disturbingly familiar about him.

10

Laura wakes up early, feels like she hasn't slept a wink. She knows she must've, of course, but her mind was whirring so much it was hard to shut it down.

Choosing the right person to share her news with was very difficult. Some girls from school lost their virginity long ago, and they saw themselves as superior beings now. Telling any of them would burst her happiness like a pin in a balloon. She had other friends who were even further behind than her, nowhere even close to a kiss. They'd only get jealous, and probably embarrassed.

She decides that Hayley is really her only option. She isn't one of her closest friends; in fact, she barely knows her – but she's funny and streetwise and she is the right person to help her deal with this. It might even make Hayley want to be one of her proper friends. Hayley has been seeing a boy in their class, Sean Talbot, for a month – but Laura knows that despite Sean's best efforts Hayley is letting him wait. Laura also knows, from the look that Hayley gave her when she told their little gang what was going on, that she didn't want to wait any longer. It might just be that Sean isn't the one she is waiting for. She scrolls down through her contacts list and clicks 'call'.

'Laura? This is a surprise. I didn't even know you had my number.'

Laura is confused. How did she know it was her if they hadn't swapped numbers? She suspects that Hayley likes to play games, to keep the upper hand. She ignores it. 'Hey, Hayley, sorry – you gave me it after we did that biology thing together last term. Anyway, this is nothing to do with school. I just needed to tell someone something, and I thought you'd be the right one to tell, what with you and Sean . . .'

'Me and Sean? Why? What've you heard?'

'No, no – nothing – only what I've heard from you . . . I wasn't . . .'

'Oh!' Hayley starts laughing. 'You must be psychic, Laura. You'll never guess what we did yesterday. Well actually, you probably can . . .'

Laura hears it in her voice. She's done it. Lucky cow. 'What was it like?'

A pause. 'You want me to be honest?'

'Er, yes . . . that's why I was calling. Well, actually, I was calling to ask you what you thought of Mark Lawrie, and if you thought I should—'

'Mark Lawrie? Bloody hell, are you going out with him? What's happening? I haven't heard any of this! Does Lizzie know? Or Karen? Or—'

Laura smiles, glad that she's had this moment. 'Well, no, it's just started really. He was eyeing me up one day at school. We *nearly* chatted at Karen's party at the end of term, then he spoke to me in the park and *then* I bumped into him down the road, and well . . . we went to Marchmont Lodge, then the shows, and later on he's coming round to take me somewhere else.'

Hayley shrieks down the phone. 'And what've you done? OMG, Laura, have you . . . ?'

'We've just kissed, but . . . I want to do more . . . I don't want to wait. But I want to know I'm doing the right thing. I want to know if this is "real" or not. You waited ages, I just—'

'Right, listen.' Hayley's voice takes on a solemn tone.

Laura imagines her face, her look of serious concentration. 'There's a question you have to ask yourself, and once you know the answer, you'll know what to do.'

Laura has a sudden flash to the fortune teller. The question she'd asked herself then. She has a feeling Hayley's question is going to be a different one, though.

'Ask yourself this,' Hayley says. 'Would you cry at his funeral?'

Laura is taken aback. 'Well . . . yes. I mean, I think I'd cry at most people's funerals . . . I don't—'

Hayley cuts her off. 'It's like the litmus test for boys, Laura. Think about how upset you'd be if he died, and then you'll know if you really want to be with him. Listen, got to go. Keep me posted, though, OK? Enjoy it. Good luck . . . oh, and don't worry. I won't tell anyone.' She hangs up.

Laura thinks there was another voice in the background. A boy. What was Hayley doing with a boy at eight in the morning? Surely it wasn't Sean. Neither of their parents would allow that, would they?

She jumps out of bed, picks up the towel that's hanging on the back of her door and heads to the shower. Never mind Hayley. She's got some serious preparation to do before Mark turns up.

11

Davie wants to murder Malkie. The fear that had gone through him when he'd gone to identify the woman who turned out not to be Marie had convinced him that he was in no way immune to having a heart attack. No matter what shape he was in. Davie's always known he's not cut out for the murder squad. He hasn't seen many corpses in his life, but he's seen enough to know that he can't cope with them on a daily basis. Malkie told him the stats not that long ago, about the number of bodies he'd had to deal with in Edinburgh and the Lothians. Mostly drug overdoses, or old people who'd died alone. In both cases, the bodies were often in a state of putrefaction, which makes Davie feel sick just thinking about it. How sad, when no one even notices that you're dead.

The woman in the hospital still hasn't been ID'd. Malkie's team are cross-checking with people recently reported missing, but, as is often the case, people go missing and no one notices. You'd hardly send out a search party if you didn't see your friend for twenty-four hours. Maybe she lives alone. Maybe she has no one to miss her. Davie worries about having no one to miss him. He's hoping Marie might change that, but it seems that after the initial enthusiasm her interest is already waning. They'd pencilled in a date for the night before and she'd called it off without any explanation.

Malkie had shown him the victim's clothing. The black skirt, the white blouse. The clumpy shoes. Not Doc Martens, but something similar. Even without the possibility of a tattoo, he'd have been able to identify Marie based on the shoes. No way she'd wear anything other than the real thing. But Malkie wasn't to know that, and the other clothing, plus the hair and the age, and the fact that she wasn't far outside the town, made her a not-unsuitable candidate. Davie shudders. What if it had been her?

Despite knowing Marie for about twenty years, he realises now that he doesn't know her at all. They'd gone out for a drink a couple of times a few years back, but he'd been the one to pull back from that. He's had no shortage of offers, but something always seems to get in the way. Marie became good friends with Anne, after joining her class at the high school – but by then Davie, and Ian – Anne's husband – had already left. Davie joined the police, and Ian started a series of nothing jobs until he was lucky enough with a win on the Football Pools that meant he was able to buy his shop.

He'd been working there ever since, and Davie had been at Banktoun Station ever since.

He's not far off being eligible for early retirement now, but who retires when they're forty-eight unless they've got something better to do? Not him. In fact, Malkie and the murder squad aside, he's quite keen on the idea of switching over to CID. He reckons he's got a good ten years left in the force, but he needs something more than local policing to keep him on his toes. His brain is starting to go stale, and he's not one for Sudoku. Luckily Malkie is more than happy to help him out. Only problem is, if he takes an official position as detective, he'll have to go and do the training at some point, and he's not sure he's capable of sitting for eight hours a day with a bunch of fast-trackers and keen recruits. Still, at least he'd be fine with the fitness part. He's been doing karate since he was ten, and running the local club is one of the highlights of his life. *You need to get out more, pal*, he thinks.

He hasn't been to a gig in over a year. Him and Ian used to go to all the Mod meet-ups on their scooters back in the day. He's too old for all that now. But he's still got the scooter.

The next morning he finds himself back at the computer, working on his original task. He wants to find the link between these drug deaths. He wants to stop them reaching Banktoun. *Time for a wee recce*, he decides.

'I'll leave you two lovebirds to man the fort.'

He doesn't wait for a response. Callum, and Lorna, his new fiancée, are through in the kitchen, apparently making tea, but Davie imagines they're up to something else in there. Something even nicer than tea. He's envious of them, finding each other. He can't even be bothered to tell them to get on with their work, as there really isn't much to do. Someone broke into the vet's surgery the other night but hadn't managed to nick anything of interest, as the medicine cabinet was locked with a key-coded lock and there is a dearth of competent safe-crackers in Banktoun. Chancers, aye. Plenty of those. They'd been caught on CCTV, and they'd had the sense to wear hoods.

All might've been OK, except Davie and Callum had already recognised one of them from his distinctive logo'd hoodie, and he was currently in the cells, stewing. They'd picked him up at home, where he'd clearly celebrated his poor attempt at a burglary by drinking half a case of Special Brew, realising that the bottles of sterilising alcohol he'd nicked would probably make him go blind – plus, he'd already sold it. But to whom, Davie didn't know. Some people were beyond desperate. The man was a petty thief, but with another break-in under his belt it was likely he'd get a custodial sentence this time. What a waste of a life. Davie has sympathy for some of those people who just never manage to make it, but Stuart Mason is a sad lowlife who'd once been caught trying to strangle a dog down by the river. Davie has no time for the man and is happy to keep him in the cells for as long as they're allowed. He might interview him when he comes back, assuming he's sobered up. Plus, his brief isn't particularly rushing to get there to his aid.

On a lamppost outside the station, a freshly tacked poster is advertising Forrestal's Fun Fair. So the shows are in town. This is interesting. Lots of unsavoury types hanging around there. Davie pulls out his BlackBerry and types himself a quick note. He might nip down there for a gander later. Maybe he'll ask Marie. It's as good an excuse as any to spend time with her, and it's something that doesn't involve them having to talk too much – give her a chance to relax in his company again. Maybe he'll win her a giant teddy on the rifle range. And maybe he'll spot something interesting while he's there. Young lads, moving around different towns, meeting different folk along the way. Selling them more than candyfloss and cheap hotdogs. In his head, he tries to map out the list of the drugs cases that Malkie has given him.

Wonders which town the shows visited last.

12

'Have you actually *made* a picnic?'

Mark grins. 'What, as opposed to going and buying pre-packed sandwiches from the Co-op? Yes, of course I've bloody made it!'

Laura is impressed. Mark gives the impression of being a bit of a lad, but underneath he's nothing of the sort. He's funny – of course – and he's gorgeous – no question about that. But, most importantly, he seems to like her. A lot. Laura's cynical demon tries to butt in, suggesting that he's only being nice to get into her pants. Half of her wouldn't mind that much. Only another year and she'll be leaving for university. He'll been leaving to do the same, then he'll go off and find his job in London. Would it be so wrong if it were only a summer fling? Surely they could manage to avoid each other after the holidays, if things don't work out. She'll be too busy with her exams to worry about stupid gossip. On the other hand, her last year at school might just be a million times better if she had an actual boyfriend to hang out with.

Laura doesn't feel the draw of London. She plans to study in Edinburgh and stay there afterwards. She has her heart set on one of those cute little cottages they call the Colonies – pretty rows of old workers' cottages, with postage-stamp gardens and cul-de-sac streets where they still hold street parties. Really close to the centre of the city, too. She just has to find a way to be able to afford one. She imagines Mark living in some new build high-rise in the Square Mile, all glass and security entry systems and space-age furniture. It's funny, she knows they want completely different things, and at sixteen she knows they're far too young to make any compromises to stay together, but she has a feeling that their relationship, no matter how long it lasts, is going to be something significant for them both. Even the stupid fortune teller hinted at that. She's hasn't told Mark what the woman said about something bad happening. He'll only say he told her so.

Mark swings the rucksack onto his back and takes hold of Laura's hand. Laura notices that a blanket has been rolled up and slotted through the straps at the back. He's put some effort into this. She has a sick feeling for a moment, wondering how many other girls he's made special picnics for.

'Am I allowed to ask where we're going?'

Mark squeezes her hand. 'Did you bring your cossie?'

'Yes . . .'

'Well then,' he says, looking up at the sky – which is a clear, bright blue, peppered with a smattering of fluffy white clouds – 'let's hope it stays warm enough for you down at Digby's Deathhole, eh?'

Laura laughs. 'Oh. How romantic.'

Digby's Deathhole is the name the locals have given to a wide section of the river where a deep cavern has become a popular swimming spot. There are various rumours about kids having drowned in there, sucked down by a mysterious vortex . . . or if you listened to some people, the ghost of Digby himself, who likes to grab onto people's ankles and drag them down into the depths – never to be seen again. Laura asked Davie about the place, wanting to know how much was true and how much was legend. Davie told her at least another three legends, before he told her the truth. One person *had* drowned in there, back in the 1950s. A local tradesman called Daniel Digby had taken a shortcut along the river after a day out at the festival raft race, where many bottles of beer were consumed. He'd fallen in and because of the river being low from a summer drought he hadn't been able to reach the bank to pull himself back out. They found him the next morning, washed up on the edge of the weir about a hundred feet downstream from the hole. His jacket was washed up on the bank there, snagged on a tree, looking like it was trying to climb out.

Laura shudders, thinking about the man, and how scared he must've been in the cold, dark water. His screams of help disappearing into the trees.

The thing about this part of the river is that it is perfect to swim in, and it's sheltered amongst the trees – so it's a popular spot for couples, even during the day – although the skinny-dippers usually wait for dusk, at least. Laura wonders if Mark has brought condoms. She thought about buying some herself, but the idea of going into the local pharmacy and having to take them to the counter where someone's mum was likely to recognise her was as appealing as having her eyeballs removed with a spoon.

'Any preferences? Shade or sun?' Mark drops the rucksack on the ground and pulls the blanket from the back. He shakes it out.

'Shade, I think. Maybe with a bit of sun poking through.' Laura looks around, trying to find the perfect spot. 'How about there?' She points over at a small clearing, where the trees seem to form a perfect circle. Sun glints through the gaps in the top of the canopy, casting starbursts of light on the mulchy forest floor.

Mark shakes out the blanket again and lets it fall softly onto the patch of ground. He kneels down and starts to unbuckle the rucksack. Laura drops her own bag on the blanket and kicks off her sandals. She walks over to the water's edge and, bending to lean one hand on the ground, sits down with her feet hovering just above the water.

'It looks freezing,' she says, turning back to look at Mark over her shoulder. He's laid out Tupperware boxes, cans of drink, packets of crisps. Something wrapped in foil sits on a floral patterned plate. He's brought plastic cups, napkins and cutlery. 'Wow,' Laura says. 'You've got a picnic set. How sweet . . .'

'Don't take the piss,' he says, pulling up a weed in a clod of earth and aiming it at her head. She ducks, and it misses, but it takes her concentration for a moment and her feet splash into the water.

'Aargh! It *is* freezing, you bugger!'

Mark grins, and takes off his shoes and socks. He jumps up from the blanket and barrels towards her, grabbing her and pushing her towards the river. She shrieks, and he pulls her away just before she slides off the bank and into the river. Then the two of them tumble back, Laura's feet still dangling over the edge, Mark straddling her, pinning her arms behind her head.

'What am I going to do with you, eh?' he says, his voice softening, cracking. He leans down and kisses her, and Laura feels like she is going to melt into the earth. Sunshine dusts her bare feet, and Mark's weight and warmth press down on her. The tingle starts again and she can't bear it any longer. She can feel his hardness, pressing into her. He pulls away, sits up. Gazes down at her before climbing off. His face is flushed. He looks like he's about to say something, but changes his mind. He crawls over to the blanket and sits down.

'I could do with a drink. Want one? There's Coke or Fanta. Or water.'

Laura sits up. 'You didn't have to stop,' she whispers.

He smiles a half smile. 'I didn't want to, Laura. Christ.' He shakes his head. 'I want this day to be special. I don't just want to . . . you know.'

Laura smiles back. 'I know.'

16th July 2015

Dear Marie,

I don't know how long it takes for a letter to arrive these days, but I'm hoping you've read the one I sent you yesterday, and that the reason you haven't replied yet is that you're busy with work. That's understandable. The people who work here are always so busy. Running around like blue-arsed flies, most of them. With some of them, I wonder if they just run around so much to avoid having to do any of the difficult stuff. It can't be easy working here. Some people are extremely difficult to get along with. You'd laugh at some of them.

Do you still listen to Billy Idol? I remember you dancing to 'White Wedding' and pulling your lip up into a sneer like Billy. You liked him, didn't you? You had a poster of him on your wall — right opposite your bed. He must've been the last person you saw every night before you went to sleep.

You were always the last person that I saw before I went to sleep. I'm not sure if you know that.

It was me who ruined that poster, but I'm sure you guessed that. Why didn't you say anything? Were you worried that Mummy would ask us why?

I'll write again soon, Marie.

I hope you'll have some time to write back.

Lots of love,

Graeme

13

Back in her flat, still spooked by the man at the pool, Marie rummages through the kitchen drawers until she finds what she needs. A multi-head screwdriver, where all the different shapes and sizes are slotted into the lid, a chisel – that she couldn't remember ever having had a use for – and a miniature hammer she'd got as a present with one of those huge bars of toffee that you have to smash up. Who'd given her that? Anne probably. No doubt one of those gimmicky things she'd bought for the shop that didn't sell.

She has slight reservations about what she's about to do – after all, it is technically vandalism – and isn't it an actual offence to take someone else's mail? Anyway, it's the middle of the day, and most people in her block have regular nine-to-five jobs, so no one is going to be in to see her. Plus, she'll make sure she fixes it back up again so they won't even notice that anything has happened.

Armed with her small arsenal of tools, she puts the front door on the latch and walks out into the hall. There are twenty flats in the block. Ten on the ground floor, ten above. Due to a numbering system that makes no sense whatsoever, Flat 9 is directly above her. She remembers thinking at the time of the fire that she was lucky that there'd been no damage to her own place. Apart from the stench, of course. No one had managed to escape that. If you went upstairs, it was even worse. The fire brigade had hosed the place down and sealed it off – apparently it was safe – but no one was likely to venture inside it. The locks had been changed, after the fire brigade had broken down the door. The man who'd been renting it wasn't in, thankfully. He'd gone out to buy bread, forgetting that he'd already switched on the pan to heat the oil for his chips. He'd bumped into someone down the street, and they'd both watched as the siren went off at the fire station and the firemen – all part-time and busy doing other jobs at the time – turned up and disappeared full pelt up his road. That was when it dawned on him. By the time he got home, the whole building had been evacuated, and he got more than a bit of abuse when he appeared around the corner with his sliced white loaf. After they all realised he wasn't dead, of course.

Marie was out at the time. Meeting a man in Edinburgh after a series of chats on an online dating website. He was at least ten years older than his profile suggested and looked like the type of person you try to avoid at the bus stop. She remembers it clearly, as it was her first and last attempt at online dating. What was the point?

She starts off with the screwdriver, using a wide, flat head. She pushes it into the keyhole, wiggles it about. Nothing. Why do these things look so much easier when you see them on TV? A thought pings. 'Oh you idiot, Marie,' she mutters. She leaves the tools on the floor and goes back into her flat to get her keys. Her mailbox key is on the keyring, along with the front-door key and a small photograph of her and Anne on a rollercoaster in Blackpool. She glances at the photo and smiles. Such a long time ago now. Not long after she'd moved to Banktoun. A school trip to Manchester where she and Anne had sneaked off on the train to the Pleasure Beach. They'd got in no end of trouble for it, but it had cemented them as friends right from the start. Marie had thought about Graeme that day, remembering when they used to go to the shows together and he'd always win her one of those mad-haired plastic trolls – what were they called again? Gonks. That was it. Marie had bitten back tears for most of the trip: no matter what Anne said or did, he was always at the back of her mind. Even in the tiny keyring photograph, she could see her red-rimmed eyes and forced smile. Anne had said to her on the train back to Manchester: 'If you ever need to talk about anything, you can talk to me. I hope we're going to be good friends.' Marie smiled at the memory, Anne's solemn face, candyfloss stuck to her cheek. Her breath all cheap cider and chewing gum.

Marie pushes her own mailbox key into the lock for Flat 9, assuming that, if not exactly the same, the keys are bound to be similar. Why had she never thought about this before? She wiggles the key and it seems to turn a fraction, and then stops. Of course it does. That would be too easy.

After a few more pokes and wiggles with various screwdriver heads, Marie has to admit defeat. She drops the screwdriver onto the floor and picks up the hammer and chisel. Still trying to remember what it was she'd ever bought a chisel for, she carefully wedges the tip of the tool into the gap next to the lock, angling it slightly to the right. Then, holding it tightly with her left hand, she whacks the handle of the chisel once, sharply and neatly, with the toffee hammer.

The door of the mailbox shudders slightly. The sound reverberates around the walls, making her wince. She does it again – this time hitting slightly harder with the hammer, pushing deeper with the chisel.

The door springs open.

Marie drops the tools onto the floor in surprise. There's an echoing clang as the metal hammer lands on the chisel and bounces against the lower level of mailboxes that line the wall. Marie holds her breath for a moment, expecting one of the other residents to open a door and come out, ask her what the hell she's doing. But there's no sound, thankfully. As she'd hoped, no one is in. Either that or no one cares.

There's a pile of mail in the open mailbox. She lifts it out and starts to sift through it. Junk, mostly. *Why am I doing this out here?* she wonders. She glances around one more time, then bends down to pick up her discarded tools. The hammer has left a small dent in the door of Flat 1's mailbox. She hopes they won't notice. Clutching the pile of mail and the tools against her chest, she pushes the door of Flat 9's mailbox closed.

It springs open again.

'Shit.'

Thinking through her options, she goes back into her flat again, dumps the pile of mail and the tools on the kitchen table. She rummages in the kitchen drawer again. Pulls out a jar of paperclips, a pile of elastic bands. Smoke-alarm battery – the square ones that her dad used to make her and Graeme stick on the end of their tongues. She pauses. Feels her heart beating in her chest.

Where are you, Graeme?

Eventually, she finds it. A ball of Blu-Tack, stuck to the back of the drawer. It's dried up, pieces of fluff sticking to it. She rolls it about in her hands, warming it up, trying to make it pliable again. She pulls little pieces off, rolling them into individual small balls. It's a basic idea, but hopefully it'll work. Will it be strong enough to hold, though? She decides it'll do until she has time to fix the lock properly.

She wanders back out into the hall, and as she starts to stick the small balls of Blu-Tack along the edge of the mailbox door an odd sensation comes over her. Something prickles down her back. Someone is here. Near her. She imagines she can hear them breathing.

Did you hear me breathing, Marie?

She pushes the memory away.

'Hello? Is someone there? I'm just sorting out some mail . . .' She lets her sentence trail off.

No reply. *Paranoid,* she thinks. *That's what happens when you start doing things you're not supposed to be doing.*

She sticks the rest of the balls inside the door then pushes it shut, holding it tight, hoping that the stickiness will find some purchase. She takes her hand away and steps back. The door moves slightly, finding its natural position. It holds fast. She watches it for a moment, listening for the sound of unsticking . . . waiting for the door to spring back open again. But it seems to be OK – for now, at least. She'll ask Anne if she can send Ian round to help her fix it. She'll have to tell them she broke it. But she won't tell them why. She won't tell anyone.

As she turns back towards her flat, she hears a noise. Something is being scraped or dragged across the floor above her. Someone moving furniture. Someone in the flat upstairs. Flat 9. But no one lives there.

Do they?

She walks back into her flat, double locks it. Puts the chain on. She never puts the chain on. She walks through to the kitchen and jumps with fright. Cadbury is on the table, licking up crumbs. The cat looks up at her and gives her one of its looks. The pile of mail has been scattered across the table and onto the floor.

'Get off the table, missy,' she says, shooing the cat. It jumps down and runs off into the living room. She scoops up the mail. She stops. She doesn't want to look. There's another faint sound of scraping from upstairs. She goes through the pile, slowly, one by one . . . pizza leaflets, people's names she doesn't recognise, junk from Virgin and Sky. Then a letter. That handwriting. Another one.

Marie drops the pile of letters onto the table. Her whole body shakes. There are at least ten letters in there addressed to her, that same looping scrawl. Marie feels the remnants of last night's rum ready to make a reappearance. She throws up into the kitchen sink.

14

When Laura was young, she was obsessed with Barbie dolls. She'd had seven or eight of them, and she spent all her time mixing and matching their outfits, styling their hair. She'd been friends with a girl called Mindy Heller back then. Mindy had a Star Wars Luke Skywalker figurine, plus two Action Men. Mindy was the kind of girl who preferred to climb trees than style hair, but at the time Laura was the complete opposite. When they were seven, Mindy told Laura all about sex, by demonstrating as graphically as she could using Luke and the Action Men and her Barbies. She described the whole thing in great detail, and Laura hadn't realised until a few years later, when they'd started biology at school, that Mindy's descriptions had been so accurate. Mindy had moved away after her parents split up, and Laura had often wondered what happened to her and how it was that she'd known such explicit, accurate details about sex at such a young age. Laura's own mum hadn't told her anything until she was nearly eleven.

'You know about how to make babies yet?' Laura's mum had asked, casually stirring a saucepan of Bolognese sauce. Laura was setting the table, glad that her back had been turned when her mum said the words all pre-teens dread.

'Yes,' Laura said quietly. 'I know about periods, about intercourse and about giving birth. Is there anything else?'

Laura's mum laughed. 'You seem to have it covered, love. You know I'm here if you've got any questions.'

Laura took glasses out of the cupboard and laid them on the table. She wondered if her brother had already had sex. She wondered if he'd tell her about it. Mindy Heller had told her that it hurt. She wondered how she knew that, if it was just something she'd been told.

Blinking away the memories, Laura lies back on the blanket. Mark is lying flat out, one arm thrown behind his head. His eyes are closed and he's snoring gently. The sun casts speckles of light across his cheeks. He was up all night playing something on his PS4 that Laura had never heard of. He's been dozing for half an hour, while Laura has been sitting looking out at the river, daydreaming. The place is so still, so quiet. The noise of the weir is a faint burble in the distance. The leaves on the trees barely ruffle, except for the occasional flutter of a bird in the trees or something scurrying in the undergrowth.

Was it going to happen today?

Laura's stomach flips, thinking about it. She's looked stuff up online, making sure she used the incognito window on Google so that her search wouldn't get saved. 'Does it hurt the first time?' 'Can I get pregnant the first time I have sex?' 'How long does sex last for?' 'How long should I wait before having sex?' 'What does spunk taste like?'

Laura wanted to ask Hayley these questions, but she wasn't sure she could trust her not to go and tell the rest of the school. Laura has changed since her days of Barbies and her sex education from Mindy. When Mindy left, Laura gradually became more like her – more tomboyish, less girly – as if trying to replace the friend who was missing. Doing karate meant she mixed with boys a lot, but in a different way – she didn't spend her time obsessing over pictures of celebrities and pop stars in magazines. She could throw a boy twice her size and weight onto the ground with a hand on an elbow and a simple flick of her wrist.

But something else changed inside her when she saw Mark looking at her that day across the assembly hall. His eyes seemed to burrow deep inside her; the small smile on his face had made blood rush to her head. Then someone had nudged him in the ribs and he'd turned away. That was it, until that night at Karen's party, when she'd been too shy to talk to him. She was glad he wasn't so timid that day he'd come up to her in the park and asked if she fancied a walk. And then a few days later when he'd been hanging around at the bottom of her street, and they'd ended up at the Marchmont Lodge and the shows . . . Had he been waiting for her? She was too nervous to ask.

Laura leans across Mark's sleeping form and takes a can of drink from the rucksack. She pops the tab on the Fanta and takes a swig. The noise wakes him up.

'Hey you . . . Have I been asleep? Why didn't you wake me?'

'You looked like you needed the rest. Besides, you're no use to me if you can't stay awake.' She flips a leg over, straddles him, pins him to the ground. She shuffles her body down until her pelvis is aligned with his; she leans forwards, staring down at him, her long hair trailing down either side of his face. He grins, and she feels him growing hard beneath her. She shifts slightly, and he wriggles beneath her.

'Am I hurting you?'

He laughs. 'Not in the way you think.' He places his hands on her bare elbows. 'Take your T-shirt off. Go on. There's no one here, and we're away from the path, if anyone turns up.'

Laura's heart starts to race. She lifts her arms above her head, crosses them back down, taking hold of her T-shirt at both sides. She pulls it slowly over her head, drops it at her side. She hears Mark take a breath. Feels him shift beneath her. His hardness is becoming uncomfortable.

'Fucking hell,' he whispers. 'Your body is . . . You're beautiful.' He curls up, pulls her down on top of him. The kiss is frantic, deep. He pushes her back up, his hands on her breasts, flips the cups of her bra down, just enough. His fingers are on her nipples and she hears herself moan. He pushes her off, climbs on top of her. She lets him slide a hand up the leg of her shorts, inside her knickers. His fingers explore her, gently, tantalisingly, until she can't take it any more. It's happening so fast. Faster than she imagined. Her face burns, her breath is coming out in small, jagged gasps.

'Can I . . . Are you ready?' Mark says. His voice is thick with lust.

'Yes. Please, yes. Have you . . . ?'

He pulls himself up onto his knees and takes a square foil packet from the pocket of his shorts, yanks her shorts down, her knickers going with them. She feels exposed, wants to cover herself up – but only for a moment. Then it passes. He looks down at her, and the look in his eyes is dark and delicious, and Laura thinks she might melt into the blanket. He pulls down his own shorts and his boxers . . . and he springs out. She's surprised at the size of it, at the colour of it . . . He rips the condom packet with his teeth, and rolls it in his fingers. Pulls it down in one swift, practised move. She knows he's done this before, but she doesn't care. She wants someone who knows what he's doing . . .

He leans forwards, places his hands at either side of her head, and kisses her again. She feels the tip of him pushing against her. He pulls away, just slightly, says, 'Are you ready? Are you sure?'

She makes sure she says it clearly, definitely: 'Yes.'

She'd thought she was ready, but she doesn't expect it to feel like this – like something too big for a small space, pushing through layers and barriers into a place it's not meant to go. There's a sharp pain, and then he pulls back a bit, slowly, carefully, before pushing back in. Then it's a delicious, numbing pain that sends her senses into overdrive. The movement, the feeling that she's doing something so intense, so . . . carnal. She lifts her legs and wraps them around his back and the feeling changes to something that she could never have imagined.

Mindy Heller hadn't told her about *this*.

It's over too soon. She was just warming up.

'Give it a few minutes, then we can do it again,' Mark says, panting. He's lying behind her, spooning her, a hand draped across her breasts.

Laura drops her hand down behind her, in between his legs.

'You sure you're not ready again, now?'

He leans in closer and starts to kiss the back of her neck. 'You're a wee nympho, aren't you? I fucking knew you would be.'

Laura flinches slightly at the change in his tone, but she's enjoying herself so she lets it pass.

15

She can't stay at home. She washes her face, brushes her teeth. Tries not to look at herself in the mirror.

The pub isn't busy when she arrives, which is unusual for this time on a Friday. But that's OK. It's busy enough to keep her distracted. Helen is delighted to leave.

'Feeling better, are we?' She looks Marie up and down, and Marie can tell that Helen knows that her illness was self-inflicted. Let her think that. She's right about the rum, but she doesn't know the reasons behind her drinking it. Fuck her.

'Have a nice evening,' Marie says, as Helen walks out of the door. 'Thanks for covering for me.'

'Nice work for some.' Sam is at the bar, a half-empty pint in front of him. It's not soda and lime.

'That didn't last long,' Marie says.

'It's Friday.'

'Take it easy, though, OK?'

'You might want to do the same. What's up, anyway? Not like you to phone in sick.'

'Yeah, well, just one of those days. I'm fine now. Thanks for asking.'

Marie leaves him to it and goes through to the other side, the lounge bar, where a few couples are sitting. The conversation is quieter through here. The music on low. Marie dims the lights, just a fraction.

'Ah, there you are!'

Bill appears from the kitchen with a box full of folded

napkins. He's wearing a pale blue shirt, buttoned to the top. His thick red neck bulges out above it.

'Sorry . . . I'm OK now. Thanks for getting Helen in.'

Bill lays the box of napkins on the serving hatch and walks behind the bar. He stands too close. He reeks of aftershave and Juicy Fruit chewing gum.

'Glad to have you back,' he says. He rubs a hand up and down her arm like he's trying to wipe chalk off a blackboard. 'Wendy is in at eight anyway. You can knock off again when she appears.'

'But—'

'No buts, my love. You look a bit peaky. Best you get some more rest, eh? Come back tomorrow.'

Bill disappears through to the public bar and she hears him greeting someone, laughing his braying laugh. Full of cheer.

She sighs. She doesn't want to go back home. Not yet.

Marie walks through to the kitchen to see who's on. Quinn, the chef, is at the far end of the kitchen, bent so deeply into the chest freezer that she can only see his legs in his black-and-white checks. She can hear boxes being shuffled and moved, swearing coming out through puffs of cold air.

Laura is in the middle of emptying the dishwasher, which is full of huge saucepans. Her face is flushed from the steamy air, and something else. She looks happy.

'Marie! Oh thank God you came in – I've got something huge to tell you.' The girl's eyes are shining; her young face is pink and damp.

'She's a dirty stop-out,' Quinn calls, from the freezer. His voice is muffled, his tone is deadpan.

'Shut up, you,' Laura shouts down the kitchen, trying to make herself heard over the noises of the extractor fan and the fryers.

'What is it?' Marie says, trying hard to sound enthusiastic.

'Well . . .' Laura picks up a tea towel and wipes it across her head. 'I've done it,' she whispers, leaning in close. 'With Mark.'

Marie is confused for a moment, and then she remembers. Yes, of course. Mark. The one that Laura has been pretending not to pine over for the last few weeks. She smiles at Laura, but she feels a sudden surge of rage course through her. Stupid girl. Stupid, stupid girl. *He will hurt you*, she thinks.

'Oh aye,' she says. 'Tell all . . .'

She swallows back bile as Laura tells her about their picnic down by the river. About how they'd 'done it' three times. About how Laura loved it. She glances round at Quinn, who is garnishing plates with little piles of salad. She sees the amused look on his face. Knows he's heard this story before. Probably more than once. He's a grumpy bastard at times, but he listens. He listens to everything.

'So he's coming to meet me tonight when I finish. Bill says I can have a shower upstairs. We're going back to the shows, and I'm going to tell that stupid fortune teller that she got it all wrong. Nothing bad is happening – it's all bloody ace. Silly cow.'

Laura is babbling away, and Marie finds herself tuning in and out of the conversation. She's about to say something, about to tell Laura that all she'll ever gain is disappointment. But she looks at the girl's eyes, and she can't do it.

'Well, lucky you, eh?' she says at last. 'He's a bit of a dish, that Mark.'

Laura laughs. 'Dish? No one says that any more.'

'What do you say, then?'

'He's hot.'

Quinn clears his throat. 'He's a ride. Do yous still say that? That'll be what he's saying to his mates about you now, anyway. "Right wee go'er, that one . . ."'

Marie turns to look at the chef. He's sliding fish onto plates.

There's a mischievous glint in his eye. He's joking, but what he says is true.

'Be careful, Laura.'

Laura throws a pot into the sink and it clatters against the sides, metal on metal. 'You two are just jealous 'cause you're not gettin' any.' She turns back to Marie and her smile has slipped, just a fraction. 'Anyway, it's not like that. He's not like that. We've fancied each other for ages. He's really nice, you know. You can see for yourself. He's coming in to pick me up at nine.'

'Better get on with they pots then, eh?' Quinn says. 'Service!' he shouts, raising his eyebrows at Marie.

Marie picks up two plates.

'Table 6,' Quinn shouts behind her, his voice fading as the swing door to the kitchen closes.

The bar is busier now. The drinkers have filled up the public bar. The place is littered with pints and crisps. The TV is switched to MTV. They're getting fired up. There is a steady hum of conversation in the lounge bar. The scrape of plates on cutlery. The occasional burst of laughter. The room smells of curry and chips.

Marie walks back through the service space and behind the bar. Wendy has already arrived for the late shift, and there's nothing left for her to do.

'Do you need me to stay?' she asks Bill.

Bill shakes his head. 'Go an' sit down and have a drink. Here . . .' he says. He shoves a small glass up under one of the optics. Repeats. Fires in some Coke from the gun. He slides the rum and Coke to the end of the bar, and Marie walks out and pulls out a stool. On the other side of the gap, Sam sits. He's still got half a pint in his glass, but Marie knows it's not the same one he was nursing earlier, before she went through to the kitchen. It hasn't had time to warm up yet. Condensation slips slowly down the outside of the glass.

'Davie was in here looking for you,' Sam says.

Marie takes a sip of the drink. It's not like her to drink like this. She can still taste it in the back of her throat from the night before. 'Oh aye. Did you not send him through to the kitchen?'

Sam downs his pint. Wipes his top lip. A smear of foam sits on the back of his hand. 'Sorry, I thought you'd gone home.'

Aye, right, Marie thinks.

She sighs. Takes another drink, then climbs off the stool to retrieve her handbag from where she's left it behind the bar. She checks her phone. Davie. 'Starting to think you're avoiding me.'

She texts back. 'I was in the kitchen.' Hesitates. 'Come back. Have a drink with me.'

He replies straight away. 'Can't now. With Ian. See you tomorrow?'

'Yes. Cool. Meet you at Landucci's for lunch?'

He replies again. 'Could do . . . Or maybe pop along to the shows? I fancy a toffee apple.'

Marie laughs, and Sam turns to look at her. She ignores him.

'Perfect. Meet you at the bridge at 1 x'

'See you then xx'

She tips back the rest of her drink just as Wendy appears through the gap from the other bar. 'Same again please, doll. Sam, another pint? My shout.'

Sam looks at his empty glass and pretends to consider it. 'Aye. Cheers.'

They chat about nothing. Marie feels the drink taking effect. Everything is a bit fuzzier around the edges. Nothing seems quite so bad any more. Fuck Graeme and his stupid letters.

She's not going to read them. She's going to take the whole lot out the back and burn them. Cadbury will like that. The cat has always had an obsession with flames, jumping excitedly when she flicks the gas on the stove. She'll do it when she gets home. Maybe just one more drink.

At nine o'clock, Laura appears. She smells of peaches and youth. Quinn must've let her away early so she could shower for her date. He's a grump, but he's a softie underneath.

'Excited?' Marie says.

Laura grins. 'What do you think? Erm, Marie . . . any chance you can sneak me a wee one in this?' She holds up her Coke glass.

'Sorry,' Marie says. 'I would, but it's too busy now. If Bill sees, he'll hit the roof.'

She watches as Laura glances around the bar. 'Aye. OK.' The girl's shoulders slump, just a bit. But then she's all smiles again when the door opens and a young man walks in. But then a girl follows, and Laura turns away.

'Fancy coming to this party, then?' Sam says.

Marie realises she's been dreaming. She's hardly aware of where she is. The sounds of chatter and the clink of glasses. The music pumping in the background. All a fuzz. A nice, nice fuzz.

She glances up at the clock. It's just gone nine thirty.

Laura is sitting at the edge of one of the long banquette seats. The glass of Coke is on the table beside her. The old men at the table are shuffling dominos and trying to get her involved, but she shakes her head. She must feel Marie staring at her. She turns, and Marie sees disappointment and embarrassment radiating off her.

She wants to say, 'See, I told you.' But instead she says, 'Want to come to a party with us?'

'No, thanks,' Laura says. She stands up, leaves the Coke on the table. 'I think I'll just go home.'

'Plenty more fish in the sea,' Sam says, as he stands, wobbling slightly. Marie punches him in the arm, then takes hold of him. They push through the small crowd to a few shouts of 'oi' and 'manners' and other pointless words that they will have already forgotten have left their lips.

'Shut up, Sam,' Marie says. 'Let's get ourselves to this party.'

17th July 2015

Dear Marie,

My scar hurts sometimes. Does yours? When I first moved here, it used to itch like mad. The doctor had a look at it. Said it was strange ... it had been healed for fourteen years by then. You could hardly see it — just a faint silvery squiggle. Much smaller than yours. He gave me some cream to rub onto it, and when I rubbed it I imagined that you were putting it on for me. I imagined your small, soft hands, running up and down my side. I hope yours hasn't given you any trouble. Like the doctor said, it's healed. Just a phantom itch. Just in my head.

Do you still swim, Marie? I long to swim, but there's no pool here. There was talk of them getting one installed once, but I think it was just that. Talk. I try to talk to the workers as much as I can. Try to get all the gossip. It's so dull here, otherwise. I'm sick of playing games. Ludo, Scrabble, Battleships. Monopoly — monotony, more like. I spend a lot of time in the library. They've got computers in there now. Some rich relative donated them, apparently. They don't let us use the internet, though. Not unless someone is watching.

There is always someone watching, Marie.

Can you imagine how that feels?

Please write.

Even just one word.

Just a hello.

Love,

Graeme

16

'You are a fucking idiot,' Laura mutters to herself. 'Total. Fucking. Idiot.'

She leaves the pub and heads towards the High Street. She's only texted him once – thank God – at 9.15, saying 'Where are you? xx'

He didn't reply. She told herself he was just running late, that he'd burst in any minute with some mad story about what had happened and where he'd been and why he was late. Then she flitted to panic. *What if he's been run over? What if he's been mugged?*

Eventually she got it . . . *What if he's not coming?*

Bingo.

'Stupid cow,' she says. She stops next to a plastic bin at the end of the street and kicks it. Hard. Not a stupid girly kick. She steps back, raises her arms into fists in a proper defensive stance, swings a sharp roundhouse kick about three-quarters of the way up and knocks the bin head clean off the top. Chip wrappers and drinks cans scatter across the pavement.

Goody Goody Laura. Nice little swot Laura. She gets good grades, she does her homework. She goes to karate three times a week. She volunteers at the library on a Saturday morning and reads stories to little kids. Laura is nice, Laura is lovely, isn't she? That's what everyone says. And today – finally today – she decides to shake that off. She does something brave, and crazy and stupid. She does something that everyone else in her year has already done. And she thinks that, yes, now she's just like everyone else.

Then she gets stood up.

What a fucking fool! Why did she think that Mark was different to every other boy in their school? And worst of all, why the hell had she told Hayley? She imagines that the news has already spread. She imagines that everyone already knows what she's done.

She stares at the overturned bin. Her first instinct is to pick it up, shove the rubbish back inside, replace the lid. No one has seen her, have they? There might be a CCTV camera on the corner, but she doubts it can see where she is now. Besides, what are they going to do? It's only a bin. It's only some rubbish.

Screw it.

She storms past, kicking a plastic bag filled with something soft that is probably dog shit into the air, and heads down the High Street. There aren't many people about – probably because they're all either in the pub, at the scuzzy party that Marie was on her way to or, more likely, down at the shows. Where she is supposed to be right now. With Mark.

Fuck you, Mark.

She stops and sits down on the steps of one of the dilapidated tenements that line the street. She takes deep breaths, tries to push the rage away. Laura isn't someone to fly into a rage. She's a well-mannered, good-natured girl. So everyone keeps saying. School reports. Her nan. Her mum. What do they know? She's changed today. She's not the same person any more. She's given a part of herself away to someone, someone she thought was special. And that person has chosen to humiliate her in return.

'Well, I'm not having it,' she says. She stands up. Down at the bottom of the street there is only one shop with its lights still on. She marches down there. Kicking at stones and any other pieces of debris that get in her way. Her face is burning. Her hands tight from balling them into fists.

She takes a deep breath before she walks in. Tries to keep

calm. She places a bottle of sparkling wine on the counter, takes a fiver out of her purse. The guy serving is two years above her. He's just left school. He tried to chat her up once, at a party at some random house out in the country. A thing in a barn where the hippy parents let the kids do what they like as long as they didn't start any fights. She rebuffed him, but gently. He still smiled when he passed her in the street. She's kicking herself now, because she can't remember his name.

'I need to ask you for ID,' he says; he's trying to look serious, but there's a smile threatening to escape. He knows she's not eighteen.

'You can just say you've seen it,' Laura says, trying to smile.

He nods and puts the wine in a bag. Rings it up in the till and gives her 50p change. 'You OK, Laura? I, er . . . I don't think I've seen you in here before.'

'I'm fine,' she snaps. Takes a breath. Smiles again, although it feels like an effort to move her lips upwards even a fraction. 'Thanks for this. Totally fine. I'm going to the shows. Might see you later.' A bell above the door tinkles as she leaves. He might've said something else as she left, but she's too preoccupied to hear it.

A hump-backed bridge crosses the river over to the common land where the fairground lies. There is a small dirt path that leads down to the river. Laura has never been there at night before, and she realises that there is no street lighting that covers the small patch of land down there. She tries not to think about what might be down there. Used needles, used condoms . . . cans and bottles. Broken glass. Hopefully that's it for the riverside props. Hopefully there are no people down there, because that's the only thing she really wants to avoid right now.

She walks carefully down the path, feeling the edge of the

bridge with one hand to guide her down. The stone is cold and slimy. The path feels dry. The loose dirt makes it slippery. *Don't fall. Don't fucking fall.* At the bottom, she finds a space on the low wall that lines the river and sits down. She unscrews the bottle. She glances up towards the street above, wonders if anyone can see her. Fuck it. She takes a long, slow drink. The wine is cold, and the bubbles catch in her throat. She stops, coughs. Savours the unfamiliar flavour on her tongue. She's had wine before. Just a little bit, now and then. Mostly when she's with her parents, having one of those excruciatingly awkward Sunday lunches. This wine is slightly drier than she's used to. Sour, like unripe berries. But it's not that unpleasant. She's already getting used to it. She has no idea how much she needs to drink to get drunk. But she can already feel it fizzing through her, hitting her stomach. The fluttering in her chest. Her head feels fuzzy. She takes another drink.

When the bottle is finished, she throws it under the bridge and hears it smash as it collides with a rock. She stands, and then realises that the alcohol has already made its way to her legs, helped along the way by the adrenalin from her rage. She feels herself stagger slightly, reaches a hand out to the wall of the bridge again. Slowly, she walks back up to the street.

She can hear the sounds of the shows now, not far. The lights are flashing red, blue, white. A laser searches across the thick, black sky. It's late now. It's dark. Navy-blue dark. She walks towards the lights.

He's there, standing next to the Waltzer. Standing with that creep from the other day. She squints. Someone else is there too. A girl, hanging off the two of them. Cuddled up to Mark. Her Mark.

She recognises the dress. The long boots. Pink highlights flashing in her hair. It's Hayley. Mark is with Hayley. This . . . this is not right. This was not supposed to happen. Why did she tell Hayley she wanted to sleep with Mark? Stupid. Stu. Pid.

Laura takes a couple more steps forward, then stops. Hayley is pointing at her. The fairground boy – Gaz? Was that his name? – nudges her and they tip back their heads and laugh. Mark catches her eye, looks away. He turns and vanishes into the crowd.

She opens her mouth, wants to shout out his name. But her mouth has gone dry. Her head is whirling. The music is vibrating across the field and into her body. The lights are flashing too bright, too fast. Epileptic. She staggers backwards. Turns away. Lurches back across the field, away from the sounds of humiliating laughter that drift through the air like an angry cloud.

17

The sun has dipped to an eerie twilight. Marie holds onto Sam's arm, and the pair of them weave through imaginary obstacles along the High Street. They cut up onto the back street, which is deserted.

'Thanks for coming with me,' Sam says. He pulls on her arm and they stop in the street at the entrance to an alleyway that leads up to the back of a row of houses where she can already hear the faint sounds of a thumping bass.

'I need this,' she says. She doesn't elaborate. Squeezes his arm.

The back gate is unlatched and they pass a small huddle of people smoking in the corner of the back garden. The back door of the house is open, light spills out from inside. They've had a barbecue, she notices. The small drum is blackened from where someone has doused the coals with water to put it out. The smell of scorched meat hangs in the air. Music pumps outside. Something dancey that she vaguely recognises.

'Sam . . . Marie . . .' A figure stumbles down the back steps. 'Nice to see yous. Hope you didn't bring anything. There's enough booze in there to sink a battleship. Jack's been on the rob at Costco again.' Laughter from the small crowd of smokers.

The man who greets them is carrying a can of cheap Polish lager. He's grinning.

'All right, Scott,' Marie says. 'What's happening?'

She feels Sam pull away from her grip, and she feels wobbly for a second, not realising that they'd been supporting each other as much as they had. She watches as he stumbles across the grass, attempting to stay on the overgrown path.

'Funny, we were just talking about you,' Scott says.

'Who was?'

'Me and Leanne. We were saying, can't believe we've known you all this time and we never even knew you had a brother.'

Marie feels the earth tilt beneath her. She stops walking. 'What did you say?'

'Didn't have you pegged as a Twitterer, either. I don't really get it myself . . . prefer Facebook. Is Twitter not just for trolling celebs and reading about *X-Factor* contestants?' He's about to say more when a shrill voice yells at him from the back door.

'Scott, come in here! Jack needs you to fix this fucking stereo.'

Marie opens her mouth to speak, but Scott has already gone back inside. The call of his girlfriend is not something he's going to ignore. Why he has to fix the stereo, Marie has no idea. But that doesn't matter now.

She feels sober. As if someone has thrown a bucket of cold water in her face. She balls her hands into fists. Feels her nails cutting into her palms. She follows him inside. *Get a grip, Marie. It's nothing. He can't know. No one knows.* She's made sure of that. And what was he babbling on about Twitter? She's never been on Twitter. Like Scott said, she'd never got the point. He must've made a mistake. Someone with a similar name, maybe. It was nothing . . . It couldn't be. Just a weird coincidence. Just like the Lego . . . and the feeling of being watched. *And the letters, Marie . . . don't forget the letters.* A small chill runs through her. She walks inside.

The air is thick with sweat. Bodies are packed close. In the hall. In the sitting room. In the kitchen. She squeezes her way through the crowd. Feels eyes on her. Girls looking down their noses, men smirking. Paranoid. *You're paranoid,* she thinks. *Too much to drink.* She pushes her way into the kitchen. She hardly recognises anyone. These are not regulars from the Rowan Tree. These are people who drink in the other pubs in town. The ones that don't have any rules. The ones that let anyone in, even if they've started fights and knocked people out with pool cues.

This was a mistake.

She manages to find her way to the kitchen sink. Tries to block out the noise. Music and laughing and screeching. Where's Sam? She wishes she hadn't come. There are a couple of glasses next to the sink. She picks up a pint glass, sniffs it. Turns on the cold tap and rinses it. Again. Fills it with water and gulps it down, trying to stop herself from shaking.

She needs to find Scott, ask him what he meant.

She fills the glass again and gulps down another pint of water. Her head is suddenly clear. She needs to stop drinking. Stop denying it. Something is going on. Graeme has sent her a letter. They've had no contact for twenty-five years. She can't keep pretending that it doesn't mean something. He's out. He must be.

He was never supposed to get out.

'Quick ... someone ... help!' A young girl in a tight blue dress fires into the kitchen as if propelled. Her face is fear. Frantic. 'Quick ... come on – it's Harry. He's having a fit or something. Fuck!' The last word is drawn out into a long, bellowing cry. The crowd in the kitchen shrinks back like a retreating tide. The girl is staring straight at Marie. *Please,* her eyes say. *Please.*

Marie blinks. Wakes up. 'Show me.'

The girl grabs her by the hand and drags her through the hall to the living room. The music has stopped. People spin out of the way like skittles. Shocked faces. No one knows what to do.

Someone – Harry – is lying on the floor in the centre of the living room. A small crowd has formed around him as if he's attempting some weird party piece for their entertainment. Someone is crying. Harry is convulsing, his body rising and falling in the middle of the floor. He looks like he's being electrocuted. A line of foamy vomit leaks from the side of his mouth. His eyes are turned back inside his head, stark white orbs bulging out of his bright-red face.

The crowd has gone into shock.

'Someone call an ambulance,' Marie says. She tries to keep her voice calm. No need to shout – an eerie silence has fallen over the room, except for the muted sounds of sobs.

'What's he taken?' she says. She kneels down next to the young man's body, takes hold of his hand. 'Harry! Can you hear me? Try to relax. Try to calm down.' She has no idea what she's doing. She's never seen someone have a fit before. Maybe on TV, but nothing she can recall. She assumes it will stop, eventually. Or else he'll die. But she doesn't know what will happen in between. 'Has someone called an ambulance?' she repeats.

Someone from the crowd replies. 'No ambulance.'

No one else speaks.

Fuck, Marie thinks. 'Fuck,' she says. 'Look, it doesn't matter what shit he's taken, but if you don't call an ambulance he's probably going to fucking die. Do you all want that on your conscience?'

A murmur from the crowd. She hears the beeps of someone pressing keys on a phone. An argument. More beeps. She tunes them out. She keeps hold of Harry's hand. 'Come on, Harry,' she whispers. 'Someone give me a cushion.' She stretches out a hand and someone hands her a cushion. She lifts Harry's head gently, lays the cushion underneath.

She squeezes his hand. His convulsions are getting smaller, spaced wider apart. She watches as they slowly fade to nothing. A final twitch. Then he is still. 'I need a cloth,' she says. Another wordless delivery. She takes the corner of the cloth and wipes gently at his face, removing the vomit. Then she lays a hand over his chest. His heart is thumping hard, but slowly. She leans her face down to his. Feels his faint breath on her cheek.

'He's alive,' she states. There are some relieved breaths. More murmurs. Still, no one has come to help. Eventually, someone crouches down beside her. A young man she vaguely recognises. Thinks he might be one of those who pops into the Rowan Tree on his way elsewhere. Quiet. She doesn't know his name. 'Can you help me turn him?' she says. The young man helps. They turn Harry onto his side, remove the cushion so his mouth is tilted downwards, in case he is sick again. She carefully folds one leg, one arm, until he is in a sideways reaching pose. She's not sure if it's quite the recovery position, but it's close. His airways are free. His limbs are in a comfortable position. She strokes his back. Whispers to him. Reassures him.

'The ambulance is on its way,' a voice from the back says. The crowd has begun to disperse. *Go home,* she thinks. *Think about this.* She notices something sticking out of the pocket of Harry's jeans. A small plastic bag.

The young man who helped her sees that she's seen it. 'Maybe I should—' He reaches towards the pocket, but Marie pushes his hand away.

'No. Maybe *I* should. No one will think to ask me.'

The young man nods. 'OK.'

'What's your name?' Marie asks.

'Lee. That was my girlfriend who came and got you. Lauren. In the blue dress? Thanks . . . Harry's my best mate. I didn't know what to do. Stupid, eh?'

Marie isn't sure what to say, but she's stopped from having to think of something as Harry coughs, and vomits up a small pool of white lumps. He murmurs something. Not words. More like a groan.

'You're OK, Harry,' Marie says. She rubs his back again. Drifting in from the back door, she catches the sound of a siren on the breeze. *Not long now,* she thinks. Hopes. He needs to be checked over, fast. She's worried about the slow heart rate. The shallow breathing. She doesn't say anything. Doesn't want to cause alarm. She glances up and sees Sam watching her from the doorway.

'Want to go home?' he says.

'Don't we have to wait? What about the police?'

'No police,' she hears someone say from the kitchen.

'The police will be here. It's a suspicious event.'

'It's an accident.'

She looks down at him again. Runs her hand down his back. 'You'll be OK,' she says. Slides her hand over the back of his jeans. Gently, she tugs the plastic bag out of his pocket. Rolls it inside her palm.

She stands up.

'Come on,' Sam says. He gestures towards the back door. 'They'll come round the front. No one will say you were here. You don't want mixed up in this shit.'

She nods. Lets Sam take her by the hand, and they run down the back path and out the gate, head up the alleyway in the opposite way from the sirens. They're screeching now. Close. *He's right,* she thinks. She doesn't want to be mixed up with something like this. She has enough to worry about. When they are far enough away, Sam stops. 'I'll let you go your own way from here,' he says. He leans in and kisses her on the cheek. 'You did great in there.'

Marie walks home. Her hand still gripping the plastic bag, so tight she thinks she might never be able to uncurl it. She tries to let her mind slow down. Takes a breath. Starts to count. Then a memory spikes her inside. *Can't believe we've known you all this time and we never even knew you had a brother . . .*

How? she thinks. *How did they find out?*

18

You could always rely on Ian to cheer you up when you were feeling down. Davie didn't see as much of his friend as he should, and the night they'd just had, just the two of them – watching *Ice Road Truckers*, getting excited about Ian's vinyl imports, not talking about anything of importance – it was exactly what he needed. He'd been tempted to ask Anne about Marie, try to find out if she'd said anything. Try to understand why she seemed to be getting cold feet so soon, and seemingly doing all she could to avoid him. But he didn't want to ruin the night, plus Anne had gone out to the cinema and she wasn't back before Davie had left.

Back home now, in his own house, the thoughts he had pushed away come back to him. He'd even popped in to see Marie at work earlier but found that she'd been and gone. Or at least that's what they said in the bar. Maybe she was hiding from him there too. Davie might not be the best with women, but he really couldn't work out what he might've done wrong.

They'd gone out for a drink the night after a great evening round at Ian and Anne's. They're moving house, and it was the last time they'd be having a dinner party there, so the four of them had made sure it went with a bang. They'd managed to drink most of Ian's wine collection, which was good at the time but not so much fun the next day. He'd had the day off though, thankfully, and when he'd met Marie that night she'd been in good spirits, carrying on from the night before. They'd gone to the cinema a few days later. All very civilised.

He'd kissed her, and had felt no resistance. But when he'd suggested she stay the night at his she'd pulled away.

'Next time, Davie,' she'd said. 'It's been a while for me. I want to get this right.'

'It's been a while for me too,' he'd said. 'But I hope it's true what they say – that it's like riding a bike . . .'

She'd laughed at his joke. Pretended to be outraged. Let him squirm when he'd tried to explain that he meant you never forgot how to do it . . . not that he was implying she was a bike. She'd laughed even harder the more he dug himself a hole.

He'd thought there was something there.

But ever since then she'd been ignoring his calls. Avoiding his texts. She finally texted him back after he'd missed her in the pub. But it was too late by then. He was already at Ian's, and he wasn't going to ditch his mate for a woman. Especially not one who was blowing so hot and cold.

Davie likes to think of himself as the sensitive sort. He has good relationships with women. They talk to him. Which is why this thing with Marie is really irking him. He senses that something is going on with her, but he doesn't want to push. Anyway, she's agreed to meet him tomorrow, so maybe he'll get a bit more insight then. If not, it could be time to cut his losses.

Going to see the woman in hospital with Malkie has shaken him. But he realises now that it wasn't because he had strong feelings for Marie like that, it was more the thought of something so horrific happening to someone he knows. There's been enough of that lately.

He fires up his computer and makes himself a coffee. He doesn't need to do this tonight, but he's curious. These herbal highs that he's been looking into at work. It's a bit of a summer phenomenon. Long hot nights, parties, that feeling people get in the summertime – like they have more freedom – not like the dark, miserable winters where you sink into depression and barely leave your house.

The thing that has come up in most of the searches is called Krackoff. Some bright spark came up with that name – probably felt quite pleased with himself. Davie's searched on the internet and found that it's quite easy to get hold of. It's described as a mixture of nutmeg, hogweed and other herbal ingredients, and it's meant to give the user a 'mild sensation of floating' when taken in the correct quantities. However, there are no suggested quantities provided, and a search through various drugs forums has yielded some more sinister results.

BlowBoy19: This drug does nothing on its own, and must be mixed with H@PEE to have any sort of decent effect. Unfortunately, it's almost impossible to buy H@PEE ready made, due to some of the components being illegal, namely ephedrine, which is banned in the UK (and most other places too). There's a workaround but it takes a bit of time. If you really want to take this shit, it might be worth finding some other likeminded folks and clubbing together to make a batch of something as close to H@PEE as you can get.

The_Bong: It can't be that hard. You got a recipe or what, bro?

BlowBoy19: Try this <u>link</u> and let us know how you get on.

PashaQueen: You can make an ephedrine substitute using wicks from Benzedrex inhalers. You have to order them from the States, but I don't think they're illegal.

PashaQueen: Sorry, clicked too soon. Amazon does them. Then you need to extract the compound. I think you boil them in lemon juice. I've never done it, but I know some people who have and they said that mixed in with the smashed up Krackoff pills is better than the real thing.

Davie scrolls down. There are forty-two pages of this stuff, and this is only one of the forums. There are endless anecdotes about people mixing stuff with various juices to be able to swallow it, as apparently it has the most disgusting taste ever – the bloggers compare it to cow shit, dog shit . . . just generic shit, in fact. He can't understand why anyone would force something so disgusting into their bodies. Is it really worth all that effort? He's about to shut down for the night when he finds a final post, right at the end. Page 42. It is the newest one, but the posts are sorted the other way. He realises he's been reading stuff from five years ago. This one's from a few months ago. It is what he needs.

Dre@mCaster: Stop mixing up those rank potions, dudes. There is a better way. Working with a good friend of mine who did chemistry at uni, we've found a way to make this stuff more palat-able. We've made it into tablets – Krackoff plus H@PEE. We've made a load, and we're looking for volunteers to test it out for us. So far we don't know how potent it is, and we don't know if it reacts with other stuff, so, not that we're going to make you sign a disclaimer or anything, but it's potentially risky . . . but then I don't think anyone on this forum is scared to take a bit of a risk, are they? PM me for more info.

There are twenty-seven 'thumbs-ups' on the comment. Davie feels a prickling under his skin. Is this it? He needs to call Malkie. Get the IT guys to take a proper look. They have experts for this sort of thing – dealing with forums and fake IDs, finding people through their ISPs.

He glances up at the clock. Well, it's a start anyway. This, plus the list of recent overdoses and the two deaths that he's pinned down to a thirty-mile radius . . . it's definitely something. He's quite enjoying this side of the work. He wonders if Malkie will let him sit in at the IT suite, see what they get up to in there. It's nearly ten o'clock. Too late to call? ·

He picks up his phone, scrolls through the contacts until he finds Malkie, and just as he's about to hit 'dial' the phone starts vibrating. An icon-sized version of Malkie's face pops up on the screen.

'Christ, talk of the devil. I was just about to call you. I think I've found something with our drugs.'

'Right, aye. Good. I'm calling about something else, though. The Jane Doe at the hospital? She's woken up. She's not said much yet, still drowsy and a bit out of it. They let me in for a few minutes but she wasn't able to tell me who she is.'

'That's good, though. Sounds like she's going to pull through.'

'Aye. Anyway, that's not what I was calling to tell you either. We've got a suspect for her attack. You know where we found her? Up at that farm in between Dalkeith and Ormiston? Well, we think now that she'd been waiting for the bus, but we don't know if she lives round there – which is unlikely, as there aren't that many houses and she doesn't look like a farmer – or if she was coming back from seeing someone round there. Only we've gone round the houses, and no one seems to know her. There's one house where no one's answered. We think they might be on holiday. We're trying to contact them. Asking them if maybe she's their housekeeper or something.'

'That'd make sense.'

'It would. Aye. Also, did ye ken there was a mental hospital out that way? I didn't, to be honest. It's not on the map. They like to keep these things secret, I suppose. It's on the NHS Trust website, though – but the location is a bit vague. I asked the guy in the farm about it, the one where the woman was found. He was angry. Said there was probably some nutter on the loose again. Well, he was right.'

'Mental hospital? As in psychiatric patients. Like Carstairs?'

'Yes, but not so secure. Medium and low risk. Anyway, they rang. There was a message for me when I got back to the station. Turns out they *do* have a missing inmate. They were being a bit cagey. Trying to downplay it. They said he wasn't dangerous . . . *any more.*'

'Christ . . .'

'Oh yes, they're going to be in some deep shit over this. There are protocols to be followed. Someone slipped up, badly. There'll be an investigation. Meanwhile, our man is still missing. They kept repeating that he's not dangerous. They sounded nervous. I got the impression that they think he's still high risk. Heads are going to roll. Looks like our Jane Doe was in the wrong place at the wrong time. I'm sending you a link to the main article. It's the ones beneath that are most interesting.'

Malkie hangs up and a moment later an email pings through on Davie's phone. He clicks on the link and the headline screams at him: SCHIZOPHRENIC TEEN MUTILATES TEENAGE GIRL.

'Fuck.' He closes his eyes.

Dear Marie,

OK, I get it. You're ignoring me. I can't blame you, I suppose. We haven't spoken for a while. A long while. Too long. We have to get to know each other again. I thought of something that might help. I've done something for you. It's a surprise. I'm not sure when I'll be able to share it with you, but it was just something I thought you might like. My wee friend in here did it for me. She did lots of things for me. You might think it was just because she felt sorry for me, but there was more to it than that. You know what I mean, don't you, Marie? Anyway. I'm not the same person any more. I don't feel like the same person. I know you didn't like it when I smoked too much weed. Do they still call it that? We don't have that here. Plenty of other stuff. Better stuff, some would say. But it's not for me. I'm clean now. I've got my ways of dealing with it. You think it's hard to hide stuff behind your tongue while they shine their little torch in there and see if you've swallowed it. They even use one of those little wooden sticks, like a lolly stick. But like I said. There are ways.

I chose one of the back molars. Not the one right at the back, because when you take those ones out the gum grows up around the others and there's no hole any more. I took one second from the back, right side, same as my scar. I was always on the right, you were always on the left. Remember? Do you have someone else on your right now, Marie? Do they hug you as tight as I did? Do you want them to? Anyway, in case you were wondering, yes, it does hurt when you pull out a tooth. I wiggled it and wiggled it, but it wouldn't budge. Apparently the roots of molars can be 3cm long. Can you believe that? Like little vines, gripping down inside your throat, anchoring themselves on the bones.

They let me have floss because I told them I didn't want my teeth falling out. They watch you floss, but sometimes you can break a piece off, keep it in your mouth. I had enough after a while to make a proper loop. I twisted it round and round. Day after day, night after night. It got looser and looser until I was able to get a grip of it. I didn't expect the pain. I had to swallow some of their drugs to deal with that. Set me back a few days. Made me numb again. But I got there in the end. I always do, don't I, Marie? Now I've got a perfect little gap to store their drugs and they don't even know. They stop paying so much attention after a while. New people start. They don't know what to look for. They don't know how clever I am.

I do remember the blood. There was so much blood.

It reminded me of that day. The way I left you.

What happened to you, Marie? What did you make me do? I should never have left you. I know that now.

That was wrong of me, Marie.

Forgive me.

Love,

Graeme

19

Marie sits in the darkness. Moonlight slices through the blinds. She heard the familiar sounds of the cat leaping out through the open kitchen window when she closed the front door. She's alone. Her heart is thudding hard in her chest. She remembers the boy on the floor – Harry – how his heartbeat had been deep, but slow. She hopes he'll be OK. Knows she should have stayed, but glad she didn't.

She stuffs the plastic bag full of what she assumes are drugs into the back of the cupboard above the sink. The pile of letters falls out, skittering across the worktop, into the sink, onto the floor. She ignores them. Opens the next cupboard. Only wine left now. White. It'll be warm, but it'll do.

She kicks the letters across the floor. Unscrews the cap. Pours herself a large glassful. Not a wine glass, a thick tumbler. She doesn't feel the need for niceties. This is supposed to be a nice wine, she remembers. One that Anne brought her from her last trip to France. Her and Ian go over a couple of times a year to restock their supplies. Whenever they come back, Ian starts the same old debate about screw tops not being as good as corks, and Anne and Marie roll their eyes. Marie couldn't care less what was used to keep the bottle sealed. She's just happy now that she doesn't have to look for a corkscrew.

At the kitchen table, Marie flips open her laptop. She waits for it to boot up. Taking forever in the lonely night. She takes a sip of the wine. Grimaces. Maybe not so nice, then. Maybe a coffee would be better for this. The light from outside has moved, just a fraction. Clouds crossing the moon. Some of the letters are highlighted in a muted glow, the others are dull. She gets out of her seat, turns the laptop round the other way, then goes and sits at the other side of the table.

The letters are behind her now. She can pretend they aren't there.

Once the Windows screen has done its thing, and the various pop-ups have been closed down, she clicks on Internet Explorer and a browser window appears. Marie has a Facebook account, but she rarely goes on there. She has nothing particularly interesting to share with her handful of Facebook friends, and she's not particularly interested in reading about people's gripes and moans, bitching about each other – or the other lot, the ones who post pics of their kids eating breakfast. Fascinating. She's thought about deleting her account before, but it hardly seems to be worth the effort. They don't want you to delete your account. They try to make it as difficult as possible.

As for Twitter, she's looked at it once. Anne called her one night when there was a documentary on about people dressed in animal masks going dogging in the woods. Apparently the Twitter commentary was even better than the show. She'd enjoyed it that night – felt like she was part of a community, all thinking the same thing – but she hadn't set up an account and she'd never been on the site again. She had even less to say to strangers than she did to her own friends and acquaintances.

It seemed you could no longer browse properly without a login, though. A Twitter handle – was that what it was called? She wants to ditch it. Give up. What's the point? It clearly isn't her on there, but she's curious to know who Scott has been reading about.

She starts to set up an account – like Facebook. It's not like she has to use it if she doesn't want to. She starts with her name: MarieBloomfield – too boring? It's the obvious choice, though. She types it in. 'Sorry – this username already exists.' It gives her a few suggestions for alternatives. She scratches the back of her head. Takes another sip of wine. It doesn't taste so bad this time. OK, so maybe her name isn't that unique after all. She settles on 'MarieBloom', decides against adding a picture. Does the minimum amount of set-up. She's in.

Suggestions appear of whom she might like to follow. Celebrities. Reality TV stars. Footballers. Footballers' wives. Alan Sugar. Jeez. Is this what people do on here? She clicks on a couple of the reality TV stars and can barely understand what they're saying, what with all the links and the heart emoticons and all the bloody hashtags. Everyone is called 'babes'. *Cheers babes, love you babes, miss you babes.*

So far, so pointless.

OK . . . so let's see who shares my name then. Who Scott thought was me. I suppose, if there's no photo, he wouldn't know, would he?

She types 'MarieBloomfield' into the search box. A few people appear. Some have variations of the name, some with numbers on the end, in the middle, using a 1 to replace the 'i'. Various tiny photos of people, animals, things like books. Slogans. The one she wants is at the top, the one with her actual name. She clicks.

The profile window pops up.

Marie takes a breath. 'No. It can't be.'

The image in the background is of a yellow wicker window box filled with daisies and busy lizzies. A small green windmill stuck in the soil at one side. She closes her eyes, hopes that when she opens them again the image will be gone. It's still there. A breeze starts up from nowhere. She turns around slowly, towards the kitchen window – left open six inches at the bottom for Cadbury to come in and out. Even in the darkness, she can see the yellow wicker shining in the moonlight. The small green windmill is whirling gently. She feels like a weight is pressing down on her shoulders, crushing her into the chair. There is half a glass of wine left – she picks it up, notices her hand is shaking. Downs the wine, barely tasting it, lets it hit the back of her throat. She feels the warmth start to spread through her.

She turns back to the screen, looks at the profile picture. Takes a closer look. Sees a child. A girl's face, with part of another face squeezed up next to her, but cropped out of the photo. Waves of panic run up and down her body. She scrolls up and down the page, but there are no tweets. There is nothing. Just the photo of her window box – which she knows is recent, because of the flowers. She only dug it out last week, tidied it up. She recognises the girl in the photograph now, and the piece of the face that is touching hers. She's not smiling. She looks scared, distracted. She remembers when it was taken. They were at the seaside with their parents. They were eleven. Graeme wanted a photo in the booth as a souvenir. When the curtain was closed, he ran a hand up her bare leg. When the flash pinged, blinding them both momentarily, his finger was under the elastic of her knickers.

'Not here,' she'd said to him. 'What if someone sees?'

'What if I want someone to see?' he'd said. He'd kissed her on the ear.

She stares at the laptop screen. There is a little padlock. 'Marie Bloomfield's tweets are protected. Please follow to request access to this user's timeline.'

She clicks the padlock. Waits. Pours another glass of wine.

There's a faint scraping sound upstairs. She looks up at the ceiling. Sees the light fitting shudder. She keeps staring at the ceiling, as if expecting a trapdoor to open and someone to jump right through. He can't be up there. He's locked up. He's never allowed to get out. If he had got out, they'd have called

111

her, wouldn't they? Someone would've warned her. He's not allowed near her. She doesn't want to see him. She stares at the little padlock. Refreshes the screen.

Still locked.

Someone is playing some sort of sick joke on her. Scott? Although why he would do that, she has no idea. Maybe it was a dare. Something stupid. The side gate isn't locked. Anyone could've taken a photo of her window box. The photo of her and Graeme, though . . . she can't explain that. She has two photos from the strip of four. They are in a box with a load of other photos under her bed. She doesn't look at them. Graeme has the other two – well, she assumes he does. If he took anything with him when they sent him away.

She refreshes the screen again. The account is still locked. She looks up at the ceiling. All is quiet. Maybe she imagined it. Maybe she's going mad. She drains the rest of the wine from her glass and snaps the laptop shut. Maybe she'll look at it tomorrow. Maybe she won't. She stands, wobbles slightly. Rights herself by laying a hand on the back of the chair. The letters are still where she left them – scattered across the worktop. In the sink. On the floor.

Tomorrow she will put them all in the metal bin in the garden and burn them without reading them. Then she will phone the hospital where her brother has been locked up for the last twenty-five years . . . and make sure he is still there.

20

Davie is sitting on the bridge when he spots Marie in the distance. He waves, but her head is down. She looks like she's reading something on her phone. It's a scorcher of a day. After a night of thunder and lightning, the air has cleared and the sun is beating down. Davie's dressed casually, in a pair of long shorts and a white polo shirt. He's double-sprayed himself with deodorant, hoping that the Lynx effect isn't just a myth. Marie is dressed in tight black jeans and a fitted black T-shirt with a purple tartan collar. Her hair is neatly combed, and she's got a small red bag slung across her shoulder. She's already dropped her phone into the bag by the time she reaches him.

She stands on tiptoes and kisses him on the cheek. He feels the stickiness of her lipstick, freshly applied. She smells of herbal soap and talc. Davie feels a sudden rush of happiness. She's made an effort for him. Maybe it's not over yet. He wants to tell her about the woman in the hospital, about how scared he was when he thought it might be her.

Instead, he says, 'You smell gorgeous.'

'So do you,' she replies, leaning in to his chest, sniffing at him. She steps back and beams up at him.

He feels a moment of panic. Her smile is there, but her eyes are dull, red-rimmed. She looks like she's been crying.

'Everything OK? I've been trying to speak to you for days. Seem to keep missing you. All OK at work?'

She waves a hand, dismissing him. 'Let's walk. Work's the same old. Nothing to report. Bill still likes to stand too close.

Wendy is still a pain in the arse. Helen's tops are still too tight. Blah blah. Oh, one thing though – wee Laura seems to have found herself a boyfriend. Getting serious by the sounds of it. I tried to tell her to ease up, but you know what it's like.'

'Young love, eh? I can barely remember.'

Davie remembered his first love like it was yesterday. They'd never even got together properly, and now she was long gone. He still thought about her. He'd never been able to find someone to fill the gap she'd left in his life when she chose someone else over him, leading to a life of unhappiness for them both. Not to mention what it did to her daughter. Talking of which, he was expecting a call from Jo soon. He'd become a sort of official guardian to her of late. The judge had been lenient because of her circumstances. She was getting weekly counselling inside. She'd need that indefinitely. There aren't many people who can kill someone in self-defence and escape mentally unscathed. Especially when they weren't the most stable of people in the first place. Being in prison wasn't the worst place for her at the moment. She wouldn't be there forever.

They walk silently, both lost in their own thoughts. Davie reaches out a hand and is glad when Marie takes it. Her hand is so small inside his own. He squeezes it, and she squeezes back. He knows she's keeping something to herself, and he's not going to push it.

The sounds of the fairground drift across the expanse of grass towards them. Davie feels a small flutter of excitement. He's glad to be walking here, hand in hand with Marie, but he's thinking about something else too. He's waiting for Malkie to get back to him on his theory about the drugs being transported from town to town by someone connected to the fair, but while he's here he's hoping to have a good snout about.

As they cut through between the Waltzer and the Dodgems, a teenage boy and girl come barrelling towards them from under the flap of a tent. They're giggling, grabbing at each other. Davie vaguely recognises the girl. He's seen her with Laura once or twice. Heidi or Hannah. Something like that.

'Having fun, Hayley?' Marie calls as they run off round the back of the stalls. The girl turns and waves. She has a pink streak in her hair that Davie quite likes. The boy turns and gives them a sneering grin. 'She hangs about with Laura sometimes,' Marie explains. 'Did you see who she was with?'

Davie shakes his head. 'No, didn't recognise him.'

'He was in the pub the other day. He's one of the fairground lads. I'm not one to judge, but he's a dodgy-looking sort. That girl wants to be careful.'

Davie watches as the couple disappear in behind another of the rides. Interesting, he thinks. Clearly a charmer, if he's picked up one of Laura's friends after only being here a few days.

Marie has dropped Davie's hand and she now has both hands shoved into her pockets. They've stopped walking and they lean against a pole in the middle of the fair. All Davie can hear are the sounds of the slot machines in the tent nearby. The music is so loud he's tuned it out. He watches Marie and sees that she's staring at the rifle range.

'Fancy a go? Come on, I'll win you something,' he says.

She turns to look at him and, for a second, the expression on her face is confusion – as if she doesn't know who he is. She blinks. 'Sorry, I was miles away. Actually, can we go on the Big Wheel?'

The Big Wheel isn't particularly big, not compared to those huge things like the London Eye or even those big old ones he's seen on TV, like the Wonder Wheel in Coney Island. He'd love to go to Coney Island, but he wouldn't go anywhere near that wheel. He'd watched a documentary on it once. About the guy who built it. No accidents since 1900, apparently. Statistics dictated that it had to happen eventually, and the older it got, the odds were shortening. Davie wasn't a gambling man, but he could imagine a disaster was imminent. It would be one of the moving carriages. The ones that slide along a rail inside as well as going round the circumference. Was it not frightening enough to be up so high, never mind in a carriage that made it look like you were going to slide off the rails and drop to the floor? Davie was terrified of heights. He managed to get away with most things in life without ever having to deal with that fear.

'Er, how about the Dodgems instead?' he says.

'You're not a scaredy-cat, are you, Davie? Big strong man like you.' Marie laughs and drags him by the elbow towards the ride. He feels his heart start to beat faster. His palms have gone clammy and he wipes them on his shorts. He can't get out of this without looking like a wimp. But he's terrified.

Marie runs off towards the ticket booth. Davie waits, watches her. Takes a deep breath and tries to calm himself down. *Get a grip, Davie.* He decides that he will do it, but he'll shut his eyes. She comes back waving a roll of paper tickets.

'Come on . . .'

He was hoping for a queue, a final reprieve. But there is none.

The wheel creaks and lurches as they sit on the seats. It's one of those with the swing seat and a bar. It couldn't really be worse, in Davie's opinion. He sits on the far side and Marie climbs up next to him. A skinny kid in a greasy T-shirt pulls the bar down in front, clicks it into place. He smacks a button next to the small control booth and the seat lifts up. It's faster than he expected and the seat swings precariously. He grips onto the bar and closes his eyes.

'Davie, I . . . Oh God, you're actually scared, aren't you? I thought you were joking. I wouldn't have made you come on if I'd realised—'

'It's fine,' he says, through gritted teeth. 'Keep talking, though. Take my mind off it.'

'It'll be easier if you open your eyes.'

His stomach lurches as the carriage loops over the top of the circle, swings forwards as it starts to descend down the other side. He opens his eyes and sees the fairground sprawled out beneath them. He can see the hidden parts that you don't see from the ground. The backs of the tents, the inner workings of things. The overflowing bins and stacks of empty boxes behind the burger vans. It starts on the second loop, and he realises Marie has fallen silent. He turns and sees that she is staring out towards the entrance of the fair.

'What do you see?' he says, sensing her bristle beside him.

Silence.

The ride descends for its third and final time, and Davie is glad to feel it slowing to a stop. The seat swings again as it pulls in to the exit point, before stopping. The skinny greaser lifts the bar and smirks. Marie still hasn't said anything.

They walk away from the ride, not heading in any particular direction. He senses a change in her. It makes him feel uncomfortable.

'Marie?'

She turns to face him, looks up. She's been crying again, or trying hard at least to hold back her tears.

'Marie. You're scaring me. What is it?'

She takes his hand and presses something into his palm.

'I want you to keep this. Please. I'll explain later. Just keep it for me. Just in case.'

He looks down at what she has placed in his hand. Two brass keys attached to a cheap plastic photo-keyring, two young faces. He barely glances at it. Drops it into his pocket.

'Marie—'

He whirls round, searching the crowd. The music sounds like it's been turned up suddenly, the pounding beats crushing his skull. There is too much laughter. The air is filled with the stench of cheap meat, onions. Candyfloss. Children are shrieking. Rifles are being fired – *pop pop pop* – against the backboard. He turns the other way, panicked. Confused. She has disappeared.

Marie is gone.

He takes his phone out of his pocket. There is a small metallic *chink* as it rattles against the keys. He clicks on his call list, finds her number. Presses 'dial'. It goes straight to voicemail.

'Fuck,' he says, too loudly. A young girl walking past with candyfloss stuffed in her face flinches, and her dad, walking hand in hand with her, throws him a filthy look.

He presses 'call' again. Voicemail.

He marches out of the fair, pushing his way through the crowds. He passes the girl with the pink streak in her hair. She's laughing again. The boy she's with stares at him. Smirks. Davie stares back. He wants to say something, but he can't. He's no reason to. He doesn't want to make a fuss. He just wants to get the hell out of this place and find out what's got into Marie.

21

It was a mistake to meet Davie. She'd tried, she really had. She knew she was pushing him away, but her mind was spinning. She'd tried to relax on the Big Wheel. She'd been about to tell Davie about what had been going on. Get his advice. She'd never told anyone about Graeme, but there were too many coincidences now. The Lego . . . the letters . . . the Twitter account with the photos of her window box. The photo of her and him.

She'd seen him standing at the entrance to the fairground. There was no mistake. It might've been over two decades since she'd seen him, but he hadn't really changed. She could tell by the way he stood. The shape of his body. Tall, skinny: so unlike her own. She knew she looked like him, facially at least, but he seemed to have gained a height and a build that was more like their father's than their mother's. Long and rangy. Narrow face with a strong chin. She was shorter, prone to putting on weight if she didn't watch what she ate. She'd lost weight recently too, could feel it in her clothes. The waistband just a bit looser.

Most of all, she could sense him. They'd always had the twin thing that people talk about. The feeling of knowing he was near, knowing what he was thinking. Even when they were apart and she didn't know where he was, she could sense he'd never been far away.

They'd moved house after it had all happened. Moved to the other side of Scotland, wanting distance, the chance of a new start. She'd taken her mum's maiden name, and her dad had changed his name by deed poll so they were all the same. The Bloomfields. She'd quite liked it. Assumed it meant she was safe. Part of the conditions of him being sent away was that he was never allowed to contact her again. At first she'd been confused. Didn't want to be apart from him. He'd managed to condition her over their sixteen years together. Managed to convince her that they had a bond that was like no other. Tried to convince her that the things they'd done together were OK. She'd wanted it at first, felt the same as him. That childlike closeness that had turned into something more. But by the time she was fourteen, nearly fifteen, she'd started to realise how wrong it was. They were brother and sister. It wasn't right.

Had he seen her on the wheel? Seen her with Davie? She knew that Davie could handle himself, but Graeme was unpredictable. Who knew what he might do. Davie was in danger just by being near her. That's why she'd tried to push him away. The instinct had kicked in as soon as she'd seen the letter. The one that she'd never have known about had she not seen the postman that day.

She shudders, thinking about that.

It was the first warning sign. Then there were others. She hadn't wanted to believe it. Hadn't wanted to accept it. But it was obvious now.

Graeme was out.

How he'd got out, she didn't know. She knew she had to read the letters. She had to find out where he was – or where he was meant to be, at least. He'd been sent to a hospital near their old town. But that doesn't mean he hadn't been moved. She knew that they would have her details, her parents' too. But they were lucky enough to be out of the country. Moving to Spain hadn't just been about starting a new life in the sun. They'd been scared.

Marie had been scared too, but she'd thought he was never

getting out. Thought she was safe. Why had no one contacted her to say he was out?

The worst part was, she actually missed him. She'd never really managed to move on. She missed their childhood, and the carefree times. She conveniently blocked out all the bad stuff. It hadn't always been bad. She'd enjoyed it as much as he had, at first. Encouraged him, even. It had felt right, special – giving herself to him. She often regretted pushing him away. She loved him.

He was her brother after all.

She drops the keys on the table. The spare set are on a plain silver ring. They look bare, with no keyring. It'd been a last-minute decision to take the spare set out with her. She'd planned to explain things to Davie. Give him the keys, tell him he was welcome any time. But then it'd all gone to shit. She'd panicked. Given him her own keys instead. She wondered if he'd bring them round. Try to get some sense out of her. Half of her wanted him to do exactly that, so she could tell him everything. Get his support. Stop feeling so damn scared and paranoid.

A horrible thought begins to mushroom inside her head. What if they hadn't let Graeme out? What if he'd escaped? Shit. Shit! He'd end up in so much trouble. Even after everything he'd done, she didn't want that for him. She wanted to see him again. Just once. Talk to him. Try to understand. The other part of her brain said, *Don't be so bloody stupid, Marie. Call the police. Get Graeme back where he belongs. Don't react. It's what he wants. He hurt you, Marie. He ruined your life. You need to forget about him. You need to move on.*

She is torn.

Cadbury is sitting in her basket next to the TV, snoozing. Purring quietly. Clearly the cat has decided to forgive her for the recent lack of attention. She needs to feel warmth now – of something that didn't expect anything back. She picks up the sleeping cat and it stirs, turns to look at her. She sits down at the kitchen table and the cat stays on her lap. Marie strokes it; the rhythmic movement is soothing and the soft fur feels nice under her hand.

She opens the laptop. She hadn't switched it off, so after a moment it opens up the windows she'd left there. The browser. Twitter. She refreshes the screen. After a moment, the timeline she'd been looking at spews out a series of tweets. MarieBloomfield's account is unlocked. Her request has been accepted. With a shaking hand, she scrolls down as far as they go. They refresh as she scrolls.

The first tweet was written nearly a month ago.

Hello World! Thought I'd come and see what all the fuss is about ☺

She starts to read them, bottom up. The first few are dull, as innocuous as the first. Nothing of interest. Someone finding her feet. There are no retweets, no replies. Just one person, typing into the void. Updating no one on things of no interest. The account has only one follower: her. The account isn't following anyone. Just spewing out a stream of consciousness, not even caring if it will be read.

Because there is only one person who is meant to read this.

She wonders how Scott had seen the tweets. Assumes that maybe they haven't always been protected. Maybe that's a new thing. Maybe whoever set up the account didn't expect anyone to contact them. Maybe Scott had sent tweets to the account, got no reply. Maybe that was why he'd seemed miffed about it at the party. Maybe that's why the others had been staring at her. Were they on Twitter? Or was she just paranoid?

It doesn't matter.

There are several pages. But it's the first page that sends a shiver down her spine. The recent messages are frantic. Someone on the edge.

What's the point of this? Why is no one talking to me?

I don't understand this thing.
It's a bit creepy, isn't it . . . talking about followers . . . #stalkeralert LOL. Luckily no one is actually following me. I'm too dull.

Anyone going to the shows this weekend? Looks like fun. I used to go there with my brother when we were kids #midgets

Maybe I should start following people. Is that what you're meant to do? Maybe I should stick to Facebook . . . anyone??

I'm going to delete this account #fucking #boring

Ha! That got me some new followers. Dirty whores with their tits out. I spose I need to protect my tweets. What's the point of that though?

I wish my brother was here. I miss him so much #bond #siblings

I skived off work today #naughtygirl

Thinking about dumping my bloke. Not sure it's working out. Lucky he can't see this!

I heard from my brother #amazing

And the final, most recent tweet. Sent at 12:00 today:

Seeing my brother today. Can't wait. So much to catch up on #siblings #love #missyou

The cat yelps. She feels its claws dig into her leg before it jumps off her lap. She's barely aware that she's been stroking it harder and harder, pressing it into her legs. Feeling the bones beneath its soft fur. She touches her leg where the cat has clawed it. She rubs at her cheek, feels an itchy tear slide down her face. Tastes salt on her lips.

He's done this.

He's set up this account. He's been playing with her, wondering when she would notice. He must've added the photograph of her window box very recently.

She wonders how long he's been out.

It was only a few days ago that she sensed someone in the pub. Found the piece of Lego. The day Cadbury was sick in the hallway.

A thought hits her. She stands up, banging her knees on the table. The bin is still under the sink. She pulls out the liner and tips the contents into the sink, frantically searching through the random crap in there. Finds it. The tissue with the hard ball inside that Cadbury coughed up. She peels back the tissue, wincing at the smell. Cat sick is never a pleasant aroma, but there isn't that much in there, thankfully. A ball of hair, bits of food. She prises it apart and finds what she's looking for. A small yellow brick.

The cat has eaten Lego.

Realisation dawns, and she walks over to the window, opens it wide. This is the way the cat always comes in and out. This is the place where the stupid cat might see something new and interesting to play with. She often finds a dead bird or a mouse in there, next to the daisies. A little present for her that she has to bury in the garden.

She leans out across the window box, looking up and down the ledge. Nothing. She leans further, until she can see the patch of grass beneath the window. A black bucket sits there, upturned. She leaves it there as a step for Cadbury, and she often uses it to transport the dead animals that are left in the soil.

She feels her heart stop.

Scattered down by the sides of the bucket is an array of different pieces of Lego. Various shapes and sizes. A small structure has been built, and knocked over. Even half smashed, she can see what it once was. A castle. Just like the one she built that day. A small flag pokes out from underneath.

Call the police, she thinks. *Call Davie. That's the right thing to do. The sensible thing.*

She slides back inside the window, barely noticing the pain in her chest from where she's been leaning down over the ledge, the frame pressing in to her. She slams the window shut.

She picks up the phone, still shaking. Takes a deep breath. They answer on the third ring.

'Marie? Is that you? Is everything all right?'

She tries to stop her voice from shaking. 'Hi Mum. Yeah, it's me. And no. It's not. I was just wondering . . . have you heard from Graeme?'

Silence. Breathing.

'Mum?'

'I'll get your father. Hang on.'

'No, wait. I want to talk to you. Mum—'

'Marie? It's Dad. We got a phone call today. We were trying to work out what to do. We should've called sooner . . . Graeme has been in a hospital not far from you. We didn't know. They sent a letter about the move, apparently, but it went to the old address. They've got our updated details now. I don't know how. Systems, or something.'

'Dad – is he still there? I'm probably being stupid, it's just, I—'

She hears her dad sigh. Hears her mum in the background, muttering, 'Just tell her, Stan.'

'Dad?'

'They can't find him, Marie. He was on a day trip. Somewhere near Edinburgh. They don't know how it happened, but he didn't get back on the bus. They tried to keep it quiet. We've told them they need to get it on the news. Warn people. I'm sure he won't try to find you, but it might be best if you went away for a few days. They think they'll find him soon. The police are on to it now. Try not to worry.'

'Try not to worry? There's only one person he'll want to see if he's out of there, Dad.' She realises she's shouting. Out of control. She pauses. Takes a breath. Feels a shiver. The cat squeezes up tight against her leg, rubbing itself against her. Mewling. The cat senses it, too.

That scrape again. Someone upstairs. *Oh God . . .*

'Dad, I have to go. I'll phone you back.'

'Marie, wait—'

She can still hear his voice, saying her name, pleading with her, when she hangs up.

She stares up at the ceiling. She takes a knife from the knife block, the sharpest one in there. Then she curls up on the couch, knife in hand. The cat jumps up and sits on her feet. Marie lies still. She is in waiting. She knows that sleep is never going to come.

Marie,

I told myself I wouldn't get annoyed with you. I never liked getting annoyed with you. But you're not playing the game here, Marie. Why the fuck aren't you replying? Do you know how difficult it was for me to get your address? Do you know how difficult it is for me to get hold of a pen and paper, so I can write these without anyone seeing? Do you know how difficult it is for me to get these letters posted? Do you know how much it pains me to suck up to that bitch in the office, let her think I like her so she'll help me do the things I need her to do? It's not like I can just pop out to the post office. Buy some stamps and an ice cream on the way back.

Do you know how difficult it is for me to be in here without you?

I read a thing about losing someone being like having a limb cut off.

That's what it feels like, Marie. I feel like someone has cut one of my fucking limbs off. The least you could do is reply.

How are Mummy and Daddy?

Are they dead yet?

I hope so.

Graeme

22

Laura stays in bed for most of Saturday. She managed to stagger home after seeing Mark with Hayley and Gaz at the shows, and, God, was she suffering for it now. Drinking that wine had been stupid. Not like her at all. Her head is thumping and her mouth is as dry as a budgie's cage.

What. An. Idiot.

Going there in search of Mark, planning to confront him . . . it had seemed like a good idea at the time. It started when she was sitting there after work, all freshly showered and excited about the night. As the moments turned to minutes, turned to 'he's not turning up', she'd felt herself get more and more wound up.

By the time she'd stormed out of the pub, she was furious. She'd kicked over that bin and left it there, rubbish strewn all over the pavement. This wasn't her. She didn't act like this. Did some sort of hormones get released after you'd had sex for the first time? Something more than the endorphins from the physical activity? Something that made you mad with rage? Apoplectic. That was the word for it. Hopping fucking mad. Not to mention even hornier. If he'd been waiting for her outside the pub, pretending not to show up to wind her up, she'd probably have punched him in the face before dragging him round to the car park and screwing his brains out up against the bins.

She'd loved being with Mark. Taking control. Watching his face. Seeing the realisation in his eyes, that OK, maybe she was new to this, but oh my God was she a quick learner. She could still taste him on her lips. She could still picture what he did to her. With his hands. With his mouth. He'd gone down on her, kissed her afterwards. Grinning, waiting for her to react at tasting herself. She'd loved it. Loved all of it. Besides, she hadn't gone in there completely naive. She'd read stuff online, read about what to do. She'd watched stuff . . . It made her cheeks grow hot, thinking about that. Being terrified of getting caught. It was part of the thrill.

But something that Mark said had given her a jolt. The way he'd looked at her when he'd called her 'a wee nympho'. It wasn't said affectionately. He'd almost said it like it was a bad thing. Like she should be ashamed. But why should she? It was fine for the boys to go and shag whoever they liked. She'd actually waited. For him.

Stupid.

Had he only been nice to her – taking her to the shows, taking her for a picnic – so that he could get what he wanted? Was he really that shallow? And was she really so stupid to have thought otherwise? Was it all about the bravado – him running off to tell his mates what a goer she was. *Go on, lads, take a punt. She sucks like a hoover. She fucks like a bunny. Her fanny's like warm apple pie* . . . She'd heard all this stuff before, about other girls. Maybe this was just how it was. A rite of passage.

Fuck him.

It makes her feel sick. She wants to cry, but she won't give him the satisfaction. And it's not just him – she confided in Hayley too. She'd seriously misjudged that bitch. She imagined her shagging Gaz, that horrible greaser from the shows. *I hope she gets an STD*, she thinks, *that'll teach her*.

Laura sighs and throws back the covers. She needs to get up. Forget about this. Luckily they used condoms, and, even luckier, there was no way anyone saw them. Imagine if he'd filmed it, or taken photos.

She picks up her phone from where she'd left it charging beside the bed. She hadn't turned it off, but she'd put it on silent and turned it away so the light flashing for new messages wouldn't bother her. Assuming she got any messages.

Yep. Three missed calls, two text messages. All from Mark. None from Hayley, which cemented her opinion that Hayley was a two-faced cow and most definitely not to be trusted. Anyway, they'd be back in school soon. Luckily this had happened in the holidays. There'd be a new scandal by next week. Things would go back to normal. She'd get on with her work and forget about the embarrassing summer encounter. She's not going to go all Sandra Dee about it. Expect Mark to fall at her feet when she turns herself into a sexy Lycra-clad vamp. If he doesn't like her as she is, then that's his problem.

He's the idiot. Not her.

She starts to feel better, mentally at least. Although her head is still pounding. Luckily her mum hasn't come up to see why she's still in bed. It makes her realise, though, that she has no one to talk to about all this stuff. Hayley was an error of judgement. The girls in her crowd at school don't talk about sex. They're *nice*, but they're boring and bookish and Laura often feels like a bit of a misfit there. Yes, she's academic, and she's sporty, but she's not dull. She's sensible, but no way is she boring. It's clearly time to expand her circle of friends. Maybe going into the sixth year will help. A lot of people will have left, gone on to college or taken jobs. There'll be a different crowd. Her registration class will change. There'll be opportunities to meet different people. It'll be fine.

She gets out of bed. Stands up too quickly and feels a rush of blood to her head. She needs sugar. Some food. A can of Sprite. She would kill for a can of Sprite. And some headache tablets.

She opens the messages on her phone. Weak apologies. No explanations. 'Meet me', one of them says. Fat chance. She decides to call someone else. Someone who will make her feel good about herself again. Davie. He'll understand. He was a boy once. Hopefully he can tell her that they grow out of it, and that not all men are pricks. Because at the moment that's exactly how she feels.

He answers straight away.

'Laura, nice to hear from you. What's up?'

The words tumble out. 'Oh God. Do you fancy a coffee tomorrow? I need to tell you something. I've been an idiot. I've no one to talk to. Please?' She chokes on the words, realising the threat of tears hasn't gone away just yet.

There's only a slight pause before he replies. 'Sure. I'll get the cakes in.'

Laura hangs up, feeling a little bit less of an idiot than she did before. She just needs her brain to co-operate now; it needs to have a word with itself about trying to bash its way out of her skull.

23

Davie orders two lattes and two cakes: one carrot with cream-cheese frosting and the little black seeds on the top, one chocolate fudge. He walks up to the back of the café and chooses one of the booths, sitting with his back to the far end of the room so that he can see everything that's going on. Force of habit. It's been a while since he's been in Landucci's, but, an occasional paint-job aside, the place has barely changed in twenty years. Good. The waitress – a smiley-faced woman in her late 60s called Hetty – has just delivered his tray with a nod and a comment about the weather, when Davie spots Laura coming in through the front door. Even from thirty feet back, he can see that she's stressed. The way she's all tightened up inside her skin. He raises a hand to catch her attention, but she's already coming his way. After all, where else would he sit? She knows him well.

With her face scrubbed free of make-up and her eyes shaded with the dark rings of tiredness and tears, Laura looks younger than her sixteen years. He's seen her dolled up at parties before, and he's torn about what he wants her to be. She's a young woman, yet he's known her since she was a kid. He feels protective of her, which seems to be a role he finds himself in more often than not these days. He might need to redress the balance at some point. Was it not about time someone started to look out for him?

Laura smiles as she sits down, but it seems like an effort for her to push the sides of her mouth up into something that isn't a frown. 'Carrot cake. My favourite,' she says. 'I hope that's for me.' She picks up a fork and cuts off a huge chunk. It's in her mouth before he can object. Not that he was going to.

'Of course it's for you. Anyway, looks like you need it. You feeling a bit better today? Do you want to talk about it?' He hoped, secretly, that she didn't. There were many things he was good at, but teenage relationships definitely wasn't part of his expertise.

Laura chews the cake for what seems like longer than is necessary. She looks away, reluctant to catch his eye. The night before, she'd told him she'd done something stupid. She hadn't said any more, but Davie already knew. Marie had told him about Laura and Mark, and it didn't take a genius to work out what had happened. There was no chance of him asking her to elaborate. He just needed to find a way to take her mind off it.

'It's nothing,' she says, eventually. 'Not really.'

Silence falls on them again, punctuated briefly by the sounds of forks scraping on plates, cups rattling on saucers. In the background, Hetty is chopping something onto a board. Cucumber, Davie guesses. Tomatoes. *Chop chop chop.* He can smell something cooking in the oven. Lasagne, maybe. A warm garlicky smell that makes his stomach flip. Maybe he'll ask for a piece to take home.

'I thought I'd made a fool of myself,' Laura continues at last. 'But I've already realised . . . it's not *me* who's the fool.' She looks up from her plate and grins. She has a poppy seed stuck in between her front teeth.

'You've got . . .' Davie gestures to her mouth, bares his teeth at her.

Laura slides her tongue over her teeth and makes a sucking noise. She opens her mouth again and grins like a monkey. 'Gone?'

'Gone,' he says, smiling.

'Thanks. Anyway, it's forgotten already. Bad day. Stupid. All good now.' She is still poking at her teeth. 'I've had some ideas for the new term at the club. I think we should start thinking about doing a demo again. I've been looking at some of those videos on the Sankukai site. Have you seen them?'

'Aye. Some good stuff on there. Seems to be an injection of new blood into the sport over in Japan. The new styles are becoming popular. Mixing things up a bit. You're right – we should think about bringing in some of the elements at ours. Maybe we can arrange a demo at the harvest fair or something? Gives us time to decide on what we're doing. Get it arranged. I've been letting things go a bit stale for a while. After we did the one-off self-defence class, I'd expected a few more new members, but nothing's really happened.'

'Things always go a bit like this in the summer. I'm blaming the weather. It's too hot. It's all gone tits-up since I went into Marchmont Lodge with Mark. That place is totally creepy, by the way. I think there was someone in there, skulking about. Bit heavy-footed for a ghost but Mark reckoned there were no junkies hanging about in there any more. Oh yeah, and then there was the shows, that stupid fortune teller . . . Remind me never to go there again, OK?'

He smiles at her rambling train of thought. 'Ha . . . I went yesterday. Got coerced into going on the Big Wheel. I hated every minute of it. Then Marie disappeared and left me with the hot dogs and the lowlife.'

'What do you mean she disappeared? Is she OK?'

'Yeah. No. I don't know. She ran off. She's fine though, I think. But she's blowing hot and cold. Starting to think it's not worth the hassle, but I need to talk to her about something and every time I open my mouth she seems to shut me down.'

'This is exactly what I mean,' Laura says. 'Relationships are just too much bloody hard work. I should've known, really.

The fortune teller told me it was all going to shit. Then I had the displeasure of meeting one of Mark's skanky fairground mates. Baz. No, Gaz . . .'

'Gaz. He the one your pal Hayley's been hanging around with?'

Laura's eyes flashed with anger. 'She's not my pal. But yeah, that's him. Greasy little shitbag. She'll probably catch something off him. I reckon he's dealing something too. Mark had a plastic bag stuffed in his pocket after we met up with Gaz the other night and it definitely didn't have a goldfish in it. Bastard.'

Davie shook his head, confused. 'Goldfish?'

'Never mind. Anyway, Hayley's meant to be going out with Sean Talbot. Maybe I should meet up with him so we can talk about how awful our partners are and how we're better off without them. I quite like Sean, actually, but he's not my type. Maybe I should change my type.' She laughs.

'This Gaz, though . . .' Davie leans forward. 'Have you got any actual evidence that he gave drugs to Mark?'

Laura drains her coffee and sets the cup back in the saucer. 'Nope. It's probably nothing. Could've been anything in that bag. I'm just pissed off with Mark. You should leave it. Sorry I said anything. I just hate the lot of them right now.'

Davie frowns. He'd hoped this was the lead that would give him an excuse to take a closer look at Gaz and the rest of the gang from the shows. Maybe not, but it's something to think about. Laura slides along the seat and stands up. She has a bit more colour in her cheeks now. Davie is pleased. Mission accomplished. This one, at least.

'See you later, Davie. Thanks for the cake . . . and the chat.'

'Any time, love. Send me some links to that new karate stuff you were looking at. We'll sort something out.'

He waits until she leaves before he goes up to the counter.

'Can I have some of that fresh lasagne to take away please, Hetty?'

She has only just taken it out of the oven. The smell is making his stomach growl.

'Well, of course, Sergeant Gray,' she says. 'I'll stick in an extra-large slice, just for you. Tell you what, though, son, you need to get yourself a woman to be making your Sunday tea for you, you know. You're no' getting any younger.'

Davie leaves the café with twice as much food as he wanted, and half as much dignity.

★ ★ ★

Back at home, Davie cuts the lasagne in half, leaves the foiled half on the side and sticks the piece he wants to eat into the oven to heat through. It's still warm, but he wants it piping hot again. Plus, he has stuff to do before he sits down with the pile of carbohydrates that will send him into a coma for the night.

He opens his laptop. The link that Malkie sent him is still there in the browser window. He'd already read it on his phone, but he knew he needed to read it again.

Graeme Woodley. The teenage schizophrenic.

The photograph, taken in 1995, on the steps of a grey-bricked police station, shows a hollow-eyed youth being led towards a waiting van. His expression is surly, his body stooped. Hands cuffed in front of him. The article has various snippets of sensationalist words and phrases peppered throughout: *Paranoid schizophrenic. Psychotic. Beast. No remorse. Dead-eyed monster.*

Woodley sexually assaulted his victim with a rolling pin and beat her half to death. The details are graphic and make Davie wince. The victim had been left in a coma, from head injuries and more than likely shock. He'd used the rolling pin on her internally as well as externally. He'd been found in a local pub, sitting calmly on a bar stool. He was covered in blood. A pint of Tartan Special in front of him, barely touched. The barman had called the police, tried not to make a fuss. He said: 'The boy smiled at me and ordered his drink. I could see from the amount of blood on him that something was very wrong, but there was something in his eyes. In the way he acted. I served him the pint, but he offered no money and I didn't ask. He was numb. Expressionless. He didn't even blink when I picked up the phone behind the bar and called the police. I could barely dial the number, my hands were shaking so much. He smiled at the police when they arrived too. He didn't put up a fight. I've seen plenty of stuff from my years behind the bar, but I don't think I've ever experienced something as chilling as this.' Meanwhile, the victim was barely ten minutes from bleeding to death. The paramedics had saved her life, but due to the unknown injuries sustained and the massive blood loss, they'd put her into a medically induced coma so they could work out what to do. She'd had an emergency hysterectomy when it became apparent that the greatest damage had been done to her internal organs.

Same as the poor Jane Doe in the hospital right now.

Davie looks at the photograph again. Shudders. Something about his face. It's familiar, somehow. He can't place it. A feeling, too. Something he hasn't been able to shake since the attack on the woman who'd led them to all this.

Underneath the article are links to others that Malkie has pasted in with question marks at the end: what happened to him (detained indefinitely under the Mental Health Act), an interview with a neighbour ('We always thought that boy was a strange one but we had no idea he was a paranoid schizophrenic'), links to articles on the effects of cannabis misuse and the triggering of mental illness. Finally, at the bottom, an article in a medical journal about 'Patient X'. It's been anonymised, but Malkie has written next to it: *This is a study by Woodley's doctor. Let's just say I had to buy a bloody expensive bottle of whisky to get hold of it. Of course, we don't have any concrete evidence that this is the guy we're looking for, but you can't ignore the similarities between the attack and what Woodley did to his victim. We've got tissue samples at the lab, so we'll know for sure soon. In the meantime, we can't use this or say anything officially, but it might give you an idea of what we're dealing with.*

He can't take any more of the brutality right now. He skims the synopsis. Scrolls down through the background sections. Patient X had a history of cannabis use and was badly scalded as a child, as was his sister. This type of trauma is a risk factor for schizophrenia, yet his sister was not affected (as far as the doctor knows, as he has never actually spoken to her and got an assessment). It's more common in boys. There is some anecdotal evidence that the boy almost drowned when he was young. Further trauma. He was a loner, very withdrawn. Blah blah blah . . . then he sees it:

Patient X was a twin.

The victim was his sister.

'Christ,' Davie mutters. He rarely drinks, but he could do with one now. He's not used to reading things like this, but if he wants to stay with CID, he's going to have to harden up.

He takes a long, slow breath. Lets it out fast.

He closes the laptop again, and as he does he spots Marie's keys sitting behind it. He picks them up and stares at the keyring. Sunlight has faded the photograph so the two faces look bleached and almost featureless. All that are left are eyes and lips. He recognises Anne. She has barely changed. The same cheeky grin. The wide smile. Marie looks haunted. Her hair is roughly cut, choppy, as if she has done it herself. As if she has tried to become someone else. Her mouth is a dark slash, the tiniest of curves at one corner, as if she is trying to smile but can't even fake it for the camera. Her eyes are deep hollows, staring at something long gone and far away. Her eyes . . .

His eyes.

Marie was sixteen when she moved to Banktoun. Anne took her under her wing. He remembers now, him and Anne drinking cans of Coke on a bench after school one day. Anne saying: 'Something bad happened to that girl, Davie . . .'

He closes his eyes. Runs a hand across his face. He can smell the lasagne burning in the oven.

Snippets of information – clues and connections – burst into his brain like soap bubbles popping in the wind.

It is all starting to make sense.

20th July 2015

Hey Marie,

Sorry. Sorry.

Is that enough?

Please write. Please.

Love,

Graeme

24

Marie wakes up crunched up on the couch. She pulls herself up on one elbow, feels the stiffness in her neck. Something sharp pokes into her chest, and she realises she has been lying on top of an eight-inch carving knife. She pulls the knife out from beneath her and holds it up, turning it this way and that. Flashes of light bounce off the surface and cast reflections on the walls.

She can't go on like this.

Graeme is missing. Except he isn't. Not really. It's obvious now, like it should have been from the start.

She has barely slept, feels stiff. Her eyes sting. But she has to go to work. Feels a drive that she hadn't realised before. But mainly, she has to get out of this flat. She will call Davie, tell him everything. She should call the police now – tell them she thinks Graeme is upstairs ... but something stops her. Despite it all, he still has that hold over her. That bond she just can't break. Even after all he's done, she *wants* to see him. She *needs* to see him. Because he is still her brother.

After shoving the knife back into the wooden block bedside the others, she dresses quickly, doesn't bother to do her hair. She grabs her swimming stuff and her work clothes and rushes out of the house before she can change her mind. Cadbury is dozing in her basket. She'll be trapped inside all day now, but it's the only option. She can't leave the kitchen window open. Not now.

The swimming pool is quiet and she manages to get back

into her usual routine. A mile, including the short wade across the shallow end to the steps at the end. The Australian lifeguard isn't there. It's a young girl that Marie recognises. She gives her a wave. She wants everything to look like normal. She imagines the girl being interviewed by a newspaper. 'She didn't seem worried to me. She swims here every day. Same routine. I didn't notice anything unusual.'

Keep calm, Marie.

At work, she arrives wearing her best smile. Chats to the couple of old regulars who are sitting at the bar. Keeps it all in. Gives nothing away.

After the lunches have been cleared, she crouches down behind the bar and starts to remove all the bottles of mixers so that she can clean the shelves.

Keep busy, Marie.

She's halfway through putting them back on the shelf when she hears the door to the lounge bar open. The sound of someone pulling back a stool. Dropping a bunch of keys on the bar.

'Oi you, missus. Where've you been? I've left you messages.'

Marie turns at the sound of the familiar voice. Pastes her smile back on. Stands up, cloth still in hand.

'Oh God, sorry,' she says. 'Just one of those weeks, you know . . .' She lets the sentence trail off. This is Anne. One of her closest friends. One she's been trying to avoid talking to for the past week, knowing that there will be only two questions asked: one, what's the score with you and Davie?; and two, are you coming to the party? Anne can read Marie like a book. She can tell when she's upset, tell when something is wrong. Marie has a tendency to retreat into her shell. She's like a porcupine; she'll stay inside and attack people with sharpened quills if they try to get her to unfurl. The only way to avoid Anne's probing is to avoid Anne altogether. Marie feels her heart start to pick up the pace.

Keep it together, Marie.

142

Anne gives her a hard stare. 'What's going on, Marie?'

Marie feels herself start to sweat. Beads of moisture form on her back and trickle down towards the waistband of her skirt. 'Let's do lunch soon, OK?' she tries. 'I'll tell you everything, I promise.' She smiles, tries to let her pulse return to normal. 'All set for the party?'

Anne looks wary, but she lets it pass. 'Ian's been to the cash and carry. The house is full of beer, wine and cheap crisps. If anyone wants anything more exotic, they can bring it themselves.'

'You sure about all this? You don't want the place getting totally trashed, do you? I've heard loads of people mentioning it. I reckon you're going to have a full house, even if it is a Wednesday night.'

'It's summertime. No one cares what night it is, if someone's supplying them with booze! Plus, I told you – it's our last big blowout. We want to do it now before we start decorating the place, and well . . . once we start the IVF, I doubt we'll be doing much partying.' She looks away.

'Hey,' Marie says. She lays a hand over Anne's, squeezes. 'You're not going to give a shiny shit about parties once this baby comes along. I can't wait for that. We're getting too old for all this boozing anyway.'

Anne smiles. 'Yeah, I know. Maybe you can convince Ian, though? I think he's worried he's never going to sleep again. Personally, I'm just worried that it's not going to work, and we're going to spend the rest of our lives pacing about in a house that's too big for us, wondering why we didn't just spend the money on a camper van and fuck off around Europe. God. Remember when we were eighteen and those houses got built and I said to you, "Oh, I'd love to live in Willow Walk when I'm older"? You laughed and said they'd look like shit in five years' time. You were right. But I'm still glad we managed to buy one of them. It *will* be lovely when it's all painted . . .'

Marie is about to say something else, when the door of the public bar slams shut. She flinches. Turns round. There's no one through there. Empty pints have been left on the bar from the two old fellas that were there earlier, but they'd already left before Anne came in. She'd have washed their glasses after she'd finished refilling the mixers shelf. As it was, half of the tonics were still lined up on the floor like soldiers. The two pint glasses were still on the bar. Anne was looking at her strangely.

'I . . . That door never bangs shut,' Marie says, trying to fight off the feeling that someone had come in, and someone had left, and she hadn't seen them. Her handbag was through there. Under the bar but not hard to find.

'Hang on,' she says to Anne.

Anne just watches her, quizzically.

Her handbag is where she left it. Doesn't look like it's been touched. She walks round the other side of the bar to the door and sees that the doorstop is lying in the middle of the floor. She opens the door, looks outside. No one is nearby.

'Marie, is everything OK?' Anne calls through from the other bar.

Marie is about to answer when she hears rustling in the store cupboard. Her heart almost stops as the door is opened. Helen walks out, looking down. Marie almost bumps into her.

'Jesus, Helen, you gave me a heart attack!'

Helen laughs. 'Shit, sorry. I knocked the doorstop when I came in and the door banged shut, then I came in here to leave my bag and this door shut behind me too. I'm determined to close all the doors behind me today, for some reason . . . I'm a bit early, but you can go if you want. Doesn't look like there's much doing.'

Marie takes her handbag from under the bar and walks back through to Anne. 'Let's go,' she says.

'See ya!' Helen calls behind them. Marie ignores her.

'What was that all about? You're a nervous wreck.'

Marie shakes her head. 'Want to walk back home with me? I, um . . . I'm just feeling a bit out of it at the moment.'

Anne stops walking, pulls Marie back. Twirls her round to face her. They are about the same size, and Marie feels uncomfortable with her friend's face so close to her own. She feels herself shrink back, pull away.

'I think you might need a rest, Marie. Forget about the party. Go home and get some sleep. You look dead on your feet. You're probably coming down with something and I'd prefer if you kept it to yourself, OK?' Anne smiles, but Marie can see the worry in her eyes.

'I'll call you tomorrow,' Marie says. They both know that she won't.

At home, the air in the flat feels thick and stale. Marie searches the cupboards for something to drink. The cat hears her come in, pads across the kitchen lino. Shoves herself up against Marie's leg, rubbing at her. Mewling. She can sense something is wrong. Knows it's not normal for Marie to leave her shut inside.

Marie takes down the final bottle of wine. Opens the cupboard beneath and takes out the pile of letters.

She'll read one or two, she thinks. That's all. Then she's definitely phoning the police. She glances up at the ceiling, expecting to hear the now familiar scrape of someone moving around up there, but there is nothing. The only sound is the hum of the fridge as the fan starts whirring. The sound of her own breathing. The quiet purr of the cat sitting on her lap.

She pours red wine into a tumbler. Drinks. Slides a letter out and unfolds it. Tries to ignore her shaking hands as she starts to read.

25

Davie knows he has to tread carefully. If his theory is right, if Marie Bloomfield is Marie Woodley, then not only is he amazed that she's managed to create any sort of life for herself at all, but there's also the real worry that she might be in danger. But he can't just storm in there and ask her about her brother. She's never hinted that she might have one. In fact, hadn't she said she was an only child? So far it's only a theory, and it's been pieced together by evidence he is not even supposed to have. The official news reports don't mention Woodley having a sister. But maybe that's because they weren't allowed to. Marie's identity as his victim wouldn't be released, regardless of whether they were related or not.

Did Graeme Woodley attack the woman at the bus stop because he genuinely thought she was Marie? Or was it just a coincidence that the first person he saw when he ran across those fields was a woman that reminded him of his sister? If Davie is right, then there's no doubt that Woodley is trying to send a message. He's not sure if it's a good thing or a bad thing that Marie hasn't received it. He's spoken to Malkie, asked if they should talk to Marie, tell her about the attack on the woman – who has now been identified as the housekeeper for the farm next to where she was found. Tell her about Woodley's escape – see if it leads her to open up. The hospital is desperate to keep it low-key, out of the papers. But it's only a matter of time. Malkie will make a statement to the press.

Once they find out that Woodley's sister is in the vicinity, it'll be a sensationalist headache for all concerned.

He has to talk to Marie.

He's not giving her the chance to avoid him this time. He knows she's off work – she'd said so during their disastrously brief day out. Before she'd run off and left him wondering what the hell was going on. And what is it that's going on? Davie wonders. Maybe this hasn't got anything to do with him at all. He doesn't really know her, not enough to understand her. He's always struggled with women. Never been able to work out what it is they really want from him.

He lets his thoughts trail off. Has he got it all wrong? Maybe Woodley isn't her brother. Or maybe he is, but he hasn't been in touch after all. It could be anything. She could be ill. Jesus, she could be ill and she's too scared to get involved with him . . . His mind is all over the place, like the tangled tape of a cassette chewed up in an old stereo.

Just talk to her, Davie.

He walks round to her flat. Rings the buzzer. No reply. He waits a moment. Tries it again. He could go round the back – that gate at the side is never locked – but he doesn't want to appear at the kitchen window and give her the fright of her life. He could use the key. Let himself in. But something stops him. It doesn't feel right. He tries the buzzer again. This time she answers.

'Hello?' Her voice sounds disconnected, far away. Tired.

'Marie? It's Davie. I was worried about you. Thought I'd pop round.'

Silence. Broken by the faint crackle of static from the intercom.

'Marie?'

She doesn't say anything else, just clicks the button to let him in. There is a buzz and a snick as the door is released. He

147

goes in, walks round the corner. Expects her to have already opened the door to her flat. The door is closed. The corridor is dark without the light from the panes on the front door around the corner. A strip light above crackles and flickers, giving out a low hum and a dim light. Davie frowns. Knocks on the door.

'Marie? It's me.'

Again, it takes too long for her to answer. He is about to knock again when he hears the rattle of the chain being taken off. The key in the mortise lock being turned. The catch on the Chubb sliding off. He feels a flutter of fear in his stomach. He's worried that he's already too late.

She opens the door, but he barely catches a glimpse of her face. She has already turned back, headed inside. Davie senses a stillness. A darkness. The curtains are still drawn, despite the sunny day that is trying to filter its way inside. He closes the door behind him, locks it and slides the chain onto the runner. In the living room, Marie is curled up on the couch, knees pulled up to her chest. Her eyes are fixed on the TV screen, where Jeremy Kyle is silently berating his plethora of unruly, undesirable guests. Marie's hair is mussed, sticking out at all angles. Her face is pale and her eyes are ringed with dark shadows.

'I'll make us some tea,' he says. He tries to keep his voice jovial, but it's not easy. The fear in his stomach has grown tendrils, and they are slowly worming their way throughout the rest of his body, making his limbs shake. Trickling up and down his spine like an annoying bug.

Davie picks up the kettle. An empty wine bottle lies on its side in the washing up basin; a tumbler, stained red, lies beside it. He fills the kettle. Ignores what is in the sink. He's never made tea here before. Last time he was round, a couple of weeks ago, he sat at the kitchen table while Marie chirped and fussed, making tea in a pot and putting different kinds of biscuits onto plates. It is very different today. The mood is sombre. Muted. It can't go on like this.

He opens a cupboard to the left of the sink. Glasses. Napkins. Nothing else. He opens one to the right. Cups, saucers. Paperwork. Mugs. He reaches in to lift two mugs from the bottom shelf and, as he does, his wrist catches the upper shelf, flicking it up off the brackets. A cascade of envelopes slides out on top of him, hitting his face, shooting across the worktop, sliding onto the floor. He tries to catch them, knocks a mug onto the floor. It clatters hard, shatters into tiny pieces.

'Shit . . . shit . . .' he mutters. He tries to scoop up the envelopes while trying to avoid standing on the fragments of broken mug. He makes a mess of both: letters slipping through his hands, pieces of ceramic crunching under his feet.

'What the fuck are you doing?'

Marie is standing behind him. He turns, looks into her eyes. Her face is blotchy. Her eyes are red with tiredness and anger.

'Sorry, I . . . I'm cleaning it up. Have you got a little dustpan and brush?'

'Have you been reading my letters?' Her voice is monotone. Hard.

'What? No. Of course not.' He glances down at the scattered pile on the worktop. He notes that the handwriting is identical on each. A franked postmark on the top right, with a crest that looks frighteningly familiar. He's seen it recently. On the website for the hospital. He picks one up, flips it over. There is no sender's name on the back.

Marie snatches the letter from his hand. Pushes him out of the way, grabs at the pile. Envelopes fall from her hands and spill to the floor. She scrabbles around, flailing. Gaining nothing.

'Marie, your feet!' Davie says.

Marie looks down. Her feet are bare. She has already stood on pieces of broken mug. Small pools of blood are peppered between her toes. She stares down at her feet until eventually her shoulders droop. She lets the remaining letters fall from her hands. He watches as her shoulders rise and fall with the weight of her silent sobbing.

He scoops her up into his arms, carries her through to the living room. Lays her down gently on the couch. He picks ceramic splinters from the soles of her feet. He sits, holds her hand. Waits for her to speak. Marie says nothing, but he can feel her hand shaking and he squeezes it tight.

'Marie . . . I know something's bothering you. I can't help if you don't tell me. Is it me? Is it us? If you're having second thoughts, I understand.'

She sniffs, pulls her hand away. 'It's not you.'

Davie laughs, he can't help it. 'It's not you, it's me? Is that what this is about?' He's trying to lighten it, inject a bit of humour. He's almost certain that Marie's spiralling behaviour has nothing to do with him, but he doesn't want to push her too far. She might retreat completely then. That isn't going to help anyone.

She turns to face him and gives him a small smile. 'That's not what I was going to say.' She sighs. 'Christ, Davie. There's so much I need to tell you. About me. About . . . lots of things. But I'm scared.'

He pulls her close and she leans in against him. 'You should never be scared to tell me anything, you know. I might not be able to help. But I can always listen. Always.' He strokes her arm. She gazes up at him, a ghost of a smile playing on her lips. Davie takes his cue. He touches her cheek, lifts a stray strand of hair and gently tucks it behind her ear. Then he bends to kiss her, takes his hand away from her arm, starts to stroke the back of her neck. The kiss is soft. Tender. And he feels her start to respond. He runs his hand down her back, kisses her harder.

She stiffens. Pulls away.

'Did you hear that?'

Davie suppresses a sigh. 'What? I didn't hear anything.'

She slides over to the far end of the couch, her hand rubbing at the back of her neck, as if she's been burned by his touch. 'That . . . there it is again.' She stares up at the ceiling.

'Probably just someone moving their living room around,' he says. 'Christ, you're jumpy. Are you going to tell me what's wrong?'

Marie crosses her arms and looks away. 'Sorry. It's not you . . . It's nothing. Just some stuff I need to deal with. You should go. *Please!*'

Davie sighs. The silence is suffocating.

Fuck it. He sits up straight. 'Who sent you those letters, Marie? What's in them? Is someone harassing you?' He stops, realises he is getting carried away, firing questions at her.

There is only the briefest hesitation. 'No,' she whispers, her voice muffled behind her hands. 'I told you. It's nothing. Please, can you go now? I just want to be on my own.'

This is a nightmare. He wants her to talk, but he can't force her. He'd thought she'd have no choice but to respond to his direct approach. He's trying to let her know that he knows. Trying to give her the chance to open up. But she's keeping it locked up. Whatever it is, she's not ready to share it. But he can't just do nothing. He can't just leave it like this. He takes a deep breath.

'Be careful, Marie. There's something you should know. There'll be a statement on the news soon, but while I'm here . . . A woman was attacked. Badly. An inmate from a local hospital has gone missing. We don't know for sure if the events are connected yet, but we're going to urge people

151

to be careful. Keep a look out for him, but don't approach him—'

'What's his name?' Marie's voice is flat. Emotionless.

'Woodley,' he says. 'Graeme Woodley.'

She stares at him, but she doesn't react. He leaves her lying curled on the couch. The cat pads into the room as he leaves. Looks at him with disgust, in a way that only cats can.

21st July 2015

Dear Marie,

I'm going to try something else. Forget about everything else I've sent. Pretend you've never read it. Take it all and throw it in the kitchen sink and burn it.

Let's start again.

Never mind me. I've got nothing to say. Tell me about you. Are you married? Do you have children? I hope you've told them about me. About the games we used to play. About the fun we used to have. Do you still watch horror films? I used to love snuggling up with you, feeling you shudder when you were scared. Feeling your warm body pressed up against mine. I know you didn't mean it when you told me you didn't want me to hug you like that any more.

What happened to that boy, by the way? Did you marry him?

He wasn't good enough for you.

I tried to tell you that.

If only you'd listened.

Your loving brother,

Graeme

26

Marie is glad that Davie has gone. When he'd turned up like that, she'd almost cracked. Almost told him everything. She'd stopped herself just in time. She couldn't tell him. Not yet. She wanted to. It was on the tip of her tongue. But she just couldn't. Telling Davie would drag him into the whole mess, and she wants more than anything to keep him out of it. She wants to keep him safe. He doesn't need this in his life. Doesn't need her. Marie is scared. Not just for Davie. For herself. Christ, she's spent so long lying about Graeme, pretending that he doesn't exist, it's become second nature.

But what Davie said just before he left had thrown her. He'd confirmed her suspicions: Graeme has escaped. He's hurt someone. He's coming for her ... Has Davie already made the connection? Does he know who she is?

No. He can't know. Not for sure. She's been so careful to hide her past. But he was definitely digging. He suspects something and he was trying to get her to tell him. It can't have been a coincidence, him mentioning Graeme like that. He is a policeman, after all. It's his job to find out things like this. But he's her friend too – her boyfriend, for God's sake – and she could see it in his eyes ... He's scared of uncovering the truth because, when he does, nothing is ever going to be the same between them. It can't be. Not if she tells him what Graeme did to her.

Despite her fear, Marie's primary instinct is to protect her brother. To tell herself that she's not in danger at all, that she's built it up into something it isn't. Graeme just wants to see her. He's trying to get her attention, but he doesn't want to scare her off. It's been twenty-five years. He doesn't know how to act around her any more. Maybe she just has to give him a chance. It might not have been him who attacked that woman. Why would he? There was only ever one person that Graeme wanted to hurt.

Her thoughts are all over the place, scattered. Torn. She can't think straight. Her head is fuzzy. She knows she's drinking too much. Not her style. Never has been. She's not sure why it seems to have kicked in now.

She sweeps up the broken mug. Stacks the letters up into a pile and pushes them into the cupboard. There's something at the back, though. Something stopping her from pushing them all the way in. She feels blindly around, pulls out a plastic bag.

She'd forgotten about it.

The plastic bag from the party at Jack Henderson's – the one she was meant to look after to avoid the kid who'd had the seizure from getting in trouble. What was in it, anyway? She opens the bag, sniffs. There are four tablets in there. Capsules. Even through the coating she can smell something strong and herbal. She'd had things like this before, stuff made of plant extracts, bought on a whim from the health food shop and never taken due to them being the size of horse pills, and the horrible aftertaste when they came back on her five times a day.

She has no idea what these are. No idea what they do – but they hadn't done much good for that kid at the party. She stuffs the bag back into the cupboard.

It's time to sort herself out. She needs a shower. She needs to tidy up. She starts by taking the empty wine bottle out of the sink and putting it in the bin. As she ties the bag, she glances up at the kitchen ceiling. Thinks she hears a faint noise. Hopes she's imagining it.

You've got it all wrong, Marie, she thinks.

But there's only one way to find out.

She walks out into the hallway. She knows it's him. She can sense him. She always could. They say that twins have a special bond, an almost psychic ability to know what each other is doing. Doubters think it's nothing but coincidence – that it happens in all close relationships, like when you find yourself finishing someone's sentence or picking up the phone just as they ring you, seemingly out of the blue.

Their mother used to joke that they were like Siamese twins, joined at the hip – literally. When they were little, they were so small that the two of them could squeeze into one baby walker, even though they had one each – hers pink, Graeme's blue. Both of them would climb into one, each sticking a leg down the opposite leg holes, and crossing the other over their laps. How did they work out how to do this? Instinct. The same instinct that's telling her that her brother is in the flat upstairs. Moving furniture.

Trying to get her attention.

Thinking about the baby walker makes her think of the scar. Of what happened that day. She wonders how Graeme's scar is now, the same as hers – a mirror image on the opposite of his body, from where the two of them had been squeezed together in the baby walker when it had happened. That scar was an accident. Their mother hadn't realised that Graeme could stand up tall enough to reach the cord on the kettle. How could she know that he could grab it, tip the kettle on top of them both, fusing them together like that. It was part of their bond. Marie has other scars too, ones that no one can see. She knows them in detail. So does Graeme.

She climbs the stairs, one slow step at a time. Knows that she has to do this. He won't come down. He's waiting for her to come and get him.

156

'Graeme? Are you up there?' She whispers it. Scared that he might actually answer her.

There's no light in the stairwell. Hasn't been for months. It doesn't really affect her, so she hasn't done anything about it. There's supposed to be a factor who does these sorts of things, but despite the monthly service charge they pay no one ever comes out to do any maintenance. The ceiling is too high for anyone to reach to change the bulb, unless they had a long ladder. It's too dangerous. People would rather walk up the stairs in the dark.

She holds her breath as she climbs further. She ascends slowly, trying to keep calm. Breathes out. What will he look like, up close? She's only seen him from a distance, and even then she can't be 100 per cent sure. She might have this wrong. Maybe it's not him.

She is scared to see him now.

Has spending years in an institution turned him grey-skinned and withered? Did he ever go outside? What did he do all day? Marie realises that she doesn't know her brother at all. He was taken away during their formative years. She wonders if he still likes to read. The two of them were always avid readers, sitting up late under a makeshift tent in one or other of their beds, shining a torch on the pages of the Secret Seven or the Famous Five, each taking a turn to read to the other. As they'd got older, they'd experimented with different kinds of books . . . Graeme had started to scour second-hand bookshops, bringing back pulpy noir with sexy women on the covers.

She can't read anything like that now. And she can never listen to a book being read. Just the thought of it brings back too many memories of them both, under those covers, shining the torch . . . learning about each other.

She shivers, although it isn't cold.

On the top landing, the hallway is even darker. There is less natural light up here: on the lower floor, the glass panels on the main door let some light in but upstairs there is nothing, just a grey carpeted hallway and nine closed doors. The tenth, Flat 9, is open – just a fraction. A spear of light cuts across the carpet, dissecting the hall outside.

Bubbles of panic shoot up through her chest. Her hands shake. What happens once she's seen him? Then what? Can she really have him back in her life? She presses her hands on the low, flat part of her belly, just above her pelvis. She pushes hard, until it starts to hurt. Remembering . . .

A figure steps out into the hallway.

'Graeme,' she says. A statement. Her voice sounds flat. There is nothing left in her now. Seeing him there, a dark shadow lit by the sliver of light from the flat where he has been shuffling around, tormenting her. Letting her know who's in charge.

They stare at each other and time seems to stop. She balls her hands into fists, feels her nails cutting into her palms. Squeezes hard to stop herself from shaking. A rush of emotion floods through her. The last time she saw him. What he did. How he left her. Why is he here now? Why has he come back? She closes her eyes.

Ten . . . nine . . .

When she gets to one, she opens her eyes again and he is still there. She'd hoped, for one crazy moment, that she was imagining all this. But no, he's real. It's all real. The nightmare from her past has come back to haunt her. Because if he's come to find her, it can only mean one thing, can't it? He wants to hurt her.

He wants to finish what he started.

Eventually, he speaks. 'I was staying down at the old lodge. But then I saw you.' He stops, clears his throat. 'I followed you.

I wanted to just come up to you, talk to you. But I was worried you'd turn me away. The postman let me in. He didn't seem to be bothered about who I was. I was just looking around. Trying to see if any of the flats were empty. It was luck, I think. Or maybe it's fate. You used to believe in fate, Marie. Me and you, two halves of a whole . . . You know, there's an old Japanese myth that says if two star-crossed lovers die in a suicide pact, they are reincarnated as twins.'

She shivers, and the fear she felt on seeing him seems to flutter in her chest before gradually fading away. His voice is slower than she remembers. Higher pitched. Softer. He doesn't sound like her brother. He doesn't look like her brother any more.

When she meets people, she tells them she is an only child.

He keeps talking. 'Can I come down to your flat? It's horrible in here. I haven't got much. I had to nick some clothes off washing lines. I'm not proud of myself.'

The initial threat has gone. She feels as if she is on autopilot. She hasn't had time to read all the letters yet. Her flat is a tip; stuff she's pulled out of the drawers is all over the place. He won't care – she remembers his room as a teenager. It stank of boy sweat, was full of dirty mugs and plates, rubbish overflowing from his bin. Clothes strewn around. Piles of crap on top of his dressing table – things he'd dismantled and tried to put back together. He had this fascination for pulling things apart: radios, watches, clocks – even the toaster, more than once – but when it came to putting them back together, he lost interest. It used to drive their mum up the wall. But then dad would come along and quietly fix things. Say nothing about it. That was how their parents had dealt with Graeme all along. Keep quiet. Sort it out. Don't make a fuss.

She feels her body tense, thinking about it. Thinking about what he did to her. She shouldn't be doing this. He is dangerous. He is unpredictable.

No. He's nothing, Marie. Not any more.

She doesn't speak to him. Walks down the stairs, slowly. Trying not to panic. There is silence, just the faint buzz of the flickering strip light in the bottom hall. She's almost at her front door when she hears the thump-thump of Graeme's heavy footsteps as he follows behind. Her mind goes into overdrive.

What now, Marie?

He tried to kill you, Marie.

He loves you, Marie.

He took your innocence, Marie.

He's the only one who knows you, Marie.

He's going to hurt you, Marie.

'He's still my brother.' She mouths the words. Over and over again, like a chant. 'He is *still* my brother.'

27

Laura is rinsing rice from the inside of a saucepan when she hears a tap at the window. She turns, expecting it to be a delivery. Quinn is through in the bar discussing menus with Bill. They're sampling some new desserts after that, which means Laura will be having a random selection of them for lunch. Neither Quinn nor Bill has much of a sweet tooth.

There's no one there.

She drops the saucepan into the sink, dries her hand on a cloth. Goes out the back door into the yard, expecting to see a delivery van and someone in the back of it pulling out boxes. But there are no vans, and no boxes.

There's only Mark, leaning against the wall next to the kitchen window. He's smiling at her. His arms are crossed. But the way he moves, fidgets as he tries to get comfortable, sets alarm bells ringing in Laura's head.

'Hi,' he says. He raises an arm in a sort of half wave, half salute, and the movement makes him stumble backwards. He's flat against the wall now. His face is confused. He steps away and takes a step towards Laura. Instinctively, she steps back, rests a hand on the frame of the kitchen door. Then places one foot partly inside the building. Away from him.

She can see it in his eyes.

Even from the few feet that separate them, she can see that his pupils are the size of chocolate buttons. It's only just gone two o'clock. She'd checked the time when Quinn had dumped the pots down at her washing-up station.

She'd been surprised it was so early. They'd not done many lunches. But Mondays can be like that.

Mark is out of it.

He stumbles towards her, arms outstretched. 'Hey,' he says. 'Hey – where you going? I need to talk to you . . .'

The words come out as intended, but his speech is drawn out. Slow. He is trying hard to enunciate every word. He's trying hard to act like he's not completely off his head on something. Laura feels sick. How could she have been so stupid, doing it with this fucking clown? He's a loser. Hayley is welcome to him – once she moves on from Gaz, of course. She places her other foot inside. She bends down to unhook the door from the metal catch that keeps it open to give them air in the stifling kitchen.

'Laura . . . wait,' he says. 'Don't go. Please. I need to talk to you. Come back out, just for a minute.' He takes another step, sways. He turns to the side until he spots another support. Sees a wheelie bin. Leans against it. A couple of boxes slide off the top of the bin and disappear down the back. Someone will need to climb in there later, stamp them flat. Something else that Bill will be asking her to do. He reckons he's too old to climb into the bin. Too fat, more like.

'Go away, Mark. Sleep it off or something.'

'No, Laura . . . wait. Look . . .' He takes his hand away, raises them both towards her in a gesture of acceptance. 'I'm a dick. I know that. I got carried away. I was spending too much time at the shows—'

'With Hayley . . .'

'Yeah. No. No!' he shakes his head violently. Falls back against the bin. 'No. She was just there. I was with Gaz . . . he's got this stuff . . .' His voice trails off, and he looks confused. Turns to face the bin, turns back.

Laura's almost had enough, but she needs to clarify something first, before she shuts the door in his face.

'Hang on . . . so you weren't with Hayley? You didn't tell her anything? About . . . about us?'

Mark shakes his head again. 'Of course not. Me not turning up . . . that was nothing to do with us. I told you. I was being a dick. I got a call from Gaz and I went to see him. I saw you at the bridge and I was embarrassed . . .' He falls back against the bin again, and Laura notices how pale he looks. His eyes seem to have shrunk into his skull. He's shaking too. His body seems to be jerking spasmodically.

'Mark . . .' She steps outside, walks towards him.

He slides down the side of the bin, lands in a heap. 'Laura. I think there's something wrong with me. I don't feel right. My head . . . lights. Turn off the lights. Laura . . .'

Laura kneels down beside him. 'Mark. Keep talking to me.' She turns towards the window at the back of the public bar. It's open just a fraction at the top. 'Quinn!' she shouts. 'Bill . . . quick!' But she can't compete with the sound of the extractor fan that is whirring noisily nearby.

Mark slumps over to the side. The smell of vomit hits her before she realises that he is being sick. She lays a hand on his back. He is retching violently, his body shaking. The stuff that is coming out of him is bilious green.

'That's good . . . that's good,' she says. She knows that being sick is what is likely to save him. His body is rejecting it. Whatever it is. 'Can you tell me what you've taken, Mark? I'm going to go and get help, but they'll need to know.'

He's in no state to protest. She pats him down, checks his pockets. Finds a small clear carrier bag. At first she thinks it's empty, but when she unfurls it she can see there is a small beige capsule inside.

Mark swipes an arm at her. Tries to grab the bag. 'It's

nothing. Just some herb thing. Don't hand it in . . . please.'

She shoves the crumpled-up bag containing the capsule into her pocket just as Quinn and Bill appear at the kitchen door.

'What's going on?' Bill says.

Quinn gives her a look and disappears inside. She knows he's worked it out. One look at Mark on the ground, the stench of vomit. Of course he's worked it out. Quinn's a recovering addict. He despises drugs. She knows he'll have some strong words for her later. She also knows that he'll be on the phone for an ambulance right now.

Bill stays back, not quite sure what to do. He is the most squeamish man Laura has ever met. He is categorically unable to walk into the gents if someone's been for a shit in there, never mind if someone's puked up. More than once she's found herself with a bit of a bonus in her pay packet after having to go in there with a bleach-filled mop bucket because Bill was more likely to add to the carpet of vomit than clean it up. It explained why he didn't have kids. He was far too much of a clean freak for that.

'Can you get me a glass of water, please?' Laura says to him.

Mark has stopped being sick. Laura is sitting on the ground, Mark's head on her lap. She's watching his chest rise and fall, making sure he's still breathing. Small croaks come out of his mouth now and then, but other than that he doesn't speak. His eyes are closed.

Bill comes back with the water. 'Is he OK?' he says. He scurries across and hands her the glass. Laura doesn't answer. She tips the glass at an angle and tries to let some touch Mark's lips.

'Come on, Mark,' she says. She is talking loudly, saying his name a lot. It was part of the first-aid training she did at the karate club. Keep them with you. Try to engage. Talk slowly and clearly. Let them know that you're there.

'Take a drink for me, Mark.'

He opens his mouth and she trickles in some water. Some spills down the side of his face, and she wipes it away. She feels the change. As if his muscles have gone into spasm. His head jerks back against her leg.

'Mark . . .' She can hear the panic in her voice. She tries to move back, but his head has become heavy in her lap. 'Mark . . .'

Bill crouches down. 'What do I do?'

'I don't know! I don't know!' Laura is panicking now. Mark's body is jerking. His eyes have opened slightly, but all she can see is white.

Quinn reappears at the kitchen door. 'Ambulance is on—' He begins to speak, then clocks what's happening. He runs towards them, bends down and pulls Mark up. Laura pulls her legs out of the way, rolls herself back onto her knees.

'Mark,' Quinn says. 'Mark, you're OK, but you need to work with me here.' He rolls Mark over, fighting with the jerks of his arms and legs. He manages to get him onto his side, and Laura sees something that looks like white foam dribbling out of the corner of his mouth. In the distance, she can hear a siren.

She's vaguely aware of Bill, ushering away the crowd that has gathered at the entrance to the yard. 'Go back inside,' he says. 'Give them some space.'

The ambulance pulls up in front of the pub. She sees the uniforms through the gap in the open door. The first one appears, with a black bag in hand.

'What's his name?' the paramedic says.

'His name's Mark,' Laura says. 'He's taken some of this.' She hands the bag to the paramedic. Feels Quinn's eyes on her. Looks away.

Dear Marie,

This is getting ridiculous now. I feel like I'm talking to myself. They tried to get me to start writing a journal at the start. But I couldn't do anything back then. Not with all the fucking medication they pumped into me. I've kept some of the letters that I wrote to you. The ones I never sent. I keep them under my mattress, inside the plastic sheet. I wonder what they'd do if they found them? If they found all the stuff that I really wanted to say. When they come in to change the bedding, I have to shove them all inside my pants. It always reminds me of you and your hair. Did I ask about your hair? It's still long, isn't it? Still dark? I can't imagine you with a different style, but then I suppose maybe you changed it for the latest fashion. I thought I would always recognise you, but maybe I won't. Maybe I have to think of your face. Your lovely pointy chin. Those big brown eyes.

I wonder how you dress. Has that changed too? Everything has changed, I can feel it. Everything has changed for you, but nothing has changed for me. I am trapped inside the body I once had. I'm not sixteen any more. But what am I? A middle-aged man with no knowledge of the world outside. I don't watch the news. It would only depress me. Those loons in the TV room watch cartoons all day. No one ever turns it over. No one stops them. They just don't do it. And that's the ones that are allowed out of their rooms. There are some people who've been here as long as me, and I've never seen them outside their rooms. I've walked past, seen them through the little window. Stared into the vacant eyes. They don't scare me, though. There's only one thing that scares me.

Never seeing you again.

I'm going to have to do something about that.

Lots of love,

Graeme x

28

Graeme has fallen asleep on the couch. He looks peaceful, his soft face relaxed against the cushions. Marie feels a stab of something inside. She's not sure if it's love, not any more. Despite everything, she's missed having Graeme in her life. He's been out of it longer than he was in it, but those years they spent growing up together shaped her into who she is.

She remembers how he looked when he slept as a boy. Peaceful, his eyes flickering as he dreamt – but what he dreamt wasn't peaceful. He would tell Marie terrible stories about the things that inhabited his mind, and how he tried his hardest to keep them at bay . . . Keep himself safe from the things he couldn't explain – things he knew were trying to harm him. Or others. Marie never really understood what it was that had driven him to harm her. She wasn't sure Graeme knew either.

She stands there, watching him. Watching his chest rise and fall. So peaceful, so calm. But the memories of what he did still scar her soul. She steps towards him, plucks a pillow from where it has slipped down behind his back. She goes to lift his head to place it underneath, but an overwhelming urge hits her.

Smother him, Marie. He shouldn't be here. Get him out of your life. He will torture you. He will ruin you. See, it's already started. See what he's making you want to do.

She drops the pillow on the floor. Runs through to the bathroom, just in time to reach the toilet. She vomits until it feels as if her stomach lining has been ripped from the sides.

This is not love, Marie. You know that. Remember what he did to you.

She cleans herself up. Pushes away the thoughts that are fighting inside her head, two fully formed entities trying for victory in a battle of wills.

Get him out of here, Marie.

He's your brother, Marie.

Call the police, Marie.

Cuddle up beside him, Marie.

She clutches her head, squeezes tight, trying to make the voices stop. Is this what it's like for Graeme? Or is it worse, somehow? She knows this is her own subconscious having a battle – but what is it like for him? He was always so alone. No one ever seemed to understand him, except her. The wild mood swings – one minute terrifying her, the next crying in her arms. Begging her to tell him what he did.

He could never remember what he did. Not when it was bad.

The bad person wasn't *him*. Not really. The *bad* person was an alien being who lived inside Graeme's skin. Most of the time he stayed quiet, hidden. But when he came out, no one could do anything to make him go away.

The bad man always left. Eventually.

And so she always felt responsible for him. For Graeme. He was her true other half. 'My wee double-yolkers,' their dad used to say. When their dad used to say things that had any affection at all. They'd coexisted before they were even *born*, and even though neither of them could ever have a way of remembering that, they shared an invisible bond that held them closer than mere siblings. When they were young, it was as if they'd almost tried to climb inside one another, to get away from a world where they didn't quite fit in. Graeme, especially. Something in him that wasn't quite right.

Something that made him more vulnerable. Susceptible. All the time he'd been away from her, she'd missed him. Every single day. He must be terrified. But she can't help him any more. This is wrong. A mistake. Right now, the only thing she can do is get out of the house.

★ ★ ★

The pub is fairly quiet when she arrives. Helen is fidgeting at the end of the bar, handbag in hand, ready to leave.

'Oh, you're here!' she says. Her eyes are gleaming with untold gossip. 'Did you hear what happened?'

Marie shrugs. Takes off her cardigan and stuffs it under the bar. 'No. What?'

'Your wee pal's boyfriend got taken away in an ambulance. Drugs, I reckon. Although Quinn gave me one of his looks when I asked what happened. Laura was a bit shaken up . . .' She lets her sentence trail off, waiting for Marie's reaction.

'Mark? I didn't have him pegged as a druggie. You sure?'

'Well no, like I said—'

Marie snaps, 'I'm so sick of people round here. Bloody gossips, the lot of them.'

'Who rattled your cage, eh?' Helen throws the strap of her handbag over her shoulder and storms off. 'Have a good night.' Her voice is sickly sweet. 'The Best and the Strongbow need changed.'

Marie says nothing. Balls her hands into fists until she feels her nails cutting into her palms.

A few of the regulars are playing darts and they glance at her, exchanging looks as she disappears through the gap into the other bar. Fuck them. There is only one couple in the lounge, sitting in the corner nursing pints of heavy, gazing at each other, deep in conversation. Oh to be like that. She collects a few glasses from a table near the kitchen. Spreads out some beer mats. She takes a few deep breaths and tries to get rid of the dark cloud that is hovering over her. When she goes back through to the public bar, she has a new customer.

'Evening,' he says. 'Pint of Tennent's, please.'

Marie pours the pint. Says nothing.

'You not speaking?'

She rings it up on the till. Turns back and offers a palm towards him. He drops the coins into her hand. Eventually, she says, 'Thought you were laying off that stuff during the week.'

Sam sighs. 'I just fancied a quick pint. Hoped you'd be here. Felt like a chat. Nothing wrong with that, is there?'

'I suppose not. Sorry. I'm not feeling myself at the moment.'

Someone quips from over by the dartboard: 'If you're not feeling yourself, you need someone else to do it for you.' They all laugh. Marie doesn't feel like laughing. Hears someone say: 'Grumpy cow.' Ignores them.

'You still seeing that copper, then?'

Marie turns away. She takes a large glass from under the optics, sticks it up. Adds a measure of dark rum. She turns back, fills it with Coke from the gun. She looks Sam in the eye, waiting for him to challenge her. No drinking behind the bar, ever. It's not the thing. One of the others does it, though. They think no one notices, but everyone does. *It's just the one,* Marie thinks. *Nothing to worry about.* Sam lowers his gaze.

'Not sure it's going to work out,' she says.

Sam looks at her again. He has nice twinkly eyes, Marie realises. She downs the Coke. Serves a round to the darts players. Then she pours another pint for Sam and another sneaky rum and Coke for herself.

Davie comes in when they're on their third.

'Hiya,' he says. 'Got a minute?'

'Sorry. I'm a bit busy right now.'

She disappears through the gap into the lounge bar. She hears the swing door open and close. Davie appears on the other side.

'Why are you avoiding me? Have I done something?' he says.

She's poured another rum into her Coke on the other side. No one has seen because the couple that were lost in each other's eyes have gone. Probably home to fuck themselves into a stupor. Or maybe just to sit in silence and watch *EastEnders* on catch-up. Who cares?

'I'm just . . . I'm not myself right now, Davie. You should probably just go.'

He's staring at her, making her squirm. Can he tell that she's been drinking? She wants to tell him: *I'm doing this for you, Davie. I'm doing this to protect you. If Graeme finds out about you . . . I don't know what he'll do.* She's had this feeling since the start, since she first suspected that Graeme was around . . . watching her. Waiting for her. She thinks that it's not her that Graeme wants to hurt now – it's whoever is with her. That's what he should've done in the first place. He made a mistake. He got it wrong. *Go away, Davie. Please.*

He takes something out of his pocket. Inspects it in his hand. He looks like he's going to give it to her and then he changes his mind.

'Call me. If you change your mind.' He walks out of the lounge-bar door. Doesn't look back.

Marie closes her eyes. This wasn't what she wanted. None of this is what she wanted. She slips out from behind the bar, locks the lounge door. Picks up the glasses from the couple that were sitting in the corner.

When she goes back through to the bar, the darts players have gone. Their empty pint glasses are lined up at the end of the bar. Only Sam is left now. He's staring at her. His eyes have glazed over. Four pints. She walks around the other side, goes to lock the door to the public bar.

'Bit early, is it not?'

She glances at the clock. It's ten thirty. They are meant to stay open until eleven, but there's no one here. It's Monday night. No one is coming in now. She ignores him. Locks the door. Pulls down the blinds. Switches the window lights off.

'Fancy something different?' she says.

He nods.

She pours them both a whisky and ginger ale. She never drinks whisky. It doesn't really agree with her. Makes her do things she shouldn't be doing. She has the two tumblers in her hands. Changes her mind, pushes them both up under the optics and makes them doubles.

'Now,' she says, pulling up a stool beside him, 'where were we?'

They sip their drinks in silence, until Sam says, 'You know, Marie, I've always fancied you.'

She feels the drink swilling around in her stomach. The fuzz in her head. She's had too much. They both have. They should go home right now. Sleep it off. She is off tomorrow. She can sleep all day . . . But no. She can't. Because *he* is in her flat. Fuck it. Fuck him. She swivels around on the stool, her knees bump against Sam's, and he turns to face her. His lips are wet from the ice. She leans forward, kisses him.

He hesitates, just for a second. Then he pulls her close. Kisses her hard. Marie feels a stirring deep inside. Something she thought was long gone. Something she always tried to push away. Couldn't cope with the memories. Seeing his face, looming at her. *This should be Davie,* she thinks. *He should be pulling me close like this. He should be the one who makes me want it like this.*

But Davie is not here. Sam is here.

She puts a hand under his T-shirt. Feels the soft warmth of his chest. He is not too skinny, not too muscular. He is not like Graeme. He is not like Davie. Sam stands up. He leans into her stool, pushes her against the bar. His kisses are urgent, but gentle. They've had too many drinks. This is a mistake. But she doesn't care any more. He pushes up her skirt, and she shuffles back on the stool. She leans forward, unbuckles his belt. Unzips him. They're still kissing. Deep and frantic now. His hands are up her shirt, in her bra, on her nipples. She reaches down, moves her knickers to the side. Grabs hold of him. Making him gasp. He pushes into her. She's pressed up against the bar, and he's pushing into her, and everything in her mind disappears. Except this.

Afterwards, he wipes the tears from her cheeks. Kisses her. Walks her home. They hold hands the whole way, but neither of them speaks.

* * *

Marie wakes to the sound of drawers and cupboards being opened and closed, cutlery being dropped on the worktop. She can smell burnt toast. Her head throbs. Her neck aches from the way she's slept, head slumped towards her chest. She's never fallen asleep on a chair before. Sofa, occasionally – if she's been watching a late film. But never a chair.

Someone is in the kitchen, clattering about. Making breakfast. What the . . . ? Then she remembers: Sam. She glances over at the sofa, which has been straightened, pillows fluffed, her fleecy throw blanket folded neatly and left on one arm.

No. Not Sam.

Graeme.

She walks through to the kitchen, rubbing the back of her neck, trying to click it back into place. The kitchen looks like a tornado has hit it. Graeme is humming something. 'Crocodile Rock', off-key. It was always one of his favourites. He turns, tray in hand. When he sees her he flinches, almost dropping it.

'I didn't hear you come in.'

'Sorry . . . I'm not used to someone else being here. I didn't mean to give you a fright.'

Graeme smiles, dimpling his cheeks. Same smile as he always had. He offers her the tray. 'I'd have made something else, but you didn't seem to have any food apart from bread. I made some roasted cheese.'

'Toasted.'

'It's roasted. Stuff's only toasted if it comes out of the toaster; this came out of the grill . . .'

'So it's grilled cheese, then.'

'Do you want a side of fries with that, ma'am?'

'Your American accent hasn't improved much over the years.'

'Not much call for it in there. I tried a few Jack Nicholson lines from *One Flew Over the Cuckoo's Nest*, but it seemed a bit close to the bone.'

She wants to laugh, but it won't come out of her. They always had the debate over roasted versus toasted when they were young. They agreed to disagree. They were both huge fans of Jack Nicholson films, too. Another thing she's tried to avoid since he went away.

The smell of melted cheese drifts across the kitchen and Marie realises she is starving. 'Bring it through then. You're lucky I even had cheese.'

'I had to cut the mouldy bits off.'

He lays the tray on the coffee table, hands her a plate and a mug. 'Two sugars,' he says, smiling.

Marie takes the cup and sips it. Yes, two sugars. That's one thing that hasn't changed. She watches him as he nibbles on the toast. Too many things are swirling inside her brain, making her head hurt even more. Davie . . . Sam . . . Graeme. What the hell was she doing, letting him in here? She lays the plate back on the tray, toast untouched.

There is a sudden movement. Graeme drops his plate. Stands up. He's standing by the side of the sofa, arms by his sides. Staring at her. His face is tight. His mouth is set in a grim straight line.

'How's your *boyfriend*, Marie?'

She feels sick. He's safe, she thinks. Davie is safe. And Graeme can't know about Sam. How could he know? Has he been following her? That *was* him at the shows. Must've been. He saw her with Davie.

Or did he see her with Sam? If he saw her with Sam, that means he's been outside. All of the windows face out to the back of the building, into the garden. Into the dark. If he saw her with Sam, he must've followed her. She shudders. Imagines him watching her. Always watching her.

'I haven't got a boyfriend,' she says. Her voice shakes. She looks at her hands. Quivering. Sets the mug down. 'You know what? I need to go out. Might be best if you just stay here and rest today, OK? I just have to pop out and do a few things. I'll come back later, make us some tea. What do you fancy?'

Graeme giggles. A horrible, high-pitched sound that she's never heard from him before. 'Don't be silly, Marie. You aren't going anywhere.'

A cold trickle of sweat runs down her back. 'What . . . what do you mean? I'm just popping out to the shop. I won't be long. You can wait here for me, can't you? We've been apart so long, what's a few more hours?' She tries to keep her voice light, upbeat, but it feels false.

He takes a step towards her. 'You know, Marie. My *sweet* Marie. In Balinese culture, it's common for twins of the opposite sex to marry each other, since they've already had sex in the womb. Did you know that? I've learned a lot of things since I've been away, you know. Things I need to tell you. That's why I knew it was time for me to come back. So why don't you sit yourself down and I can tell you some more?'

Marie is frozen. 'I . . . Look, we can talk more when I get back. I told you, I won't be long.'

He takes another step towards her, then stops. Smiles. A wide, forced grin that turns his face into a terrifying mask. Marie takes a step backwards, her hand grappling wildly behind her for something, anything she can use as a weapon.

His face goes blank. He seems to be staring right through her.

'Graeme?'

He sits back down, starts fiddling with the TV remote. He won't look at her.

A bead of panic fizzes inside. He's calm again, but for how long? She can't do this. She needs to get out. Call the police. Get him back where he belongs. Sort things with Davie. Talk to Sam – does she have to talk to Sam? Just a one-off. Sam has a wife. Kids. Nothing is going to happen.

She needs to get rid of Graeme. If she can get him out of her flat, she can try to work out what to do. 'Maybe you should go upstairs and get your stuff. You can put it in the spare room. Let me know if you need anything new and I can get it for you.'

He ignores her. He's pressing the on-off button on the remote.

On. Off. On. Off.

'Graeme?'

'Whatever you think, Marie. You know best. You always did.'

Marie can't bear it any longer. She walks through to the bathroom, locks the door behind her. Takes a deep breath. A flood of anger hits her. Her cheeks burn. Hot tears roll down her face.

I'm not letting you ruin my life, Graeme, she thinks.

Not again.

29

'Are you sure you want to walk down by the river? Bad memories and all that,' Mark says. He is still pale, but other than a night on an IV drip he hadn't needed any serious treatment. He was lucky. Luckier still that despite the doctors not being able to work out what he had taken, their standard treatments for overdose had worked: pumping him with fluids, giving him charcoal to help eliminate the poison from his system. His blood tests showed that there was nothing left behind, although they did stress that they couldn't know if there would be any long-term effects.

They've sent the capsule off to toxicology for testing, Mark told her. Because no one actually knows what it is. Laura watched a TV documentary about legal highs. It was horrific. People injecting stuff into their groins. People convulsing on the ground while their mates filmed them. According to the show, the problem with these drugs is that every time the lab develops an assay to identify them, the manufacturers come up with something new. Laura realises how lucky he was. Lucky that he'd come to see her. Lucky that she hadn't ignored him and let him wander off. Things could've been very different.

Laura and Mark are walking side by side. Occasionally, his hand strays towards hers, but she pushes it away. She hasn't forgiven him just yet.

'I've no bad memories of *that* day,' she replies. 'Just what happened after . . . and yesterday, obviously – when you scared me half to death.'

He lets out a long, slow sigh. 'You know . . . or maybe you don't. Maybe you don't ever feel like this. But sometimes – don't you just wish you weren't one of the good kids? Just for a while? Imagine what it might be like to swear at old people at bus stops, skive off school and go drinking . . . take a few risks now and then. It's so fucking boring being the one who does well at school. The one that your parents like to boast about in their Christmas cards to Auntie Pat, who I really don't think gives a fuck one way or another.'

Laura laughs. 'Have you actually got an Auntie Pat?'

'No. But you know what I mean. It's not just me, is it?'

Laura takes his hand. He grabs hold of it, tight. 'Why do you think I did what I did, with you . . . what we did?' They pass by their picnic spot. Tucked away in a corner, they can make out the edge of a rug. The faint sound of voices. *Ah well,* she thinks. It was hardly a unique choice of venue. They stop walking and he pulls her close.

'I'm sorry,' he says. 'You've no idea how much. I thought I was being wild and crazy hanging out with Gaz, taking that shit. I could've died. You saved me.'

'Quinn saved you. And don't think he'll be letting you forget it. He wasn't happy with you for standing me up the other night. Said something along the lines of "liquidising your bollocks to put in the pâté". It's put me right off that stuff now, I'm telling you.' He pulls her closer, and she enjoys the feeling of his arms around her again. She feels a stirring inside her, but she pushes it away. They'll both need to wait a bit longer for that. 'Did your mum and dad go mental?' she says into his chest.

He leans his chin on her head. 'Not yet. They were mostly just scared, and shocked. I was hooked up to the drip when they arrived. I think my mum went a bit hysterical. They were quiet this morning. I think I'm going to get the "we're disappointed" chat later. I'm just glad they let me come down to see you first. I wanted to make sure we're OK. I mean . . . I totally get it if you don't want anything more to do with me, but I wanted to explain at least. I don't want you to think I'm a total dick. I'm not like Gaz . . .'

Laura pulls away. 'Talking of Gaz – what's going on with him and Hayley? I'm done with her, but I don't want her to end up in a ditch somewhere.'

Mark laughs. 'He's a drug-dealing creep. He's probably shagged half the girls in the county. I reckon she'll get the clap. If she's lucky. I'd try to tell her to stay away, but she won't listen. She's off the rails, that one. You're right to be wary. I feel sorry for Sean, though. He did actually like her. It'll be interesting to see what happens in a few days' time when Gaz and his dodgy mates have moved on to the next place, looking for new pickings.'

'Are you going to talk to Davie? About the stuff you took . . . Gaz made it, didn't he?'

'Enough about Gaz.' He leans down, places a hand under her chin, lifts her face up to his. She likes the move, although it feels a bit rehearsed – like something he's seen in a film or something. She lets him kiss her, just a gentle brush of his lips against hers. Then she pulls away. She has to ask him this now or forever wonder if she's making a big mistake.

'You know . . .' she says, making it sound like she's pondering some great truth.

'What?' He is smiling. Anticipating.

'You did do something the other day that pissed me off a bit, actually.'

'Oh?'

'You called me a "wee nympho" . . . and I didn't really like the way you said it. Like it was bad, that I might be enjoying it. Enjoying *doing it*. You made me feel cheap.'

'Isn't that a line from a film?'

She punches him playfully in the ribs. 'Never had you down as a fan of *Pretty Woman*. Seriously, though, what was that all about?'

Mark sighs. 'Just me being a dick. Honestly, Laura. I've fancied you for so fucking long. I was starting to think it was never going to happen. The amount of times I thought about you . . . when I was in bed on my own, late at night. Imagining what it might be like to kiss you, never mind anything else.'

She turns away so he can't see the big fat grin on her face.

'Well, OK then. I guess I should be flattered.' She kicks at a stone. 'There is *one* more thing though, since you asked . . .'

'Oh yeah?' He looks sheepish, waiting for her to hit him with something else that'll make him squirm.

She leans up and whispers in his ear: 'You still taste of sick.'

30

After sending the information to Malkie about the drugs forums and the possibility of a link to the fairground, Davie is at a loose end. He's not working for CID officially, so he can only do what Malkie asks him to do. Which was fine for a while – dipping his toes in without the responsibility. But he's already starting to feel bored again.

He knows what he has to do – the options are simple. He can stay here and be in charge of a station that effectively does nothing and will remain on the brink of closure until someone higher up makes the final decision. Or he can take control of his life and take a position in CID. It'll involve on-the-job training and he'll be part of a much bigger group. And at some point he'll have to go and do the residential part and sit an exam. It's that part that puts him off, but Malkie is insistent that this won't be an issue. It's nice that his friend and colleague has so much faith in him. In fact, he'd probably have more faith in himself if it wasn't for all this stuff with Marie. It's clouding his judgement, and he knows he should stay away from her, or tell Malkie his suspicions about the link between Marie and Woodley – but it's hard for him to move away from the informal community policing style that he's so used to.

He doesn't know another way.

He's managed to turn the previous inhabitant's office into his own. Gordon 'the Big Ham' Hamilton has been gone for nearly a month, and oddly it doesn't seem to have made much difference to the place. Apparently Gordon is moving to

Spain. Getting away from it all. A new start for his retirement. Davie's not convinced. He thinks there is more to it. Money, for example. Gambling debts due to the wrong people. Other stuff too. There were always rumours about Gordon's murky past. Him and dodgy councillors. But nothing ever held up.

There are a couple of shelves full of old ring binders that Davie has to get sent off to archiving. It was all before his time, but there are some old cases. He's sure there's some interesting reading in there. It's a shame to archive the files without having a chance to read them, but it's hardly a priority. He's in the middle of packing the files into boxes when there's a knock on the door. Callum sticks his head around the corner.

'Someone here to see you, Davie. He reckons you'll want to talk to him.' There is a smirk on Callum's face that he is clearly unable to shift.

'Who is it? Can you not see I'm busy?'

'Stuart Mason. Says he's got information for you. Want me to bring him in? He's at the desk trying to chat up Lorna for a cuppa.'

'Fine. Get him a cuppa. Bring one for me too, would you? And bring him through. This'll be interesting, I'm sure. What's he doing anyway? I was hoping he'd be back inside for a bit after last week's wee stunt.' He sighs.

'I heard a new word down at the school the other day. I reckon it was made for our Stuart. Cockblanket. What d'you think, Davie?' Callum laughs, quite pleased with his own hilarity, then shuts the door without waiting for a reply.

'*Cockblanket*,' Davie mutters to himself. 'Aye. Sounds about right.'

He slides the box of files under the desk. There are still a few on the shelf, so he lays one on its side to stop the rest from tipping over. He sits behind the desk, shifts some bits of crap out of the way. He's putting pens into a pot when the door opens and Stuart Mason slithers in, like the wee snake that he is.

'Stuart. To what do I owe this pleasure? Let you out, did they?'

'Just gave me a fine, boss. Big man says there was nae point me going back in. They're gi'en me a chance, I think. I've tae go doon the job centre the morn. They're gonnae sign me up an' all that. I've hud one oh they things . . . what dae ye call 'em again? When there's the flash o' light and it all just comes tae ye in yer heid?'

'A migraine?'

'Naw! An episcopacy, something like that . . . ye ken what I mean?'

'An epiphany, Stuart. Is that what you've had? Sounds painful.'

'Dinnae take the piss, or I'll no bother telling ye what I came here tae tell ye.'

Davie is stopped from saying more by the arrival of Callum with two mugs of tea. He's got a packet of digestives tucked under one arm. He lays them on the table and walks back out without a word. Davie can see his shoulders shaking. Bastard's laughing. He should've got him to interview Stuart. The bloody time-waster. It's all a big joke, but Davie has an issue with Stuart Mason. Apart from not trusting him as far as he could throw him, he thinks there's more to him than just a daft wee wannabe burglar. No one ever got to the bottom of why he tried to strangle his dog. Obviously drugs were suspected, and the dog was fine, taken away, rehomed with people who didn't have plans to strangle it . . . but it was a thing that made Davie uneasy. Someone who was capable of something like that could be capable of a lot of things.

At the moment, though, he looks happy enough, dunking his biscuits into his tea and humming away to himself quite the thing, as if the two of them are out for an afternoon jolly, not sitting in an office in a police station. Davie takes a mouthful of tea. A bite of his biscuit. He's not a dunker. Mushy biscuit floating about, ruining the tea. There is something fundamentally wrong with dunkers. It's surely no coincidence that Stuart Mason is a dunker *and* he once tried to strangle a dog . . .

'Right, Stuart. I've not got all day. What is it you wanted to tell me?'

Stuart lays his mug down on the desk. He links his hands together. Cracks his knuckles. Davie doesn't react. 'You asked me, after the vet thing. Aboot why I took the bottles of alcohol. The stuff that ye cannae even attempt to drink or you'd go blind on the spot – even I ken that.'

Davie sits up straighter. Shuffles forward in his seat. 'Go on.'

'Well, it was nicked to order, you see. Somebody requested it. Said it was urgent, and that they couldnae get it anywhere else.'

Davie frowns. 'You can get that stuff in any chemist, Stuart. Nothing special about it. It's bog-standard medicinal-grade ethanol. You can probably buy it in five-litre containers. In fact, you can get it in DIY shops too.'

'No' the medicinal stuff. It's extra sterilised, ye ken.'

'And how would you know any of this?'

'Customer telt me. He said it was important. Said he couldn't buy it anywhere, and there was no time to get it online.'

'Why couldn't he buy it anywhere?'

Stuart rolls his eyes. 'Because it would look dodge, wouldn't it? He'd already been buying loads of the stuff. He'd been to all the chemists in the area, gone as far as he could. Even as far as Duns and Hawick, he said.'

'Hang on . . . so he'd been buying up loads of this stuff?

Not just in East Lothian, further afield? What was he doing with it?'

'He said it wiz a solvent but that it had to be medical grade. He was specific about that. Medical grade. I wouldnae forget that. Why do you think I went to the vet's? I'd have just tapped the paint shop down the street if I could've got him the usual stuff, ken, like they use to clean paint brushes.'

'So, what was he doing with it?'

Stuart shrugs, looks away. 'He didnae say.'

Davie is losing patience. He bangs a hand on the desk and Stuart's tea jumps out of the mug and sloshes down the sides.

'Hey . . . Hey, boss. Take it easy. I'll tell ye. Just wondered what was in it for me, like?'

'What's in it for you is that I don't find some way to get your weaselly wee body locked up for a month in Saughton, that's what's in it for you. Bloody job centre? That's a bloody joke, that one. Stop messing about, Stuart. Tell me what he wanted all this *medicinal-grade* ethanol for, and then tell me who your *client* is, or I swear I will find a reason to get you cuffed and back in a cell before you can finish your second biscuit.'

'All right, all right. He wanted it so he could make his party drug – that thing they're aw taking now. I dunno how he makes it. He'd hardly tell me, would he? I just know he needed that stuff and he needed it quick. Orders to fill, I reckon.'

'Who's "he", Stuart? And, out of interest, why are you telling me all this? What exactly *is* in it for you?'

Stuart sighs, crosses his arms across his chest. He shakes his head, looks at Davie as if Davie is the mad one. 'Is it no obvious, Sergeant Gray? The wee nyaff hasn't paid me, has he? That wee shite from the shows. Gary McKay, his name is. Everyone calls him Gaz.'

Nice, Davie thinks. Although he already suspected that Gaz was behind all this, he didn't have all the pieces in place.

'Well, thanks, Stuart. I'm sure you know I can't do much about you not getting paid, but how about you take the rest of that packet of biscuits with you, eh?'

Stuart picks up the biscuits, turns the packet over in his hand as if he is inspecting the quality of a rare diamond. He tucks the biscuits into his jacket and stands up. 'Cheers, boss. Mind, though . . . I've scratched your back. Maybe next time you could give me a wee tickle, eh?' He winks.

Davie shudders. 'See you later, Stuart.'

He waits until the door closes, then picks up the phone. 'Malkie? It's me . . .'

23rd July 2015

Marie, Marie, Marie,

Listen – I've got a plan. Hear me out. I know you're reading all these letters thinking, what a fucking loon, but I'm telling you. I'm fine. I'm better than fine. They've been having meetings about me. I think they're going to let me out. Maybe not permanently, but I think they're going to take me on one of the trips that they take some of them on. A white minibus pulls up outside. I can see it from my window. They take ten of them at a time. When they come back at the end of the day, they're happy. They've had ice cream. Fish and chips. They take them on trips, and then after a while they're gone. Vanished. Whoosh!

They actually get to leave!

I've got a plan though . . . I'm getting out of here, one way or another. The girl who works in the office really fancies me, you know. It was her that gave me your address. She gave me Mummy and Daddy's, too. Next of kin. One letter each, she told me. I know what you're thinking – why didn't she just let me write the letters and she could've written the envelopes? I persuaded her. You know how persuasive I can be, don't you, Marie?

I let her kiss me. I could tell it was giving her a thrill. She's always got books on her desk in there. True-crime stuff . . . all that. She told me she used to write to a prisoner on death row. She's sick, this girl. I don't know how she got the job.

Lucky she did, though.

I think she's going to help me get out of here.

She's going to get me a phone. You get internet on phones now, you know. Did you know? It's amazing what's happened since I've been in here. I just need to bide my time. Just a little bit longer. You can wait though, can't you, Marie?

You've already waited twenty-five years.

What's a few more weeks?

Are you excited? I am.

Love,

Graeme

31

It's Wednesday morning. Marie should be excited about Anne's party but she is numb. She'd stayed in her room all day yesterday. Pushed a chair up against the door, wedging it under the door handle. She could hear Graeme skulking about. He seemed to flip so easily from light to dark, and she'd been scared he was ready to lose it completely. She had no real idea how to deal with him. His episodes seemed to start without warning, and afterwards it was almost as if he had no idea what had just gone on. That slack, vacant expression on his face was almost as terrifying as the horrible things he said. Not to mention that bubbling undercurrent of what he might do next. Sooner or later it was bound to turn physical. He'd tried to get in, just once. Then he'd gone quiet. She heard the TV. Heard the cat, scratching at her door. Then nothing. Sometimes she thought she could hear him breathing. Imagined his face pressed up close to her door. His eyes blank and staring. She'd barely slept.

She stares at herself in her dressing-table mirror. She looks like shit. Everything is falling apart. She thinks about texting Davie. But what is she going to say? Part of her wants to tell him everything. Ask for his help. But it's too late for that. It was stupid of her to let Graeme into her flat. Ridiculous to think she could handle this herself. She's a fool. An embarrassment. She's made the whole thing worse for everyone. She wishes she could tell him. She *wants* to tell him. Everything. But she made her choice.

She chose her brother.

Even after all that he's done, he still has that hold over her. That bond that she can't seem to break. *Idiot. You're such an idiot, Marie!* Disastrous clichés tumble through her mind: the wheels are already in motion, she's created a rod for her own back, she's made her bed . . .

She can't ask for help. Not now.

The day passes in a blur. The lunchtime shift is busy. Quinn shouts at her when she drops a plate of steak pie, chips and peas, smashing it on the floor. Bill asks her if she is OK, and she says nothing. Just nods.

She's not OK. She needs a drink. Hasn't got anything at home. Didn't dare touch anything in the pub.

She thinks about going straight to the party. Trying to block it all out. But then she remembers. Cadbury. She hasn't been feeding the cat. It's quite capable of sorting itself out, but she starts to worry about it being there around Graeme. Worries about what he might do. He'd never liked animals. They'd had hamsters as children, but they'd always died out of the blue when they were barely weeks old. She suspected at the time that Graeme was responsible, but like her mum and dad she'd pushed the thoughts away. *Not Graeme. Not my brother.*

He loves me.

Graeme is sitting on the couch, his face directed towards the TV. He doesn't even flinch when she walks into the room. One of those crappy antiques programmes is on, where people flog their dead relatives' jewellery for the price of a couple of CDs.

'Hey. I'm back,' Marie says, standing in the doorway.

Nothing.

'Graeme? Are you OK?'

He turns around slowly, and he looks confused for a moment, as if he can't work out who she is or what she's doing there. 'Hi,' he says, eventually. Blinks. 'Do you want a cup of tea?'

He's retreated back to the placid man she met in the hallway upstairs. The dark, accusing eyes and the disapproving tone from the day before have disappeared. She wonders how long it will last. 'Tea would be lovely,' she says. Marie feels a strange sadness washing through her. Feels herself regressing back to her younger self. The one who gave in. The one who let Graeme do what he wanted to her. The one who wanted it as much as he did . . .

They'd become as close as two people could be, and it had felt right. Once. Until it didn't. Until it felt wrong. Sordid. Graeme disagreed. Graeme felt rejected. She knew that now. But what was she supposed to do? She could've told their parents. Should've. But she'd wanted it as much as he did. That word . . . that horrible word . . . *incest*. It made it all sound so dirty. So wrong. But it hadn't always felt wrong. That word didn't explain how they felt. That bond. That closeness.

That love.

She thought she'd done a good job of growing up, moving on – but his very presence brought her right back to the past.

She sits down on the sofa, where Graeme has clearly slept again. The blankets are folded up at the end, but different to how she left them.

She remembers the last time they shared a bed.

'Can I get in? I've got us a video to watch. You'll like it,' he'd said. 'It's scary.'

Marie pushed her nightie under her legs. She was wearing knickers underneath – something she'd taken to doing since she'd started her period. It felt weird to be naked under a nightie now, even though it was only her in her bed and it wasn't like anyone was going to see her. Graeme hadn't been coming into her bed for a while, and she realised she missed it. She always enjoyed the warmth of another body squeezed up next to her in the narrow bed. Touching each other. Keeping her eyes squeezed shut while he guided her hand, gently spread her legs . . .

Things hadn't been the same since the night they'd watched that dirty movie and Graeme had got a hard-on. Marie had felt a wave of disgust. Suddenly, things felt different. It didn't feel right that he should be sitting next to his sister like that. The memories of what they'd been doing together since they were young slithered through her, making her flesh creep. They'd joked, but Marie had felt something strange and scary wash over her, and for a while afterwards Graeme had spent most of his time on his own. He'd started to smoke weed, usually in the shed at the bottom of the garden. She didn't know where he got it from, didn't ask. But when he was spaced out on it, his eyes went straight through her, and she didn't like it at all.

He'd pushed the video into the player under her TV then climbed into bed beside her. He wriggled around, plumping up the pillows and getting himself comfortable. The video had trailers on it for a couple of horrible-looking slasher movies and Marie knew she was going to be terrified.

'What film is it?'

'*Carrie* . . . you know, teenage girl with telekinetic powers goes on a rampage after she gets bullied for being a freak. Right up your street.'

Marie punched him in the arm. 'What're you trying to say?'

'That you're a freak, Freak.'

'What does that make you, then? Double Freak?'

He threw an arm around her shoulder and squeezed her tight. Kissed her on the head. She could smell the musty smell of cannabis coming off him and felt herself pull away.

'Have you been smoking?'

He shrugged. 'Yeah, why? You should try it some time, little sis. You might even like it.'

The film started. The girls in the shower room. Naked. Graeme's hand went under the covers. She heard him groan. He moved in closer to her again and Marie tried to shift away, but there was barely any space left on her side of the bed.

'Graeme, I'm pretty tired actually. Can we watch this another time?' She tried to keep the fear from her voice, but she heard it shake. She tried to push away the images that burned inside her brain. Little hands rubbing and tickling. Exploring. Graeme put a hand on her knee, pushing her nightie up – just a little bit, but still too much. 'Graeme . . .' She pulled her leg away, and she went too far, slid off the edge of the bed onto the floor.

Graeme jumped out of the bed. She could see a hard lump straining through his thin pyjama bottoms. He thrust a hand inside and pulled it out, shaking it, tugging it. Marie turned away. She was glad she was on the other side of the bed from him. Glad that he wasn't standing right next to her like that. She turned back to face him, trying not to look at what he was doing. 'Please, Graeme, can you just go?'

He leered at her. 'You didn't used to be so shy, Marie. You used to love playing with Mr Wiggle once upon a time, didn't you?' He continued to touch himself.

'Please . . .' She was crying now. Curled up on the floor on the other side of the bed, terrified of what he might do next. His eyes were wild, his hand moving faster and faster until eventually he groaned. Spurted over his clenched fist, let it drip down his hand and onto her bed.

She held her breath. *Thirty . . . twenty-nine . . . twenty-eight* . . . She closed her eyes tight. By the time she got to zero, he was gone.

'Marie? Here's your tea. Are you OK? Seemed like you were miles away . . .'

Marie blinks. Back in the present. She takes the mug from his outstretched hand. It's shaking slightly and she wonders if it's because of his medication. Or because he isn't taking his medication. Or because he'd been sharing her thoughts. It wouldn't be the first time.

'I think we need to talk,' she says.

'What about? Have you got any biscuits? I'd like a biscuit—'

'Forget the bloody biscuits, Graeme. You scared me yesterday. Like, really scared me.'

'Why? What did I do?' His face softens and that vulnerable little boy peers out.

She blinks. Did she imagine it? No. He'd definitely tried to stop her from leaving. His tone had been threatening. His words hurt. 'You told me I wasn't allowed to leave, Graeme.' Her voice is barely a whisper.

He stares at her. He blinks, and then the hard, glazed look is back.

'It's your fault! If it wasn't for you acting like a stupid little girl, everything would've been fine. I wouldn't have had to hurt you. They'd have never put me away.' He pauses, and she can see his chest heaving. His breathing has quickened. 'I don't think I'm safe around you, Marie.'

'What do you mean?' She can feel her heart beating through her chest, trying to push its way out. She needs to get away from here.

She walks past him, through to the kitchen. Takes the carrier bag with the pills from the cupboard, stuffs it into her pocket. She glances at the knife block, the knives are all in there, lined up correctly. Small ones at the front, large ones at the back. She runs a finger across the handles. Selects the carving knife. Pulls it out, hears the metal shearing against the sides. Slides it back in. Her hand hovers over another.

'What are you doing, Marie?'

He is standing behind her. Too close. She can smell him. Sweat. Unwashed.

'I'm going out, Graeme. Stay away from me.' She turns around slowly, edges along the worktop. He is too close to her. She can smell his sour-milk breath.

'Aww, Marie . . . *Sweet Marie*. Don't be like that.'

She feels the edge of the worktop digging into her back as she recoils from him. 'Get out of my way.'

He pushes against her, and she can feel the hardness pressing through his trousers. The hardness at her back. Panic rises in her chest, spitting and hissing and trying to choke her.

'You used to like this . . .' He pushes his face up to hers and she turns her cheek, bites back tears. She needs to be away from him, but she is scared to push him. Doesn't want to provoke him. He will kill her one day. She is certain of it.

'Please . . .' she whispers. 'Don't do this.'

His grubby paws grab at her breasts, rubbing and mauling, until finally she snaps.

'No! I said no!' She shoves him hard. He stumbles backwards across the small room, crumples and slides down the wall at the other side. He looks up at her, and his eyes are wide with surprise. He didn't expect her to stand up to him. He glares at her. He didn't expect it, and he doesn't like it. Anger flashes. His face contorts with rage.

'Where the fuck do you think you're going?' He stands up straight, his hands are raised in front of him like claws. He is an animal. A wild cat, ready to pounce. Ready to tear her to pieces.

A single tear runs down her cheek and she closes her eyes. She holds her breath. She stands, paralysed.

He makes a small whimpering sound.

The air shifts around her. The storm has passed. She opens her eyes.

He slumps into a kitchen chair. He has his head in his hands. A low whine is coming from somewhere deep inside him. His hands rub at his head. Frustration. Agitation. He starts to methodically pull out great clumps of hair. She hears the sound of flesh ripping. Sees the blood on his hands.

She has to try hard to stop her voice from shaking.

'I want you out of here when I get back, or I'm calling the police.'

She doesn't give him a chance to reply. She scoops up the cat, who protests by spitting out an annoyed mewl and scratching her on the arm. She walks calmly out of the flat. Gulps in mouthfuls of fresh air. She turns back. He hasn't followed her. She hesitates, waiting for him to appear at the front door. After a few minutes, it's clear that he's not coming out. She exhales a long, slow breath. Wipes a solitary tear off her cheek. She's safe. She's free.

She drops the cat on the grass.

'Off you go, puss,' she says. 'Off you go and play. Mummy will be back later. Don't you worry.'

The plastic bag is still in her pocket. She pulls it out, drops it into her bag. Walks to the party, stopping at the off-licence on the way. She needs a quick livener. Something to lift her up and calm her down. The little angel inside her head says, *Call Davie. It's not too late . . .*

No, she thinks. *I can handle this by myself.*

32

Davie won't be ridiculed. He's been worried about Marie, but she's thrown all his attempts to talk to her back in his face. She'd been like a different person last night in the pub. That little scrote Sam hanging around, smirking. Something's going on between the two of them. Sam and Marie. Davie can sense it, the awkwardness. But Marie won't say anything.

He knows this has nothing to do with him.

There's still no sign of Woodley though, and that *is* a problem. He's going to text Marie the link to the article. See if he can draw her out like that. He wants her to talk, but she won't. What else can he do?

He drops a packet of diced chicken into a pot, covers it with a jar of madras curry sauce. Slams the lid on. He opens the pouch of Uncle Ben's basmati rice and wanders through to the living room, scrolling through his phone. He's got a Paul Weller album playing low on the stereo. That's him in for the night. Settled. Marie can sort herself out. He's not running after her any more.

He's about to ring Malkie for an update when the phone buzzes. It's Malkie. Funny that. Twice that's happened recently. Davie doesn't believe in coincidences, but sometimes it does spook him when things like this happen. It's not much of a shock, though. They have been talking most days.

'Was just about to call you . . .'

'Aye. I've been down at that hospital. Still no sign of Woodley, but they've been investigating the "situation", as they're calling it. Fucking balls-up would be a more accurate description. They've discovered that Woodley was using someone in there to help him with stuff on the staff computer. One of the admin girls. Young. Impressionable. Apparently Woodley could be quite charming. Quite funny. Anyway, she's gone AWOL. They can't get hold of her. I can't work out if they're worried about her safety or just pissed off that she's done a runner. They can see that's she's accessed Woodley's next-of-kin information. I'm waiting for the warrant for them to confirm the details. Should be any time now. And Davie . . .' Davie hears him take a deep breath. 'I've got some news for you, and you're not going to like it. Woodley's sister . . . It's Marie.'

Davie feels an icy cold hand gripping the back of his neck. 'Shit. Listen, I've been doing a bit of investigating of my own. I didn't want to say anything until I was sure because I had nothing concrete. Just a feeling. Marie's got a stack of letters in her kitchen cupboard. There's a crest on the postmark. I thought it looked familiar but I wasn't sure . . . And she gave me her keys. There's a photo on there of her when she was sixteen. They've got the same eyes. Jesus.'

'Christ, man. Why didn't you say anything before? The link has been there since the beginning. Our lookalike Jane Doe . . .'

'I tried to ask her about them but she all but threw me out. She's all over the place. I don't know how to talk to her. But I get the feeling that she's torn . . . So now I know Woodley is definitely her brother. Her twin brother. And, er . . . I think she might know where he is. She hasn't said as much, but she's knows something. I'm sure of it. I'm trying to be supportive, but—'

'You need to take a step back here, Davie,' Malkie interrupts. 'Forget about any relationship you might or might not have with her. You need to talk to her. Properly. Bring her in. Have a chat at the station. Make her realise this is serious. Tell her about the poor cow that Woodley attacked. Tell her the details. Go round and see her. If you genuinely think she's got any inkling of where Woodley might be, we need to know. If it *was* him, then he needs to be up on an assault charge. He needs to be back in high security. It drives me mad the way these places work. They're dealing with the most manipulative people in society and they let them go on day trips!'

'Graeme Woodley is schizophrenic, that's not the same as a psychopath, Malkie. We don't know if he's manipulative. He's mentally ill. He'd been assessed and downgraded. They didn't think he was dangerous. That's all we know right now.'

'Don't give me that. You've seen those articles. You must've read the one written by that fancy-pants heid doctor. He said that Patient X had most likely been manipulating Victim Y for years. He had some sort of control over her. There were hints of there being a sexual element too – it tied in to what he did to her, and the fact that she had a boyfriend at the time. Woodley was jealous. He tried to damage her so no other men could have her. Tell me that's not manipulative. As for what he did to that poor woman who just happened to be in the wrong place at the wrong time. People like him should be locked up . . . And there shouldn't even *be* a bloody key!'

Davie sighs. 'I'll go round. But I'm not expecting her to talk to me. It's gone past that now. I think you need to come down tomorrow. I'll ask her to come into the station. We'll tell her everything. I think she'll talk. She just doesn't want to talk to me.'

'You're too close to her. She's embarrassed.'

'No, that's not it. She's been pushing me away recently, just doesn't want anything to do with me. She doesn't trust me. I don't know what more I can do.'

'All the more reason to get her in then, eh? Get her to tell us where he is. Talk to you tomorrow. I'll be down about nine. Oh . . . wait. We've been following up on that stuff with the ethanol. Your theory looks sound. All the overdoses and the two deaths have all been in places within five miles of where the funfair has been. Your one there is due to close up after Thursday night. They'll be moving on Friday morning to set up elsewhere. We're going to leave it until then. I don't want to chase them away too soon.'

'You know that a local lad called Mark Lawrie was hospitalised after taking some of that shit. Are you sure you want to leave it until Friday?'

'Aye. Speak to the boy, if you can. More we can get on them, the better. This is part of a bigger thing, Davie. I want the whole thing sorted out, not just this one fair and this one amateur chemist. He's small fry. He's not behind the whole thing, but he's going to lead us to them. The IT boys have got some info from that forum thing you sent, but they're having to jump through hoops. Masked IP address and all that. There's an operation behind all this. I want all of it, not just a wee segment.'

'Right then. I'll go and see Marie. Talk to you tomorrow.' Davie hangs up.

He walks back through to the kitchen, where the pot of curry is bubbling hard on the stove. Turns it off, leaves the lid on. It'll be cooked by the time he gets back. He takes the scooter. He's there in five minutes.

The side gate is blowing in the wind, banging against the latch. He presses Marie's buzzer. It took a few goes the last time before she answered. Buzzes again. Waits. Tries it twice more, then knows that she's either not in or she's not going to answer. Wednesday night, she should be back from work. He takes the keys out of his pockets. Hesitates.

He remembers.

Ian and Anne's party. He was invited, of course. But he'd forgotten all about it. He'd heard someone mention it in the pub the other day when he'd popped in to see Marie. Someone asked if he was going. He stands at the door, thinking. Weighing up his options. He could go to the party, have a few drinks. Try to forget about what's going on, if only for a few hours. But it wouldn't work. If Marie is there – which he knows she will be – it'll only be awkward. He won't be able to talk to her there.

Tomorrow then.

He'll ask her to come down and chat to him and Malkie at the station. He'll leave her to it tonight. He should probably go to the party and get her, but she's with Anne. She's with Ian. What harm could come to her there? If she has been in touch with Woodley, she's hardly likely to take him with her. Wherever he is, he's staying under the radar. Out of sight. Marie's not alone tonight, and that's all that really matters. Let her have this night. Let her have some fun. Tomorrow she'll have to answer some difficult questions. Davie just hopes she will cooperate. Tell them where Woodley is. Help them lure him in. They don't know for certain yet if he was responsible for the attack on the housekeeper, but he needs to be brought back in. For his own safety, as much as for anyone else's.

It was all going to kick off tomorrow, he could feel it. Marie . . . Graeme Woodley. Then the next day would be a very different visit to Forrestal's Funfair. He'd have pleasure watching that unfold. The little scumbag that was supplying the Banktoun residents might only be a small fish, but he was a slimy, repulsive little fish. Davie would be delighted to get him hooked and gutted.

He arrives back home, looking forward to his dinner and a quiet night. He turns off the engine. Climbs off the scooter and wheels it in through the gate. His head is down, and he's humming to himself. One of those songs that's always on the radio. Something annoyingly catchy about a secret potion to make you fall in love.

He hears a faint rustling noise. The song dries up in his mouth.

He's not alone.

Someone is leaning on the wall next to his front door.

The figure has his hood up, arms crossed over his chest. Even in the dying light, Davie can see that the expression on his face isn't a happy one.

Davie stops walking. 'Hey. . .' he says, his voice uncertain.

The man pulls his hood off and drops his arms to his sides. 'It's me, ye daft shite. Where've you been?'

Davie sighs. Tries to cover up the fear. The stupidity. Who had he expected it to be? 'Jesus, Callum. What're you doing skulking about outside my door? You scared me half to death.' Davie pulls off his helmet, relieved.

A cloud passes across Callum's face. 'Wasn't sure you'd be home, Davie. Listen – I need to talk to someone . . .'

33

Marie almost changes her mind when she hears the music pumping out on to the street. She can see through the window that the living room is already full of people. Laughter escapes through the open front door. The smell of cigarette smoke wafts outside and down the path to the front gate.

'Oi, out the back, I said.'

She recognises Anne's voice. Smiles. Glad that her friend is managing to keep things under control. But it's only nine thirty – still early. If it's anything like the party at Jack Henderson's, it'll be barely kicking off yet. She takes a breath to calm her nerves. She feels sorry for Graeme, wants to help him. But she's scared. She'll let him stay one more night, and then she'll call the hospital. Get them to come and pick him up. Davie doesn't need to know any more about it. No one does.

She feels bad about how she's treated Davie. Eventually he'll guess that she slept with Sam. He's no fool. But she'll talk to him. She'll sort it out. She's had a blip. Messed up. He'll understand, won't he?

She slides the half bottle of rum back into her handbag. She's only had a few nips, but she feels the comforting warmth of the alcohol hitting her bloodstream. Her cheeks have grown pleasantly hot. She feels calm.

She takes the rum back out of her bag and takes another small swig. The bottle is half-empty. She's fine now. Warm. Relaxed. As she slips the bottle back into her bag again, she feels her phone vibrate. New message. It's from Davie. She hesitates. Doesn't want to get involved. Not tonight. She'll reply saying she'll see him tomorrow.

She opens it: 'Marie, I think you should look at this.' There is no kiss. Just a link and 'Davie'. As if she didn't already have his number in her phone. As if she didn't know who he was. Maybe it's spam? Her finger hesitates over the link.

'No,' she mutters. 'Tomorrow.'

Nicely buzzed from the rum, the house feels like a welcoming place. She sees plenty of people she recognises – a lot of regulars from the pub. People nod, raise their glasses. Their cans. A few shout 'All right, doll!' She smiles back. Feels herself sway, just a little bit. She's up for it. She's going to enjoy herself.

Ian appears from the kitchen. 'Hey, you!' He leans in to kiss her on the cheek. 'No Davie?'

'Working,' she says. Shakes her head. She squeezes his arm and shifts past him before he can ask her anything else.

'Marie?' she hears him say behind her.

She pretends not to hear. She's too busy trying to make her way through the ridiculous number of people crammed into the small space. People try to talk to her, a hand on her elbow, a hand on her back. She feels like she's not really there. Observing from afar. Looking down on it all from the ceiling and seeing herself shoving her way through. Someone grabs her arm, pushes her into the kitchen.

'There you are,' Anne says into her ear. Anne's arms wrap around in a hug, but Marie's return is lacklustre. 'Ian says you're being weird. Are you being weird? What's up?' Anne is trying to keep her voice light, but Marie can hear the questioning tone underneath. Anne is good at reading her. Needling at her. Buzzing around like a fly.

'I'm fine. Just need to blow off a bit of steam. Gimme a break, eh?' She can't be doing with this. The doe-eyed

206

concern. Marie nudges her friend out of the way and opens the fridge. Takes out a can of cider, pops it, drains half. Anne is staring at her. Waiting. Marie locks eyes with her. Doesn't blink. Marie can hold a stare for as long as she can hold her breath. Something else she used to do with Graeme.

'Fuck's sake,' Anne says, eventually. 'I can't talk to you when you're like this.'

'Good. Don't talk to me then. I can't be fucking arsed anyway.' Marie takes another can of cider from the fridge and pushes past Anne, walks out the back door and into the garden. Anne says nothing, but Marie knows she's just storing it up to have a go at her later. 'Tomorrow,' Marie says. 'Save it for tomorrow.'

She hears Anne swearing at her.

Feels like laughing.

Feels like crying.

The drink. It's just the drink. She'd hoped she could just turn up and get quietly wasted without drawing any attention to herself. Why did people have to be so bloody *concerned* all the time?

'Fuck!' she shouts, out towards the grass. She's trying to pretend that everything is OK, when clearly nothing is OK. Maybe nothing will be OK ever again.

'All right, Marie? Someb'dy pissed on your chips, hen?' It's Scott. He's leaning against the back wall of the house, smoking.

'Got a fag I can have?' Marie hasn't smoked since she was eighteen, but as she's already activated her self-destruct mode, what's another vice to add to the mix?

He shakes the pack at her, letting a cigarette stick out from the top. 'Couple of lovebirds down in the shed,' he nods towards the bottom of the garden.

Marie glances at the shed, where a flickering light is visible through the plastic window. A candle, probably. She looks at

Scott. Takes him in. 'Where's your missus, then? Thought you were on a tight leash.'

Scott laughs. 'Just how I like it, doll. Nah. She's working lates this week. Says she might try and nip away early. Tell them she's got a headache or something. They always send folk home when they're sick.'

'What, is she a nurse or something?'

He chuckles. 'You've met Leanne, haven't you? Not exactly got a bedside manner. She works in a call centre for RBS. On lates, she basically answers the phone to drunk folk who've left their cards behind bars. She's cancelled the wrong ones before – husbands and wives with joint accounts. Some of the stories . . .'

Marie looks away, bored.

'Aye, well. Maybe it's only funny if you work in financial services.'

Marie ignores him. Takes a final drag of her cigarette. Grinds it against the wall. She takes another swig of cider and feels it hit her stomach. She's already quite drunk. Not really sure what she's doing here. She slides the bottle of rum out of her bag. Grips it tight.

'Oh, aye,' Scott says, still trying to engage her. He's lit another cigarette from the butt of the last one. 'I had a good chat with your brother the other day. He was coming out of the front door just as I was coming in. Didn't know who he was, so I just says "All right, mate?" and we got talking.'

Her hand tenses. Her fingers go numb. The bottle slips through her fingers and smashes on the paving.

'Whoa!' Scott says. 'Watch yourself there.'

She doesn't react, but she can feel herself shaking. 'The other day,' Scott said. Before she saw Graeme. Before he came down to her flat. 'What did he say to you?' she wants to ask, but she doesn't. She's too scared of the answer.

The door to the shed opens and Laura pops her head out. 'Everything OK?'

'You got a brush and shovel in there?' Scott shouts. 'If you're not too busy . . .'

Laura reappears a moment later with a long-handled broom. She trots across the lawn, Mark following close behind.

'Thought you weren't speaking to him?' Marie nods towards Mark. She is glued to the spot. Broken glass at her feet.

Laura scowls, but her expression changes as she gets closer. 'You OK?' she says to Marie. She starts sweeping up the glass.

'Will everyone please stop fucking asking me that?' Marie kicks at the head of the broom and shoves past, knocking Laura onto the grass.

'Hey,' Mark says.

'Someone needs to take a chill pill,' says Scott.

She heads straight for the downstairs loo. Locks herself in. Her heart thumps in her chest. The rum might be gone, but the night's not over yet. Those fuckers out there. Pissed up, drugged up. What do they know about anything? She sits on the toilet, rummages in her bag. At the bottom, hidden under her purse, tissues, phone and all the other handbag detritus, she finds the plastic bag. The one she took from Harry at Jack Henderson's party. Three capsules still inside. She takes one out, rolls it between her thumb and forefinger. Inspects it. Sniffs it.

'Just one,' she mutters. Harry took too many. So did Mark. Stupid boys. Too greedy. Just one, and this party might get started. She catches her reflection in the mirror as she lifts the capsule to her mouth. *What are you doing, Marie?* She glares at herself. Smirks.

Someone thumps hard on the door. *Bang. Bang.*

'All right, all right. I'm coming,' she says. Impatient bastards. She drops the capsule back into the plastic bag. Scrunches it into a ball and shoves it to the bottom of her handbag. She flushes the toilet. Turns the taps on full blast. *Maybe later.*

She yanks the door open. She's fired up. Ready to shout abuse at whoever's outside.

He's leaning on the wall opposite. Hands in pockets. Smiling. Waiting for her. Just like he used to do at school all those years before. That stare.

Eyes like glass.

'Hey,' Graeme says. 'I think you forgot my invitation.'

Hi Marie,

Sorry for the delay. My friend in the office was on holiday for a few days and there was no one else to post the letters for me. I don't trust anyone else. The doctor came to see me yesterday. Asked me if I was feeling myself, or if I felt like I was slipping away again. I asked him what he meant, but he couldn't explain. He asked me all sorts of questions. How long did I sleep for? What did I do between breakfast and lunch? What was my favourite game? Did I want to do an Open University course? They've asked me that a hundred times over the years. I've always said no. Remember when we used to watch that on the TV? That bearded man in the lab coat talking about Newton and particle physics and stuff that you didn't need to know about protons and electrons. Did you go to university, Marie? Did you meet boys there? I wish I could've been there with you. We could've shared a flat. One bedroom. One bed.

Me and you.

I'm still waiting to hear from you. I ask the girl in admin if I've got any letters and she always says no. But I'm starting to wonder if she's lying to me.

It wouldn't make sense, me writing all these letters to you, and you not writing any to me, would it?

I love you, Marie.

Graeme xxx

34

The party is becoming raucous. Laura has sent Mark in twice to get them drinks, but this time he insists that she goes to get them. She leaves him lying on the picnic blanket on the floor of the shed. He's got his eyes closed, an arm thrown back behind his head. Just snoozing, after their recent attempts to rekindle their romance. They haven't had sex. Not this time. Just snuggled up in there with cushions and candles and spent the night chatting and drinking – trying to zone out the sounds of the party that are spilling from the house into the garden.

Someone keeps changing the music. A couple that she doesn't recognise are laughing and rolling about on the grass. They're drenched, after turning on the sprinkler. Smokers are huddled by the back door, downing beer from cans. She slips past them and into the kitchen. Marie is standing by the sink.

'Hey, you! You OK? You seemed a bit rattled earlier.'

Marie glances at her before going back to what she's doing. Mixing something up in a glass. Crushing ice cubes with the back of a heavy spoon.

'What are you doing?'

Laura opens the fridge and takes out two cans of cider. There are jumbo packs of crisps on the worktop nearby and she picks up a bag of onion rings and shoves it under her arm. Pushes the fridge closed with her elbow.

'Making cocktails?' she tries.

'Yeah. Something like that.' Laura hears the sound of a

spoon rattling off glass as Marie stirs her drink. 'You back on with Mark, then?' Marie says, turning round to face her.

'I know, I know . . . don't say it,' Laura says. There is laughter in her voice. 'He's apologised. I got it wrong, anyway. He wasn't with someone else. Hayley is just being an idiot.'

'So's Mark, messing around with those drugs and that arsehole from the shows.'

'Yeah, well, that's over now. He's talking to Davie about it all tomorrow. He's going to tell him where he got the drugs.'

'What?'

'He's going to tell Davie about Gaz. Get it all sorted out. It's not illegal anyway. But the police are looking into it all.'

'That so?' Marie takes a can of cider from the draining board and takes a drink. 'You been in the living room yet?'

'No . . . trying to stay outside. It's all a bit mental in there.'

'You're telling me. Irish Tracy has commandeered the stereo. If I hear "Drops of Jupiter" one more time, I'm going to throw the thing out of the window.'

Laura laughs. 'Good song, though.' Irish Tracy is called that to distinguish her from the other Tracy that they all know. Tracy Bennett – unfortunately known as Tracy 'Bent It' after an encounter with someone who ended up having to go to casualty following a prolonged bout of what Tracy called 'Drunken Carnal Monkey Sex'. Laura can only imagine.

'Maybe the first five times . . . Everyone's pissed, anyway. You're not missing much. Better get back to your love nest, eh?'

Laura is about to leave when someone walks into the kitchen. Someone she doesn't recognise. Yet there's something oddly familiar about him. Laura wrinkles her nose. He seems to have brought a strange smell into the room with him too. It's noticeable even above the sticky stench of spilled beer and burnt pizza. He looks grubby. He smells off.

'Hi,' he says.

'Oh, er. Hi,' Laura replies, smiles. Tries to be polite. She glances over at Marie, gives her a 'who the fuck is this?' look.

Marie puts an arm behind her and picks up a pint glass. Hands it to him. 'I made you a cocktail,' she says. 'I think you're going to like it.' To Laura, she says, 'Sorry, where are my manners? Laura, Graeme. Graeme, Laura.' She takes a slurp from her can. 'Laura, this is my brother, Graeme. He's been, er . . . working away for a while. He's just got back. Excuse his appearance.'

'Hi,' Graeme says again. He takes the glass from Marie.

'I didn't know you had a brother,' Laura says. 'How come you never said?'

'How come you never asked?'

Marie and Graeme are both staring at her now.

'I, uh . . .' She feels uncomfortable. Doesn't know what to say. 'You're very alike.'

Graeme takes a sip of his drink. Chuckles. 'We're twins,' he says.

'No way! Marie, I can't believe you never told me this before. In fact, I'm sure you said you were an only child.' She watches a glance pass between Graeme and Marie.

'I don't think so,' Marie says. She tips back the can and drains the rest of her drink. 'Pass us another, will you? In fact, is there anything stronger kicking around? This stuff's making me feel sick.'

'Maybe you should take it easy,' Laura says.

Graeme laughs.

Marie crosses over to the other side of the kitchen, where she's spotted a few bottles of spirits. She pulls a bottle of vodka from the middle of the collection. Inspects it. Tucks it under her arm. Lifts a bottle of cheap fizzy wine. A four-pack of Red Bull.

Laura is about to say something when a couple of girls

come bundling into the kitchen. 'Yay, ay, ay, ay, ay, ayyyy,' one of them is singing. Tracy Cavan, aka 'Irish Tracy'. Laura knows her from coming into the Rowan Tree, where she is usually seen huddled in a corner having a deep and meaningful with someone or crying down her phone. While her friend Susan Pola, a quiet blonde girl who Laura has never seen taking a drink, sits and observes. Susan looks rosy-cheeked tonight. Having fun. Tracy starts opening cupboards, pulling stuff out. 'Sangri-a-a-a,' she chants. 'Anne said there was some Martini Rosso somewhere. Her and Ian have fucked off out to the camper van. Her last words were: *do what ever you like*. So that is exactly what I intend to do.'

Laura puts her cans and her crisps down on the side and goes over to help. 'I could go a sangria,' she says. 'Don't make it too strong, though.'

Tracy laughs. 'Oh, little one . . . You have much to learn.'

She finds a jug and starts pouring things into it. Laura finds some oranges and a knife, starts chopping them up. It takes her a few minutes before she realises that Marie and Graeme have disappeared.

25th July 2015

Marie,

Here's something I've been working on:

The prettiest face I ever did see,
The loveliest girl, one half of me.
The widest smile, her biggest gift,
Touched my heart, gave me a lift.
The day I lost you, my heart broke in two,
When I became me and you became you.
I hope that one day I'll see her again,
Not so much if, just a matter of when.

What do you think? Don't take the piss. It's my first attempt, but I'll get better. Things always get better when you keep doing them. Don't they, Marie? That's why I never really understood why you wanted to start it all again with someone else.

I promised myself I would never ask you this, but what did I do wrong? I don't know if you realise this, Marie, but I can't remember a thing about the night I got taken away from you. They've told me stuff. They've told me what I did to you. But it can't be true. Can it?

Love,
Graeme

35

The morning after.

Four bodies. Vague shapes. A stale, sticky smell. Spilled beer and vomit. Cigarette smoke. Weed. A sudden flash from the night before: a couple behind the sofa, bangs and thrusts. An audience looking on. The girl riding and bucking. Big grin on her face, eyes closed. Oblivious.

Marie walks slowly towards the sofa, crouches down. Peers around the back. They're still there, arms wrapped around each other. Totally out of it. A mist of sex lingers. Something else. Something stronger. She knows who they are: Scott and his new girlfriend, Leanne. Leanne had looked down her nose at Marie at Jack Henderson's party. She didn't even know her. She knew Scott a bit, just from him coming into the pub. They might've been good together. Too late now.

That makes six.

Marie is in shock. She recognises the feeling. She's been there before. Everything feels unreal, even when the truth of it all is staring her in the face. Her head spins as she stands up. Her eyes sting. She has a vague memory of waking up in darkness, peeling contact lenses off her parched eyes, tugging at dry eyeballs. She can barely see without them, everything fuzzy-edged and hard to decipher. She squints, stumbles against the sofa. A head lolls against her.

'Shh, sorry,' she says, low, under her breath. No response. Why would there be? It was an instinct – that was all. She's seen this man before. Not even a man, still a boy. Sean.

Hayley's boyfriend. The one she dumped for that boy from the shows. Silly girl.

A girl is draped at an awkward angle. Long, dark hair trailing on the floor. She is wearing a blue dress. Same one she wore to Jack Henderson's. Must be her favourite at the moment. It is stained now. Ruined. Poor Lauren. Sean sits, head leaning off one side of the sofa, his soft hair tickles her hand. She nudges him gently and his head rolls back onto his chest as she moves carefully away.

Try not to wake them.

On the other side of the room, a skinny figure lies splayed across an armchair, head hanging off one side, legs off the other. She steps closer, but she can already see who it is. Sam. Her heart lurches. She feels responsible. If he hadn't come . . . if they hadn't been together . . . if he hadn't thought he had a chance with her. Marie moves away. She can't look at him. Under the window, a girl is curled up and facing the wall. Her fair hair is matted and spread out around her like the head of an old mop. Susan Pola. She remembers the name. Unusual. Not from the area. An incomer to the town, like Marie. She remembers her from the night before – dancing, singing. Laughing.

The room shifts. Tilts.

Marie feels sick. Brings up bile and swallows it back. The syrupy taste of Red Bull burns the back of her throat. Memories of vodka and cheap fizzy wine whirl around her head and her stomach like an aspirin fizzing in water. What was she doing? Why had she gone to the party? Her head was all over the place. She'd wanted to get away. She needed to escape from Graeme.

Where is Graeme?

What has he done?

She walks around the room in a haze. All around, there are shadows. Dark patches and pools. Spilled things. Dirty things.

She squints, faces swim in and out of focus. She holds her breath . . . *thirty* . . . *twenty-nine* . . . *twenty-eight.* Her head thrums. The smell is getting worse. Body odour. Piss. Carnage and decay. Bottles and cans everywhere. Discarded bits of clothing. Upended ashtrays.

Her stomach lurches again. She has to get out. Now.

It is too quiet. Too claustrophobic.

Wings of panic flutter in her chest. She feels like she is being attacked. Birds flapping and slapping around her head, her body. Hitting her, scratching her.

Ten . . . nine . . . eight . . .

She lifts the latch. The door opens with a squeak and she flinches. Hears a soft thud from somewhere behind her. She turns back. Sees that Lauren's hand has slid off from where it had been resting on her stomach, and it now flops uselessly on the laminate flooring. But she hasn't woken up.

Of course she hasn't.

There's a faint banging sound. *Tap. Tap. Tap.* A draft. Someone has left the back door open. Maybe someone is out there now, having a fag or a morning sup from one of the cans of warm beer she imagines to be littering the kitchen worktops. She hesitates. Should she go through? Offer to help clear up? Sort out the drunken mess of bodies scattered across the lounge like a pile of coats?

They're not drunk, Marie. They're not asleep.

She squeezes her eyes shut and sparks flip and leap across her vision. No.

No.

She has to get out. She needs air, water and sleep. She needs a wash too. A long hot bath, to get rid of the stink that seems to be seeping into her pores from the toxic air. She needs to shake off the memories of the night before, threatening and bothering her like tiny pinpricks jabbing at her skull.

Something happened. Something went wrong.

I wasn't there . . . I passed out.

What happened? WHAT HAPPENED?

She walks out into the early morning sun, shielding her eyes. She takes a gulp of fresh air and feels the nausea subside – for now, at least. A chorus of blackbirds twitters in the trees. Anne and Ian's camper van is parked on the road outside. The awning has been popped up. The curtains closed. Marie hopes they are in there. Hopes they haven't seen . . .

Marie wonders if she will manage to walk home without bumping into someone, or something . . . or getting knocked down by a car as she stumbles, half-blind, down the road. She hugs her jacket across her chest.

What now, Marie?

She bangs the door shut. Hard. Starts walking. Fast.

Something pings at her. *Get away from here. You need to get away.*

Behind her in the house, no one flinches. No one stirs.

No one breathes.

She has to find Graeme before the police do. She has to find out what happened. What went wrong.

This is *all* wrong.

This is not what she wanted. A tear runs down her cheek, tickling, itching. She rubs it away.

Four . . . three . . . two . . . one.

She's gone.

36

Davie is busy whipping up eggs with a fork. He's stuck four slices of bread under the grill. The kettle is boiled. It's not often he sits down to breakfast like this, but he's enjoying looking after his house guest. They'd shared the beers and the curry. Chatted into the night until he'd fallen asleep on the couch and Callum had passed out on the chair. Despite the beers, and the half bottle of vodka Davie had found at the back of a kitchen cupboard, Callum is bright and breezy this morning, and Davie is glad to have him around. He's barely been in the station lately. He realises he misses it. Or maybe he just misses the banter.

'Thanks for last night,' Callum says.

Davie laughs. 'Some men might take that the wrong way,' he says. He pours the egg mix into a frying pan. The smell of eggs frying in butter makes his mouth water.

'Ah, you know what I mean. It's not that I've got doubts about Lorna. Not really. It just seems to be happening so fast. Her mother asking about table decorations and floral chair-backs. That's what set me off. What the hell's a floral chair-back anyway? Why do we need to cover up the chairs? I don't get it. I think you're right, though. The wedding is just a day out. Lorna and her mother can deal with that. I'll do the rest of it. The being-a-husband bit – I reckon I can just about manage that. Anyway, cheers. I appreciate it. I needed someone to talk to, and I knew you were the one. You've known both of us for long enough.'

Davie flips the eggs. Scrapes the crispy bits from the bottom of the pan. 'Yet I didn't even notice you'd got together. Some detective I am, eh?'

'Do you think that's what you're going to do? Stick with CID? I don't fancy it myself, but I don't know what we're going to do if they close the station. Lorna said an email came in yesterday. There's a meeting planned for next month to discuss it. I reckon that'll be our marching orders . . . relocate or take a package. And I can't imagine it being much of a package. Not with the cuts and the way things are now.'

Davie is about to reply and tell him about his plans, but their chat is interrupted by Davie's phone ringing. He takes the pan off the heat, checks the caller display. Malkie. He thinks about not answering. Having his breakfast first. He can't do it. He has to tell him that he still hasn't spoken to Marie. He's going to suggest they go round to see her together. A bit later, though. Let her sleep off the party hangover.

'Morning,' he says. 'What's fresh?' He's not expecting anything major. They've already planned to go to the shows the next day. The woman in hospital is recovering. The hospital is being cooperative about Graeme Woodley. It's only a matter of time before he turns up.

'Something's happened. I need you to keep quiet. Keep calm. Go round to Marie's. Now. Keep it low-key. Call me when you get there. Don't let her go anywhere. I think she knows where Woodley is.'

Davie's stomach flips. 'What's happened, Malkie?' He stares longingly at the pan of eggs. Callum is already buttering toast. Davie has a feeling he's not going to get anything to eat after all.

'Just find Marie. Then call me. I'll need you to come round to Willow Walk.'

A spike of dread pierces him. 'Willow Walk? What number?'

He already knows what the answer will be.

'Twenty-three,' Malkie says. He hangs up.

Davie tries to fight the panic. That's Ian's house. Where they had the party last night. Ian had texted him in the afternoon, asking him if he was going. Davie said he'd make it along if he could, knowing he probably wouldn't bother. Shit! What has happened? Ian and Anne are his closest friends. He's no idea how he'd cope if anything bad happened to them.

'Callum, I have to go out. Finish your breakfast. Make yourself at home. I'll call you at the station later.'

'What's happened? You're as white as a sheet. Can I—'

'Just stay here. Please. I'll call you later.'

He leaves him with the scrambled eggs on toast. His appetite has vanished. His stomach is churning. He has a very bad feeling about this.

Marie is not in. Or at least she's not answering the door. Davie walks round the back to her kitchen window. It's pulled shut. Underneath it, there's a black bucket. Something else. A pile of Lego bricks. Something has been built and smashed on the ground. Lego. What was it with the Lego? The woman in the hospital . . . Shit.

He texts Malkie: 'No sign of Marie. I think Woodley has been here.'

He gets back on the scooter and floors it around to Willow Walk. He's not alone. The street has been sealed off with crime-scene tape. Several vehicles are parked in the middle of the road. Police cars. Two ambulances. A white van. There is an eerie silence. Why is no one out on the street? He parks the bike. Scans the windows of the houses on both sides. Sees faces, staring out. He lifts the tape and walks into the street.

'Sorry, you can't come in here.' It's a uniformed officer that he doesn't know. Someone from another station. Why wasn't he called?

'DI Reid sent for me,' he says. 'Sergeant Gray.'

'Right. OK. Go through.'

Davie walks along the pavement. As he gets closer to Ian's house, the churning in his stomach gets worse, giving him sharp cramps. The back doors of the ambulances are open. He can hear the faint sounds of sobbing. He watches as crime-scene investigators clad in white protective suits slip in and out of the front door. Silent. Solemn.

'Where's Malkie?' he asks one of them. She's carrying something in a plastic bag. Looks like a shoe. The plastic bag is smeared with blood.

'Inside,' she says. 'You'll need to get suited up if you're going in.'

Davie is numb. Feels like he is in a trance. He walks to the CSI van, finds a box of suits and shoe covers in the back. Pulls them on over his clothes. He has never done this before, but his instincts have kicked in. He knows what to do. He sees Ian and Anne's camper. The doors are open. No one inside.

He walks into the house.

'Jesus Christ,' he says. He has no more words.

The place is a scene from a horror film. Pools of blood. Smears. Spatters across the chairs and the couch. There are remnants of the party still around, but the CSIs are quietly and diligently putting everything into evidence bags.

Malkie walks out from the kitchen.

'What happened? Is anyone . . .' Davie doesn't know what to say. He takes a deep breath, ignores the smell. Tries to short-circuit his brain into action.

'Six have been taken to the Infirmary. Four were dead at the scene, two clinging on, but I don't hold out much hope. Couple of witnesses out there in the ambulances. Not very helpful so far. Seems that the whole lot of them were pissed up and high as kites. They were passed out in various places.

Didn't hear what went on in the living room, but they can hazard a guess. Someone went kamikaze with a kitchen knife. It must've been utter carnage in here a few hours ago.'

'Why didn't you call me earlier? Who called it in?'

Malkie pauses. Considers his reply. 'Your friend Anne. Her and Ian slept in their camper. Said the party was out of hand. They left them all to it.'

Christ, Davie thinks. *Why didn't you call me, Ian?*

'Where are they now?'

'Been taken to the hospital. Both in shock. They'll be OK, though. As for the rest of these poor buggers . . . this is one of the worst things I've ever seen. This is going to rock the whole community.'

'Why did you ask me to find Marie?' His stomach has tied itself into a knot. He can barely get the words out.

'It's not her we need, Davie. It's Woodley. He was here last night. She was introducing him to everyone. She was hammered, apparently. Caused a bit of a scene. One of the witnesses said she and Woodley had a screaming row, but she doesn't know what happened after that. We don't know when she left. No sign of Woodley, but he can't have gone far. Not in the state he's in.'

'What do you mean? What state is he in?'

'Well, it's only a guess. But I think he might be the one who carved the place up. Something happened with him and his sister. Tipped him over the edge. We're searching for him now. Wondered if you might have any insights. Local places he might hide out.'

'He's not local, though, is he? He won't know anywhere in the town any better than you do.' He pauses. Tries to think. Is there anywhere to hide up by the Track? Probably not.

'No derelict buildings or anything around, then?' Malkie asks.

The thought smacks him on the side of the face. What Laura said. She'd been rambling on, and he'd meant to ask her, but then they'd been talking about the shows . . . 'Jesus. Yes. Marchmont Lodge. It's an old children's home. Not quite derelict, but it's a place where people hang out. Lots of rooms, plenty of dark nooks and crannies. It's meant to be getting developed soon. The new owners have managed to scare away the usual druggie inhabitants, but the kids are still hanging out down there. Someone mentioned to me the other day that they thought there might be someone in there.'

'Right. Let's go. Mike, Simon – get the details from Davie. We're going to check out this place. Get Louise. If you find Woodley, be careful – he is considered armed and extremely dangerous. Take him in if you can, but if there is any problem whatsoever, do not take any risks. We have specialists for this kind of thing. I don't want any heroes. The main thing is to locate him. Try not to spook him. We need him in one piece.'

Davie watches as the officers disperse. Sees the expressions on their faces. Excitement. Determination. Despite the worry swirling in his stomach, despite the danger his friends are in, he wants to be part of this. His mind is made up.

'What can I do?' he says.

'We need to find Marie, Davie. That's the best thing you can do to help right now.'

Davie feels ice run down his spine. What if she *was* still in the flat? He'd assumed she had left. But what if she was inside? What if she was hurt?

Or worse.

37

Marie fumbles with the lock. The walk back from the party was fuzz and noise. Luckily it was early enough that no one was about. What time did she leave? She pushes the door open and walks into the welcoming coolness of her flat. She checks the time on the kitchen clock: 5.30 a.m. Even at this time, the sun is threatening to make it a sweltering day. Anne's house will be heating up. The stink of the party giving way to something else, something much worse.

Marie isn't stupid.

Despite her clouded vision she could see that the people who were slumped around the sitting room weren't just comatose from a night that got out of hand. And it did get out of hand.

She knows that now.

She has a vague memory of Anne grabbing her by the shoulders, shaking her, saying, 'Why Marie, why didn't you tell me?' When, though? And tell her about what? About Graeme? That he *exists*? Or what he did to her all those years ago? What he's doing to her now, back in her life? Manipulating her again, controlling her. Making her think that what he wanted to do with her – *to* her – wasn't completely abhorrent. But what the fuck happened? Graeme wasn't one of the bodies slumped in Anne's sitting room in a pool of dark, congealing blood.

He's disappeared – again. Only this time he can't hope to get away with it. Maybe he's seen sense, killed himself before the police turn up. She doubts it.

He's not brave enough for that.

Marie plugs her phone into the charger. It's not totally out of life, but hanging by a thread. The burst of power revives it and a series of beeps shows that she's got missed calls, messages. Anne, ten minutes ago: 'Where are you, please call me!' Anne. Not dead then. Marie realises that something has changed within herself. Nothing will ever be the same again. Forget Anne. Forget Davie. She wonders if Anne has been in the house, called the police. She wonders if they've found Graeme already.

No.

She can sense him. He's still out there. He's scared. He's vulnerable. If there was an electric chair in this country, he'd be next in line. He's fucked. Marie is fucked. She has to find him. She goes through to the bathroom, splashes water on her face. Rubs at her eyes before sticking in a new set of contact lenses.

She doesn't look at herself. Doesn't want to see what she's become.

In the kitchen, the empty slot in the knife block where the carving knife should be glares at her accusingly.

*   *   *

Graeme was always a creature of habit. He told Marie where he'd been before he turned up at her flat – the old children's home. He'd seen her when she'd walked past that day. He was up in one of the top-floor rooms, watching her, waiting. He's in there now. Stupid fucker.

Marie drags a broken milk crate in front of the broken ground-floor window that she knows is the entrance. She places a hand on the ledge, flips herself inside. The room is dimmed, shadowed. It smells of stale beer and teenage sex. She thinks of Laura, fumbling with that boy. Getting hurt. Wanting him back. Stupid girl. Marie was just like her once. Except she wasn't. Because any chance she'd had at innocence, at finding herself with a nice boy, had been crushed by Graeme, with his twisted games, his heavy hands and feet. Her body ruined by his vicious revenge. If he couldn't have her, no one could. Marie was lucky, if lucky is the right word. She didn't die. The doctors managed to patch her up inside, as best they could. But she'll never bear children. She hasn't enjoyed sex since. Her body feels dead to her from the navel down. It's a mental thing. She knows that. But that thing with Sam . . . she'd almost felt like a different person. Like she was floating above herself, looking down. Maybe it's because she knew there were no strings with Sam. No need to think about it. Just feel it . . .

She listens as the floorboards creak above her. If she gets rid of Graeme once and for all, does she get to have her life back? Too late for that. It's revenge now. Pure and simple. She walks across discarded crisp packets, kicks empty drink cans out of the way. She looks down at her sandals and realises that they are crusted with something dark, sticky. Blood. She is complicit now. The police will see her footsteps in Anne's house. She wonders if Anne will move out now that her dream house has been tainted like this. She ascends the stairs, slowly, carefully. They are old stone and several are crumbling at the edges.

'Graeme? Where are you?' she calls out in a sing-song voice. This game is over now, one way or another. 'Come out, come out, wherever you are . . .' She walks along the dark corridor in the direction of a faint muted light that leaks from the room at the end. The door has been kicked in, hangs half off its hinges. She hears movement inside. Whimpering. She imagines him in there, crying, rocking. Blood dripping onto the floor. *Drip, drip.*

She takes a deep breath. *Ten . . . nine . . .* pushes the door

229

open. He is there, but he is barely human. She recoils at the sight. His curled figure, jerking, humming sadly, whimpering. He's coated with blood. He *is* blood. It splatters his face, like freckles. Covers his hands, like fresh paint. His clothes are saturated. His hair sticks to his scalp. His eyes are fixed, unfocused.

Marie is jolted into reality. It is much, much worse than she imagined. What did he do to those people? Are they *all* dead? She can see them, slumped and sprawled. Strewn across the living room. Discarded. They were the last ones standing when she went to bed. The last few stragglers who were too off their faces to remember that they didn't live there. Her heart starts hammering. She should call Davie. She can't deal with this now. Not now. Not when she realises what it is he has done.

What *she* has done.

She crouches down next to her brother and takes his hand. It's warm, sticky. She swallows back bile. 'It was only meant to be you, Graeme,' she whispers. Tears fall. 'None of this . . . this wasn't meant to happen . . .'

'They were coming for me,' he says. His voice is barely a rasp.
'Who?'
'The zombies. They were coming for me.'
'What zombies? What are you talking about?'
'They came for me, came at me. I didn't have a choice.'

Light glints off the blade of the knife. He is holding it loosely, dangling it from his grip. If he lets it fall, she will be faster than him. She will get to it before he does. She edges closer to him.

'You killed them, Graeme.' She chokes back a sob. 'But they weren't zombies. They were people at the party. You know that, right? You had an episode. It's my fault. I put stuff in your drink. I thought you'd just . . . fall asleep. Not wake up.' She pauses. Swallows. 'You were supposed to die, Graeme. Just you.'

Graeme lifts his head, stares at her. His eyes shine. He blinks.

'You're the same as me, Marie.'

'What do you mean?'

He's more alert. His hand grips the knife more tightly and he shuffles back in his seat, putting distance between them. 'You. Me. I always told you . . .' He lowers his voice to a whisper. 'You're a monster too.'

Marie lunges at him, but he is too fast. Had he been bluffing? Luring her in? He jumps up and the seat falls back behind him. He holds the knife out in front of him, waves it at her.

'Don't come any closer.'

Marie takes a step back, her heart is racing. She thought she was prepared for this, but she isn't. He overpowered her once before. How could she have been so stupid? Coming here, confronting him on her own.

'Give me the knife.'

'Why? So you can try and kill me again, Marie? You didn't do very well the first time.'

'No. No.' She slides down the wall. She drops her head into her hands. Starts sobbing. Pushes her shoes off her feet. 'It's over, Graeme. Please. Just put down the knife.'

'You're not giving up, are you?'

She hears the confusion in his voice. Hears the sound of sirens in the distance.

'They're coming for you, Graeme,' she says, looking him straight in the eye. He stares back. There is only darkness. 'Do us all a favour.' She stands up slowly, edges towards the door. 'Kill yourself, Graeme. What choice do you have? They'll lock you up again . . . and this time you'll never get out.'

'So what?' he says. 'I'm not supposed to be out now, am I? I should thank you for the little holiday. It's been fun. Anyway, I don't think you'll be getting off lightly either, *sweet Marie*.

They're probably knocking on your door right now.'

'Let them,' she says. 'I don't care any more. I realised today – and, Jesus, it's taken me a long time – I don't love you, Graeme. I don't even like you. In fact, I *despise* you.'

Graeme picks up the knife, holds it to his throat. His hand is shaking. 'Say . . . Say you don't mean it.'

She smiles at him.

'Marie!' His voice is thick with desperation. 'Say you don't mean it, Marie.'

She opens the door and walks away.

Marie,

This has got to stop. You need to write back I can't keep on this one-sided conversation into the fucking abyss.

Sometimes I hope the reason that you're not writing back is that you're dead. Then I think about that, and it makes me sad. They'd tell me if you were dead, wouldn't they? I think they'd tell you if I was ...

Not that you'd pay any attention to their fucking letters. Would you, Marie? I get it — I do — it was a shock to hear from me. But you need to get over that now. You need to fucking write back to me, because I am going to be seeing you soon ... very soon ... and wouldn't it be fucking awkward if we had nothing to talk about? I am trying to help you, Marie. I'm trying to make you realise that I am still me!

You can't ignore me forever.

I won't let you.

G.

38

The scooter doesn't want to start. He fires the ignition. Again. Kicks the front wheel in frustration. 'Come on. Not now.' He sits back, adjusts the strap on his helmet. Tries again. The bike comes to life and Davie turns, heads away from Willow Walk and back down into town towards Marie's flat.

He slows down, glances up side streets. Peers at anyone he passes on the way. Looking for Marie. Looking for Graeme. The streets are quiet. It is still early in the morning. A few cars are starting to appear, people heading off to work. People going about their day. No one knows yet. The town is small, but news has not yet spread. The residents are being kept in their homes, asked to stay calm. Be vigilant. Try not to spread their fear.

It won't be long before everyone knows what has happened. If they can find Graeme – find Marie – maybe they'll have a fuller picture of what went on before the hysteria starts. Because it will start. There is no doubt about that. Davie turns at the bottom of the back street, heads up towards the estates. No sign of Marie.

He's almost there, two streets away, when the engine whines and the scooter sputters to a stop. He veers off the road, almost hits the kerb. Manages to right himself just in time.

'For the love of God, not now.' The bike has been due a service. He had the letter from the specialist garage in Edinburgh over two months ago. He's been putting it off. Trying to find time to get it done. Too late now.

He climbs off the bike, flicks out the kickstand. Leaves

it sitting there at the side of the road. He could wheel it to Marie's, leave it there, but he doesn't want to waste any more time. He pulls off his helmet. Starts walking. Turns it into a jog. He glances down at his feet, realises he is still wearing the white shoe protectors.

'Christ,' he mutters. He stops, peels them off. Balls them up and shoves them inside the helmet that he is carrying by the strap like a basket of flowers. He picks up the pace. Jogs along the street, turns into the next one. He can see Marie's flat up ahead. Nearly there. He passes a couple of people in suits, faces fixed on phones, fingers scrolling, texting. No one pays attention. No one knows what he knows.

Not yet.

He'd forgotten about the keys. He'd meant to give them back to Marie in the pub, but something stopped him. She'd asked him to keep hold of them. He hadn't known why, but he was starting to realise. She'd been planning something. She knew something was going to happen.

Visions of Marie lying in the bath, wrists dripping blood onto the tiles. Marie slumped in a chair, a bottle of pills and a kicked-over bottle of whisky on the floor near her feet. *Please,* he begs, *please don't let me be too late.*

He should've seen this coming. He should've known that something was very wrong. Marie's behaviour had been erratic. Nonsensical. He'd put it down to him not really knowing her. Maybe she was prone to mood swings. Maybe she was a flake. He realises now that he got it wrong. She was all over the place.

She was terrified.

He tries the buzzer. If she answers, then he'll know she's OK. Nothing. He tries once more. Realises he is wasting valuable time. He sticks the key in the lock. Nothing. It doesn't turn. Wrong key.

'Fuck.'

His hands are shaking. He tries the other key. Turns it the wrong way. *Fuck!* Eventually, it turns.

He walks into the dim hall. Turns the corner to Marie's flat. Braces himself for what he might find. He knows which key to use now. It turns on first attempt.

'Marie? Are you in here? Sorry for using the key. I tried the buzzer first but there was no answer.'

Silence.

The flat is empty. He can sense it. But there's something hanging in the air. A faint imprint of someone. Marie. She's been here. But she's not here now. He walks inside slowly, pokes his head around the kitchen door.

'Marie?'

Nothing.

The kitchen is a mess. Plates and mugs lying on the worktop. A carton of milk left outside the fridge, the top lying on the draining board. There are envelopes scattered across the floor. Balled-up paper. The knife block is lying on its side. Four knives are stuck in it. A fifth has slid out, lies nearby. There are six slots.

One knife is missing.

Davie swallows. Tries to push the thoughts out of his head. The state of Ian and Anne's new house. The blood.

The living room is empty. A blanket is crumpled up on the couch. The room smells musty, as if someone has been sleeping in there. Sweating. The window has been kept shut.

In the bathroom, he sees two small plastic containers next to the sink. Drops of liquid inside. Contact lens packets. The disposable ones. He's seen these before. Knows that the liquid inside evaporates after a while, once they've been opened. The lenses shrivel up when exposed to the air. They've been opened recently. He steps closer, pokes at one with his knuckle. No lenses inside.

Marie has been back. Put new lenses in. But where is she now?

He goes back through to the kitchen. He's about to pick up some of the letters. Thinks better of it. He takes his phone out of his pocket, photographs the kitchen. Tries to capture the scene. A pair of pink Marigolds is draped over a small metal sink caddy. He pulls them on, squeezing too-big fingers into narrow rubber tubes. Feels slightly foolish, but knows he needs to avoid contamination. He knows that the CSIs will have to come in here, search the place. Look for things. He doesn't know what. Not yet.

He scoops up the letters that have been strewn across the floor. Unfolds one of them carefully. It's dated 15 July. Only three weeks ago. The date sticks in his mind: Marie's birthday. He starts to read. His stomach starts to churn again. *I hope you haven't cut your hair.* Something about the line sends a chill down his spine. Marie has had short hair for as long as he's known her. He takes the keys out of his pocket. Stares at her chopped hair. He swallows. Takes a deep breath, and picks up another . . .

17th July. There is always someone watching, Marie.

Another . . .

19th July. How are Mummy and Daddy? Are they dead yet? I hope so.

And another.

21st July. If only you'd listened.

26th July. You can't ignore me forever. I won't let you.

29th July. I miss the feel of your skin against mine.

30th July. I love you, Marie.

He drops the letters and the envelopes on the table. Bends down to pick up one that has been scrunched into a ball. It is creased and torn, dated 31 July: *Did you hear me breathing that day, Marie? Did you feel me watching you? I always loved watching you . . .*

Graeme sent her a letter every day, from their birthday to the 31st. The day before the woman was attacked. The day he went missing from the day trip.

'Oh Marie,' Davie says. He wants to cry. Wants to grab hold of her and shake her. 'Why didn't you tell me? Why?' He takes off the gloves and hurls them against the wall. Then he sits down at the kitchen table and calls Malkie.

39

Marie keeps walking. She doesn't pay any attention to where she's going. She's outside her body, looking down. Can't feel her feet. Can't feel her body. Everything has unravelled. Leaving Graeme in that house was like being pulled apart at the seams. He is broken. He doesn't even know what he did. And it is all her fault.

Moments of clarity burst through the clouds of her mind. Crushing up the pills. Mixing them into his drink. She thought he'd just slip away. That lad at Jack Henderson's had been lucky – he'd convulsed for a bit, but then he'd thrown up and the stuff was out of him. Those other kids that she'd read about in the paper – they weren't so lucky. One of them had been taking steroids for a bout of acute asthma. The drugs hadn't agreed with each other. Another one had taken his with half a bottle of Jaegermeister. Heart attack.

Graeme's had been mixed with alcohol. And with his troubled mind. She hadn't expected the outcome. She'd wanted his heart to stop. It was the only way to stop him from taking over her life. But that's not what happened.

Marie doesn't really know what happened. Doesn't want to. Memories spin inside her skull and she can't shake them away. When he'd turned up at the party, she'd panicked. She tried to push him out of the door. She'd begged him. Screamed at him. He'd just smirked. She remembered someone coming into the hallway, remembered screaming at them too – *fuck off, just fuck off, leave us alone* . . . and later, with Anne. Another argument with her best friend, the one she'd never been able to share her darkest secret with, despite her being the only one to give her a chance when she'd turned up in Banktoun all those years ago, all badly shorn hair and unrelenting anger. Scott had said something, and the news had spread. *Marie has a brother* . . .

'Why didn't you tell me?' Anne had begged, gripping her shoulders, trying to shake the words out, hurt shining in her eyes.

There was nothing else for it. When she'd put the pills in her bag, she'd fully intended on taking them herself. Using them to forget all the shit that was going on in her life. But when Graeme had appeared, clearly having followed her there, he'd taken her choice away.

She'd drunk too much. There are gaps. Blackouts. Time seemed to slow down and speed up. The place was packed with bodies, and then it wasn't. The party was winding down. After giving Graeme the cocktail, she'd gone upstairs with the vodka and the wine. Passed out in one of the spare rooms. Laid herself down in a corner. Covered herself with coats.

Had Graeme come looking for her?

There must be witnesses. Some of those people in there were sleeping it off. Someone was in the garden.

Someone must've seen something.

What Graeme did.

What *she* did.

Even without her contact lenses, she'd known what she was walking through in that room. She'd known that the coppery tang in the air was blood. Recognised the dark-brown stains on the rubber soles of her shoes.

She left her shoes with Graeme. She doesn't know why. Her plan was to finish what she started, but when she saw him there in that room, she knew she couldn't do it. She'd wanted to curl up, go to sleep. Wanted it all to be over.

She finds herself on the railway bridge, the first one along the old line that they call the Track. It's a popular walking spot. Other stuff happens along there, too. Good things. Bad things. Strange things.

She stands on the bridge and looks along the path towards the stagnant pool that lies hidden amongst mossy boughs and tall reeds. Hidden from the sun, it is a dark and frightening place. From her viewpoint on the bridge, she can just make out the edge of the water. She can see a flash of white from the statue of the fairy with the water lily. She'd found the pool when she'd first moved to Banktoun. She'd stood too close to the edge, reaching out to touch that statue with its cold, blank eyes. She'd almost slipped in, caught herself by grabbing onto an overhanging branch.

She wants to go back there now. She wants to soar from the bridge, dive into the pool. She wants to sink to the bottom. How deep is it? How dark?

What's in there?

She feels the statue calling to her. Beckoning her. *Marieeeee . . .*

There's a faint rustle of wind catching leaves. No one else is around. No one has come looking for her. Not yet.

She strains her ears, listening for the sounds of police sirens. Nothing.

Graeme . . .

She lays her hands flat on the cold stone wall and pulls herself up. She rolls onto her knees, positions her feet on the wall and stands up, slowly, carefully. Tries not to wobble.

Her feet are cut and bleeding. Her blood now. No one else's.

There is too much blood.

She has to get away.

She stands up straight and tall. Holds her hands out at her

sides. She wonders if anyone can see her – from a distance, she must look like she's on a giant cross.

Marie the Martyr.

She leans forwards slightly, gets a better view of the pool. She can see about a quarter of it now. Bright-green scum coating the surface. If she leaps . . . if she soars . . . will she make it to the pool? She imagines herself sinking through the soft, slimy surface. Feels it enveloping her into its depths.

She takes a breath. *Sixty . . . fifty-nine . . . fifty-eight . . .*

Do it, Marie. It is Graeme's voice.

Do it.

Jump!

She jumps.

Dear Marie,

Sorry. Again. I don't like to get angry with you. I never liked to get angry with you. But sometimes you do stuff that is just so infuriating. I don't think you can help it. I was thinking about you at breakfast this morning. The way you always put three sugars and half a sliced banana on your cornflakes, and then you threw the other half of the banana away. Why didn't you eat it? Do you know I used to take it out of the bin? I imagined you biting it. Your lips around it. Sometimes I used to rub it on myself, then eat it. Imagining it was you. Wishing you would touch me just one more time. I never wanted it to stop. No one said it had to stop. Only you, Marie.

You wanted it to stop.

You tried to replace me with that boy. Why?

I realise my mistake now. It was him I should've taught a lesson. Not you.

Love,

Graeme

40

Laura is shaking. She's sitting in her living room, a blanket wrapped around her shoulders. Mark was taken home. She wants to be with him, but her mum is refusing to let her leave the house. She's fussing over her, bringing her cups of tea with too many sugars. But Laura is still shaking.

She knows what she has to do. But if she's right, then the consequences are huge. Devastating. She's not sure if she can be the one to make this choice. She wanted to tell Mark, ask him what to do. But then the police had turned up, found them there in the shed. They'd taken them out the back gate, driven them home. A young detective called Louise kept trying to ask her questions, but Laura felt like her throat had closed up. She couldn't speak. Shook her head.

'So, you didn't hear anything?' Louise Jennings had asked her. 'Nothing at all? No shouts . . . screams . . .'

'Louise,' the other detective had said. Simon, his name was. Maybe. There had been a warning in his voice. Louise had stopped asking questions after that.

Laura had questions, like: why are you here? Why didn't you let me go inside to use the toilet? She heard it on the radio. Simon and Louise had looked at each other, Simon had tried to turn it down, turn it off. But it was too late.

'Suspect is an IC1 male, name of Graeme Woodley. Suspected armed and dangerous. Do not approach.'

'What did he do?' Laura said. Her voice was a croak. A whisper.

'Are you sure you didn't hear anything?' Louise said, one more time.

'We were in the shed. We had headphones on. The music they were playing was shit. People were screeching in the back garden. We just wanted to drown them out.'

Louise caught her eye in the rear-view mirror. Her face looked pained.

'Let's get you home,' she'd said.

Laura is still shaking. She picks up her phone. Knows that she's got no choice. She saw it. She thinks she saw it. What if she's wrong?

She starts texting. She writes in short sentences, trying to get it all across. Trying to explain: 'I saw Marie at the party. She was mixing up a drink. Crushing stuff up. She kept stirring it. I asked her what it was, but she ignored me. She gave it to him. Her brother. I don't know if he drank all of it, but I saw him drink some of it at least. There was a brown scum on top. It stuck to his upper lip. I think she put something in there. But I can't be sure. Please don't say it was me who said anything. I might be wrong. Maybe it was just some scuzzy cocktail.'

She puts her finger at the end of the line. *Delete. Just delete it,* she thinks. *You don't know. You don't really know.* She takes her finger off the screen. Checks that she's picked the right contact. Closes her eyes and counts to three.

Hits 'send'.

28th July 2015

Marie,

I've written a letter to Mummy and Daddy. I've told them I don't want to speak to them, but I wanted them to know that I am still here, still breathing. I know that they will never reply, but I hope that when I see you, you can tell me about them. Tell me if they did anything interesting with their pathetic, miserable lives. Do they ever talk about me? Does anyone ever talk about me?

Do I still fucking exist?

One day, Marie. One day, you will fucking answer me.

Your brother,

Graeme

41

Marie's ankle burns. Jumping backwards down onto the bridge in her bare feet like that had been a stupid thing to do.

But not as stupid as if she'd jumped the other way.

It might have only been thirty feet high, but she would've never made it as far as the pond. There would have been no quiet release into the soft green water. Only the pain of broken bones. A crushed skull.

She limps home, left foot almost dragging behind her. She doesn't know if it is broken or sprained, but she knows that it hurts, and that the hurt in her ankle has taken away the hurt in her head. Classic distraction technique – like curling your toes when the nurse sticks a needle in your arm. Her version is more extreme, but it works. It's stopped her head from pounding, and momentarily, at least, she is thinking about her ankle, and her cut and bloodied feet, and not about all the other things that she needs to face.

She lets herself in, closes the door carefully behind her. Something feels wrong. Disturbed. There is a chink in the curtains, and sunlight is funnelled in like a laser beam, specks of dust dancing inside. She didn't open the curtains when she'd come back earlier. She'd splashed her face with cold water, forced contact lenses into her tired, dry eyes. She hadn't changed. Hadn't washed any of the party away, and now she feels clammy and grubby. She can smell herself through her T-shirt. Sweat. Fear.

Someone is in the house.

'Hello? Who's there? If you're here to burgle me, you'll find slim pickings. Better just let yourself out the back door and we'll say no more about it.' She hears the wobble in her voice. Her bravado is just that. A front. She knows who it is. Knows how he got in, too. After all, it was her who gave him a key. She had a premonition that day at the fair. She knew this moment was going to happen, one way or another. If it hadn't been to sit in wait for her, it would have been to save knocking the door down when they saw her through the kitchen window, dangling from the ceiling.

A familiar figure steps out of the kitchen.

'Hello, Marie,' Davie says. 'Hope you don't mind me letting myself in. I've been meaning to give you your keys back. Wasn't sure why you wanted me to have them. I think I know now. Are you OK? Where've you been? We've been looking for you.'

'We?' Marie says. She sits down on the armchair. Another figure appears from the kitchen. He's dressed in a grey suit and a slightly crushed white shirt. She recognises him, vaguely.

'Marie, you remember Malkie, don't you? You met at the barbecue at Anne's last summer.'

Malkie doesn't smile. 'Detective Inspector Malkie Reid.'

Davie sits down on the couch, facing Marie. Malkie stands nearby. He looks angry and bored, but Marie suspects this is just his usual look.

'What's going on?' Marie says. She knows why they're here, but it doesn't harm to try to put it off for just a bit longer.

'Let's not beat around the bush, Marie,' Malkie says. 'We know what you did. Davie?'

Davie stands, and she notices that his hands are shaking slightly. 'Marie Bloomfield—'

Marie steps back, raises a hand. 'Wait,' she says. 'I need to tell you what happened. I need you to understand—'

248

'Marie, stop. Don't do this now. We need to take a formal statement from you. We need to make sure we get this right. I know there's probably a lot of stuff you want to tell us—'

'I *need* to tell you . . . I need to tell you why . . .' She lets the sentence trail off. Davie looks uncomfortable. Gives her a tiny shake of his head. Tries to communicate through his eyes. *Shut up, Marie. I can't help you if you start talking now.*

He won't be able to help her anyway. She's beyond help. She knows this. She thought she could cope, living her life the way she did. But she got complacent. She should have always realised that there was a possibility that Graeme would get out. That he'd be back to torment her. She'd thought taking him in would protect him. Protect herself. But it had backfired. Badly. She wasn't mad. She'd known exactly what she was doing. But what now?

She sighs. Clears her throat. 'You'd better do it then, Davie. I'm not going to stop you. Just . . . just remember this. I did have feelings for you, you know? I still do. I thought you might be the one to help me. But I realise now that could never happen. You can't run away from your past, Davie. I . . . I'm sorry.'

Davie glances back over his shoulder at Malkie, and the inspector nods, once. His mouth fixed in a tight, straight line.

Davie takes a set of handcuffs from his pocket. 'Marie Bloomfield, we're arresting you on suspicion of assisting in a multiple homicide. We have information that indicates that your actions were indirectly responsible for the serious events that took place at a party at Willow Walk yesterday evening. You do not have to say anything, but anything you do say . . .'

Marie tunes out the rest of the caution. Stands up. Says nothing.

'We've found Graeme,' Davie continues. 'We know you just

came from seeing him. DC Jennings has taken him in. DI Reid and I will be joining her later to commence questioning . . .'

Marie offers him her wrists, ready for the cuffs. He closes his eyes. Opens them again. Takes her by the elbow.

'I don't think we need the cuffs.'

Marie lets Davie lead her out of the door. She is still limping, but he doesn't ask her what happened. She hears Malkie following close behind. Then another sound, a scratching, a quiet mewl.

'Wait,' she says, spinning back round. 'The kitchen window . . . Cadbury . . .'

'Who the fuck is Cadbury?' Malkie says, impatient now. He turns and Marie knows he can see the brown ball of fur with the angry eyes, staring at them through the window.

Davie ushers her through the hall and out the main entrance. Marie hears the door slamming behind her. She's about to say something about the mailbox. The letters. She keeps quiet. They'll find them soon enough, if they haven't already. Outside, Malkie overtakes them both and opens the door to the back seat.

Davie leans in close as he helps her into the car. He places a hand on her head. Whispers into her ear. 'I wish you'd come to me. I could've helped you.'

'I'm sorry,' she whispers. 'Please, Davie. Look after the cat.'

Davie pushes her door shut. Stares in at her through the window. He nods once, and then he turns away. He climbs into the driver's seat. Malkie is already sitting in the passenger seat. He doesn't look back.

Davie catches her eye in the rear-view mirror.

It's her turn to look away.

Marie leans back in the seat and realises she's not scared.

Not any more.

29th July 2015

Dear Marie,

I know, I know. I'm blowing hot and cold here. I don't know what else to do. Help me out. Please. Tell me about life. Tell me what it's like to live a life and be free to do whatever you want, to go where you want, to eat where you want. Tell me about a bedroom with pictures on the walls, books on the shelves. A window without bars. How many times have you been to a pub, do you think? Do you know how many times I have? Four. Three times with you, Mummy and Daddy for Sunday lunches – remember they made us get dressed up, like we were going to the bloody Oscars or something? And the roast was always tepid, the gravy thin and weak. Daddy always had a pint of bitter and Mummy had a small port.

We were fourteen, Marie. We had Babycham. Do you remember? That little prancing deer on the side of the bottle. I don't know who decided to stop taking us, but three times ... that's pretty low, I think. I only went one other time, on my own. That day I left you. They served me a pint of lager, even though they knew I was underage. I think they were scared of me.

Maybe it was the blood.

I remember thinking, when the police walked in: 'That was quick.' I didn't get a chance to finish my pint, so technically I have never even drunk a pint.

Can you imagine that, Marie?

I liked it when we went into the woods with the cans of shandy from the corner shop. We thought if we drank enough, we'd have to get drunk eventually. We never did, but we had fun, didn't we? Just the two of us.

I miss you, Marie. I miss the feel of your skin against mine.

Please write back. Please.

Love,

Graeme xx

42

Davie watches her on the monitor. He's sitting in a small room that isn't much more than a broom cupboard, but it has a large screen and three chairs. She is in another room, just along the corridor. She has a beige cup on the table in front of her. He has one just the same, sitting next to the keyboard. The machine said it was café au lait, but it smells of burnt tyres. Like his burnt-out scooter that he left on the side of the road. Louise Jennings sits beside him. She's zooming in and out of the screen. Trying to get the best position so that they can see Marie, as well as those on the other side of the table. Malkie Reid and Simon Richards.

Simon was recently promoted to detective sergeant, according to Louise. Her tone suggests she's not happy about it. He imagines that she wants to be in there, taking the centre stage. He can see the gleam in her eye. What an exciting case this is, she is probably thinking: *I'd love to be involved. That should be me.* He wants to be angry about it, but he sees a bit of himself in her eyes. He can almost *smell* the buzz coming off her and he wishes he could feel like that now. Eager. Enthralled. *Involved.*

Davie is involved, but not in the way he wants to be. He aches, looking at her there in that room. Sitting on the plastic chair. Her hands clasped in front of her. She has refused a solicitor. She will need one eventually, but it's her choice to be interviewed without one. Davie wishes he'd had a chance to talk to her. He has no idea what she is thinking. He still doesn't know exactly what she did, or why. Before her arrest, Marie was ready to tell them everything. But, sitting there in the interview room, she seems to have retreated into a shell. She is answering with one-word replies. Giving them nothing. Davie can sense that Malkie is getting annoyed.

Let me in there, Davie thinks. *She'll talk to me.* Then again, though, would she? She had plenty of chances to do it before. Before her brother turned up at her flat. Before he followed her to the party and stabbed six people.

All six of them are dead. Two hung on for as long as they could, but they'd lost too much blood. The knife had been driven in too deep. The pathologist said it looked like the knife had been plunged in like a sword. There were a few defensive wounds here and there, slashes to palms and suchlike, but they had been attacked in their most vulnerable state. Off their heads. They never saw it coming. Were too slow to fight him off. They probably thought they were having a bad trip.

He hopes so. He hopes that they didn't know what was really happening.

'Marie, it'll be easier for us all if you can just tell us everything now. If you'd prefer, we can still call in a solicitor for you. We strongly advise that you listen to us on this. Your brother might be the one who stabbed them, but something triggered his psychotic episode. The doctors have taken samples. They'll find out what he took. You can save us a lot of time if you help us out.'

Marie shuffles in her seat. Looks up at the camera. Davie knows that she can't see him. Doesn't even know that he's there. But it feels like she is looking straight into his eyes.

'Wow, she's creeping me out now,' Louise says.

Davie wants to say: *Shut the fuck up. You don't even know her.* But he realises there is no point. Louise isn't doing anything wrong. Marie is a suspect now. No one is going to cut her any slack. Not if she's responsible for this. Not if she gave something to her brother that set him off. Davie knows what she did. He knows she somehow got hold of some of that shitty herbal drug that's been doing the rounds. He wants to burst into the room. He wants to save her. But it's too late. He wants to take her in his arms and squeeze her. He wants to say he's sorry. If he'd acted sooner. If only he'd got to her before she went to that party . . .

Marie is staring into the camera. Staring into his eyes. He shivers.

'I just wanted him to go to sleep,' she says. 'I just wanted him to leave me alone.'

43

After several hours, they take her to a cell. They leave her there, with a plastic cup of water. They have given her a pair of shoe covers to wear over her feet, as they were scraped and bloody from walking. She hadn't thought to put on shoes when Davie had taken her away from the flat.

She's asked them for some paper and a pencil, so that she can write everything down. They hummed and hawed about the pencil, worried she might stick it through her eye and puncture her brain. She hadn't even considered that as an option, but it will stay in her head now. A possibility.

Eventually, they allow her a pen, but only if someone sits with her.

'It'd be quicker if you just told them in the interview room, love,' the young detective says. Her name is Louise. Marie sees glee in her eyes when she talks to her. She is desperate to know the full story.

Marie smiles at her. 'I'm not in a hurry. Besides, I don't want to miss anything out. I want to make sure you understand. You need to understand it all.'

Louise shrugs. 'You know they've taken your brother to Carstairs. He won't be getting out. There'll be an inquiry. About why he was downgraded to medium risk. About how he ended up on that day trip. He hasn't confessed to that attack yet, but we know it was him. DNA. He's never getting out again. He can't hurt you any more, Marie. It'll help you out if you tell us everything now.'

'What'll happen to me?' Marie says. Her voice is barely a whisper.

'I don't know. DI Reid is finalising your charge sheet. Might be conspiracy to commit murder. You did want to kill your brother, didn't you?'

Marie says nothing.

'Or they might charge you as an accomplice for the six that your brother killed. Depends on your mitigating circumstances. Might be time for you to think about getting that solicitor . . .' She lets the sentence trail off.

Marie can tell that she doesn't know. It's conjecture. She'll find out soon enough. In some ways, getting sent to prison would be a blessing. She won't have to worry about Graeme in there. Won't have to continue her attempt at a normal life.

Marie picks up the pen, starts to write.

My name is Marie Stephanie Bloomfield. My date of birth is 15th July 1974. I live at Flat 7, Marnie House, Colbert Road, Banktoun. I've lived there for twenty-five years, most of those on my own when my parents moved away to Spain. They'd had enough, they said. Felt like they were looking over their shoulders all the time. Waiting for someone to work out who they were. Make their lives hell.

It was me who should've been worried about that. My life was hell from the minute I was born, three minutes and forty-four seconds after the screaming lump that was my twin brother. They put us in cots next to each other and, if I didn't know better – if I didn't know that babies had no memory – I'd swear he started watching me from the very minute we were born.

Sometimes it was fun, growing up. We could read each other's thoughts. We knew what each other liked and hated. We played games, and we made up worlds. It was our world. Graeme and Marie. We even made up our own language, so we could say things to each other and no one else would know.

It was just a temper he had, sometimes. Nothing to worry about. Everyone gets annoyed about stuff. But it started to happen more. Things seemed to trigger it. Mum blamed herself, for that time when the two of us got scalded in the baby walker. Said he was never the same after that. But we were only two. How could she know? I think she always knew. Dad too. They just didn't want to admit it. Couldn't accept it. I know now that if they'd got help for him sooner none of it would have happened.

That's their burden. Their guilt.

I saved him that day in the pool when he nearly drowned. He tried to hold his breath for too long. He passed out. I dragged him up from the bottom, gave him the kiss of life. He woke up, choked up pool water into my face. Smiled at me. Told me he loved me. I kissed him again then, even when he wasn't choking any more. I could taste the chlorine on his lips. Felt the warmth of his mouth against mine. We'd been close all our lives but something changed that day. I realised that I loved him too. Properly. More than a sister should love a brother. A stronger love. Deeper. One that only the two of us could understand.

It was our little secret.

When he started to smoke weed, that's when I lost him. That's when he changed. The tantrums became rages. He broke things. Threw things. Mum was scared of him. She told me that one day. Told me she couldn't wait until we were old enough to leave home, so he could go away. So I could escape.

I think Mum knew.

She caught us once. In Graeme's bed, under the covers. We were just cuddling then, but I think she knew what we were doing. She could smell it. That musty stink of bodies too close.

When I was fifteen, a boy from my English class asked me to go out with him to the cinema. We went to watch Ghostbusters. It was in one of the arts cinemas, a special double bill. We ate popcorn and he put his arm along the back of the seat behind me. I didn't see Graeme until we were back outside. He was standing in a dark space in the corridor near the toilets. He smiled at me, and I realised then he was never going to let me go.

He wanted me.

But I didn't want him any more. Not like that. Not like the things we used to do when we were kids. We were just children. We were experimenting. Was it really so wrong? I knew that it had to stop. I pleaded with him one day. Begged him to stop following me. Stop waiting for me outside my classes. Outside the toilets. No one liked him. They liked me, but I think a lot of it was pity. 'Poor Marie, her brother's a weirdo.'

I waited until I was sixteen. I was in love with Howie. He was pleased that I'd waited for him. Lots of other girls had already done it, he said. He didn't know that I had . . . and I would never tell him.

Graeme walked in on us. He'd followed us home. We were having a party that night. Our 16th birthday. Mum and Dad had gone out to buy balloons. He started on Howie. He hit him with the rolling pin, smashed it over his head. No. No. I begged him. Please, it's not his fault. I shouted at Howie, told him to run, get help. Graeme let him go. It wasn't Howie he wanted to punish.

He started on my face. I tried to fight him off, but in the end I just gave up. I'd already passed out by the time he started to shove it inside me. I think he tried to wake me up. I have vague memories of him slapping me, spitting on me, shouting in my face. 'How do you like this, sweet Marie? How do you like this?'

He stopped, eventually. Jumped out of my bedroom window onto the roof of the outhouse at the back. Disappeared. They found me, then they found him. They thought I was dead. There was so much blood. The whole place had to be bleached down and re-carpeted afterwards. A specialist team came in to do it. Crime-scene cleaners. Who knew those things even existed?

I stayed in hospital for six months. They patched me up. Let me convalesce. When I came out, Mum and Dad had already sold the house. They'd enrolled me in a new school. Given me a new name. I liked Bloomfield. It reminded me of my gran. But the best thing was, it was something that Graeme would never have. He would always be Graeme Woodley.

They'd managed to prise us apart.

I missed him at first. I know that probably sounds strange. But before he hurt me, I loved him so much. He was my best friend. He taught me everything. I never laughed with anyone as much as I did with him.

Therapy helped. They taught me that it wasn't my fault. That Graeme had developed an obsession with me. It wasn't natural. He wasn't well. They'd diagnosed him a schizophrenic. It explained a lot of the things he'd done over the years. The paranoia, the delusions. The nightmares that turned out to be hallucinations.

When he came back, I didn't know what to do. Part of me wanted to see him. Talk to him. Ask him why he did it. I wanted him to be better. I wanted him to be the old Graeme, the brother I loved.

But it became obvious that he wasn't better. He would never be better. He was still obsessed with me. He would always be obsessed with me. I didn't have a choice. I'd seen what that drug did to Harry. I knew it could kill – especially if it was given to someone who had other issues. Other problems. Someone who hadn't drunk alcohol for more than twenty years.

I just wanted him to go to sleep.

I'm sorry for what happened. I never thought it would react so badly in his system, sending him into a frenzy like that. I thought he'd have a fit. Choke on his own vomit.

I thought he would die . . . I didn't even know he had the knife.

Maybe he's told you now, what he had planned. But I think I know. He took that knife and he followed me to that party. He wanted to kill me. Just me. Kill or be killed. He's not stupid. He must've known I wasn't going to let him stay with me any longer. If only I'd called the police. If only I'd told Davie. Forgive me.

Marie lays the pen on the plastic mattress. Folds the sheets of paper in half. Louise is still watching, waiting.

'I'm done,' Marie says. She offers Louise the papers. 'Here. I suppose you're getting the exclusive.'

DC Louise Jennings tries to suppress a smile. She takes the papers from Marie, picks up the pen from beside her. She walks out of the cell, leaving Marie on her own. With just the plastic cup. The water inside is cloudy. Lukewarm.

Marie lies back on the narrow bed. Throws her arms back behind her head. She is tired. So very tired. She takes a breath.

Sixty . . . fifty-nine . . . fifty-eight . . .

Closes her eyes.

Waits for whatever is going to come.

30th July 2015

Dear Marie,

Remember when we used to go swimming? I loved those days with you. I loved the shape of your body inside your costume. That shiny pink Lycra with the silver stripes on the sides. The way your hip bones jutted through the fabric. I loved your hair when it was wet, slicked back smooth and flat over your head. You reminded me of a baby otter. Flipping and swimming and popping your head up out of the water. Remember how we used to hold our breath and sink to the bottom of the pool? I used to love to sit there on the bottom, looking up at you, watching your legs scissor-kicking up above me. I could make out the shape of you beneath the fabric. Every last shape and fold of your skin. I longed to touch you there, but I stopped myself. I know we had to keep our little secret.

You saved me that day. The day I stayed down for too long. One hundred ... ninety-nine ... too much. Too long. But I couldn't help myself. I wanted to watch you. I don't remember you coming down there to get me, but I know you did.

I woke up when you kissed me.

I could taste your lips.

I love you, Marie. I'll always love you, Marie. No matter what. We're one, Marie. One being, split into two. Fused together, split apart. But we don't need to be apart any more.

Ever.

I'll always be watching, Marie.

With love,

Graeme xx

44

They arrive quietly. Davie takes the lead. Malkie follows close behind. There are three squad cars parked around the back of a disused warehouse next to the river. Waiting. The strategy is simple. They've given no indication that they know anything. As far as everyone who was able to has reported, Gaz was not at the party. He didn't supply any drugs there. He has no reason to suspect that they are on to him. Unless someone has tipped him off, and Davie can't see who would gain from that.

Davie walks across the grass towards the fairground. Most of the machinery has been taken down, folded up and packed into sections. Tents have been flattened, poles lie on the ground. There don't seem to be many people around, yet everything is getting done – quickly, efficiently. It is a well-oiled machine. It's almost a shame to upset the flow.

Somewhere inside the perimeter of the fair, a radio is playing. The tinny sound of a recent pop song that Davie vaguely recognises. This time there is no smell of food. The burger vans are closed up. Piles of rubbish are loaded into trailers ready for them to take to the dump. He can't complain that they're not leaving the place tidy.

They're due to drive down to the coast now. Next stop: Dunbar. Davie hates to think of the kids being disappointed, but he's thinking more about the older kids now – the ones who just might live a bit longer if Gaz and his dodgy legal highs don't make it down their way.

Legal highs. Not the best name for some of them. Herbal

highs. Yes. The one that Gaz has concocted is herbal, but the herb that it contains – a disgusting, sharp-flavoured South-east Asian plant called Kratom, or *Mitragyna speciosa* – is not legal in the UK. It's not even legal where it comes from. There will be measures taken to shut down the suppliers; new government legislation will soon be in force, making sure that all psychoactive substances are regulated – but it's complicated, and the problem isn't going to go away overnight. So they have to take baby-steps.

First, they're going to take Gaz – and then Gaz's boss. And hope it leads them to whoever is making this particular batch of stuff, which has unpredictable consequences, and has become popular primarily because someone has made the stuff into a capsule that can be swallowed. There aren't many people who would buy the herb themselves, not with all the hassle of making it palatable. Most of these kids are lazy. Alcohol is easy to get hold of. Weed, coke, whatever. Not really a stretch. But there's a horrific new appeal of these herbal things. They can justify it to themselves that they're legal and therefore they're safe. But they're neither. Far from it. Without instructions on dosage, they are dicing with death every time they touch one. These kids are kidding themselves. It's a bleak reality, but maybe they might've learnt a few lessons from recent events. Two overdoses . . . then something that no one could have foreseen.

Graeme Woodley's reaction was a massive psychotic episode. Hallucinations. He was only trying to protect himself, the doctors said. He didn't realise he was waving a kitchen knife at real people. Hacking them down like weeds in a potato field. He says he got the knife from Marie's handbag, but it's his word against hers on that. Marie's not denying it's her knife. But she's not admitting to taking it with her to the party. No one is ever going to know the truth about that.

Davie spots him. He's rolling a huge tarpaulin on the ground. A younger boy is standing nearby, holding a rope. Davie ushers an arm behind himself, wants Malkie to hurry up.

They walk in through a gap between two dismantled rides.

'Gary McKay?' Davie says.

Gaz turns to face them, a scowl on his face. Ready to have a go at whoever is here disturbing him from his work. The kid with the rope drops it on top of the tarp and runs off towards one of the caravans.

'What do you want?' Gaz says.

'Not very polite, is it?' Malkie says. He takes his badge out of his pocket. Davie takes a step back.

Gaz stands up. A smirk plays on his lips. Davie watches as his eyes dart this way and that. He's looking for an escape route. Hedging his bets. Davie crosses his arms and gives him a look.

'I wouldn't bother, if I were you,' Malkie says. 'We're not here alone.'

Gaz scans the remnants of the fairground. Stands up on the rolled tarp and puts a hand to his forehead as if he is a captain of a ship, looking for pirates in his midst.

'You sure about that?' Gaz says.

Malkie's radio crackles. He takes it out of his pocket. 'Be ready,' he says.

Gaz's expression changes. The smirk fades away. Just for a moment. Then it's back. 'I think I asked yous what yous wanted,' he says.

'What do you know about a robbery at the vet's surgery on the High Street on Monday last week?'

He shakes his head. Looks confused. He wasn't expecting this. 'I wasn't here. We were still in Ormiston on Monday.'

'I know that,' Malkie says. 'I didn't ask where you were. I asked what you knew about it.'

Gaz barks out a single beat of laughter. 'Well, nothing. Obviously.'

'What about the thirty litres of medicinal-grade ethanol that was stolen. Know anything about that?' Malkie says.

'Or this?' Davie says, stepping forward, holding up a small plastic bag with one capsule in the bottom. The bag that Laura had handed in. The one Mark got from Gaz on their first night at the shows. It had already been dusted for prints. Mark's were on there, Laura's . . . and a third set. Presumably belonging to Gaz.

Gaz shrugs. 'You've got nothing.'

'Fair enough,' Malkie says. 'You'll have no objection to coming down to the station with me then. I've got a few more questions. And I've a couple of people there who've agreed to look at an identity parade. Be in your interests if we could eliminate you from our inquiries.'

'I doubt there's much I'd be able to help you two gentlemen with. As you can see, I'm a bit busy at the moment.' At that, the young boy from earlier comes running back from the caravan. Behind him three men follow. They don't look happy.

Malkie sighs. 'I offered you the easy option,' he says. Then, into his radio: 'Come in, please. All units. Assistance required.'

Davie watches as the men form a barrier around Gaz. None of them speak. Someone in one of the cars switches on the siren. The noise is loud as they appear from behind the warehouse, making their way across the grass.

Gaz's face is beetroot. He knows there's no point in running. He knows they wouldn't have brought back-up if they weren't sure they had something worth bringing in. As it was, they have several witnesses from around the county who are happy to identify Gaz from a line-up. News of what happened at the party and a last-minute article in the *Evening News* had prompted a bout of mild hysteria. People were handing stuff into police stations, asking for amnesty if they helped find who was behind it all. It had all come together quickly. The intelligence had been building and the recent events in Banktoun helped whip it all to a soft peak.

The other officers are out of their cars. Gaz doesn't put up a fight. Jennings cuffs him and pushes him roughly into the back seat. She nods at Davie. Says to him and Malkie: 'Nice work, fellas.'

'Thanks, Louise. See you back at base,' Malkie replies.

Davie leaves them to it. He's on his way to offer help setting up the cordon – they want to search the place before the fair is allowed to leave, they want to question everyone on site to see if more arrests are required – when he spots a familiar figure crouched down behind one of the lorries. A strand of pink hair blowing outside her hood gives her away. He walks over. He can hear her sobbing.

'Hayley, can you come out from behind there, love?'

'No. What's going to happen to me?'

Davie takes a few steps closer. 'If you haven't done anything wrong, then nothing's going to happen to you. Have you done something wrong?'

'No.' She stands up, walks around so she is at the side of the lorry now, still some distance away.

'How about I take you home then? If there's anything you need to tell me, you can tell me in the car. How does that sound?'

'Will I get in trouble?' Her voice is small, quiet. She's not so bold and bolshie now, all on her own, in the presence of twelve policemen and a group of massively pissed-off fairground workers who're set to lose a lot of cash if they don't make it to their next gig.

Davie wonders how many of them knew about Gaz's little extra-cash earner. He imagines that some of them won't be best pleased. There's a code of honour amongst these people. They try to stay under the radar, within the law. Gaz is not going to be popular at the moment, that's for sure.

'Come on,' he says.

Hayley walks towards him, her head bowed. Hands shoved deep into the pockets of her jeans. Davie rests a hand on her back and guides her across the field. There are crackles of radios. Car doors slamming. Several conversations going on at once. Gaz is in the back of Jennings' car. He taps on the window. Davie and Hayley turn. He blows her a kiss, and she looks away. Embarrassed.

'I'm such an idiot,' she says.

Davie smiles. 'There's a lot of that going about.'

Epilogue

Two Weeks Later

It was a joint decision by all the families involved. There could be six separate funerals, six days of grief. Or there could be one for them all. A memorial event. Something to mark the event with the gravitas it deserved.

There hadn't been a tragedy like this in the town in the town's history. It was something that no one could have predicted, something that would never happen again.

It was right to mark it. Remember the victims.

All six.

Sam Murray
Lauren Reeves
Scott Philips
Leanne Baxter
Susan Pola
Sean Talbot

The last one to die had been Sean. He'd stepped in front of Tracy Cavan and taken a knife to the heart. His was the cleanest kill of them all. He'd fallen back onto the sofa, looked like he was sleeping. Tracy had passed out from the shock, and when she'd woken she'd refused to believe that the whole thing wasn't some sort of alcohol- and drug-induced nightmare. They'd found her huddled in a corner. Singing to herself . . . something about heading to the Milky Way.

She's here today, with her sister. She's wearing oversized sunglasses, has her hands clasped in front of her. Most of the girls are the same. Black dresses, solemn stances. Hayley is here, standing alone.

Things will be different after this.

The boys and the men are all in black suits. There was talk of going informal, T-shirts and jeans, skirts and tops. But the consensus was that some ceremony was required. They'd make up for it in the pub afterwards, no doubt. Ties would be removed when the pints started to flow.

Davie sits next to the central aisle in the last pew, right at the back of the nave. He's in dress uniform, something he hasn't worn for a while. It feels good, feels right. Malkie sits directly in front of him; he has managed to find a suit that isn't crumpled and ripped. He actually looks smart. Davie glances around at the congregation, a sea of bowed heads. So many young people. They are hurting, unable to stop their tears. But there is a lesson here too, as much as they might not want to see it now. It wasn't only Marie that led them to this day. It was Gaz, and Stuart Mason, and everyone else who was involved – buying the legal high, spreading its buzz. Taking it to the party.

He knows that Laura, too, feels responsible. She saw what Marie did, but she didn't act. She was too wrapped up in herself, desperate to be back with Mark, hidden in their love nest – and Davie couldn't blame her for that. But he knew Laura would struggle with it. She would need help. Wouldn't they all?

Laura sits quietly to his left. Next to her is Mark. Head dropped low to his chest as if in deep contemplation. Davie can see he is trying to hide his tears. He's clearly feeling the enormity of it all. What could've been. It could've been him. His knuckles glow white where he is gripping Laura's hand.

Davie looks away. Stares down the central aisle towards the chancel. He thinks about the dead. Scott. The downward spiral from losing his job to splitting up with his fiancé, Jo, to where he is now, has been rapid. He'd taken too many chances, too many risks. He wanted some fun – to break away from the norm. Doesn't everyone? His only crime was being in the wrong place at the wrong time. Scott and Leanne were the first ones to die. They'd been the trigger. What had Graeme seen there? A young couple having a bit of fun, a quick shag in a place where they thought no one would bother them. Was it a reminder? A snapshot of him and Marie, from a different time and place?

Davie closes his eyes. The minister stands at the altar talking in low, soothing tones. His magnified voice seems to float through the air. He has given the eulogies – the relatives of the deceased too distraught to stand up there themselves – and he's listed their names, over and over, like a chant. Davie opens his eyes as the old man begins the committal:

We have but a short time to live.
Like a flower we blossom and then wither;
like a shadow we flee and never stay.
In the midst of life we are in death;
to whom can we turn for help,
but to you, Lord, who are justly angered by our sins?

He's not religious. He's never believed that a higher power has the ability to govern a person's life. But words said inside a church seem to take on a deeper meaning, even for the atheists and agnostics, and the plain-old apathetics: *to whom can we turn for help*?

A wave of loneliness washes over him. Coldplay come on the sound system, telling everyone to look at the stars, and the crowd starts to filter outside, squinting into the bright daylight. Davie follows, to the small area set aside at the back of the churchyard where six new graves wait patiently. There'd been a special council meeting about all this. The section they'd dug up wasn't part of the original graveyard. It was a small garden at the back, a peace garden. They'd rearranged it, replanted the flowers and shrubs into the borders, and left the space in the centre, three by two. The workmen had been fast. Efficient. Davie hopes that the memorial garden will help bind the community even more closely. Make them realise what they have. Davie scans the crowd. Most of the faces are familiar, some more than others. He senses someone at his side.

'Have you seen who's here?' Callum says.

'You'll need to give me a better clue than that.'

'Over there, standing under the willow. Maybe you won't recognise her. It's been years since I've seen her, but you never forget a face. She was in my year at school. She's Sean Talbot's cousin. I couldn't work out the connection at first, but when I saw her talking to Sean's mum, I remembered.'

Davie looks. Sees a tall, blonde woman standing with her arms crossed. Her face is cold, distant. A man is talking to her. He can't hear, but he can see his lips moving, fast. Hands gesturing. The blonde is trying to tune him out. She must sense his gaze, and her eyes shift. She stares at him. Looks away.

'That's not . . . Polly McAllister?'

'Yep,' Callum says. 'Never expected to see her back in town. Wonder if I should go and speak to her. She keeps glancing over at me, trying to catch my eye. It's like she wants me to recognise her.' He pauses, waiting for Davie to say something, but he just shrugs.

'Maybe she's just here for the service, Callum. Leave it.'

Davie wonders if Polly's here to stir up trouble or to make amends. Anyway, he's not getting involved. Best to keep the rumour mill shut for the day. It's the least they can hope for.

'Maybe she's planning to stick around,' Callum persists. 'People seem to gravitate back here. It's like a magnetic pull. You can try to escape, but it'll drag you back eventually. Look at Graeme Woodley. He wasn't even from here, but somehow he was drawn in . . .'

'He came here for Marie.'

'Yeah. How is she, Davie? I can't believe the life she's had. Poor cow. Saying that, though – you're becoming a bit of a magnet for nutters.'

He's right. But Davie is struggling, too. He isn't without blame. He's not as innocent as Callum thinks. If he'd gone to Marie when he found out that Graeme was her brother . . . stopped her from going to that party. Maybe Graeme could've been safely locked up, unable to hurt anyone again. But now Marie's life is ruined, and any chance they had of a life together was lost the minute she mixed those drugs into that drink. But he can't say any of that. He can't let anyone know how he really feels. *Responsible.* This is a burden he's going to have to carry alone.

Forever.

'She's coping. She's at Cornton Vale on remand. I'm not sure what's going to happen to her.'

'Do you think you'll stay together? She might get out – if the judge takes her circumstances into account?'

'He might. But Marie's going to have to live with what she did, whether she's in prison or not. I don't think she'll want to be with me. I'll only remind her of how it all went wrong. I think I'm destined to be on my own, Cal. I think it might be easier that way.'

Callum looks like he wants to say more but changes his

mind. He pats Davie on the back, then makes his way into the crowd that is huddled around the graves. Davie glances across towards Laura and Mark. They have their arms wrapped tightly around each other. She senses him looking and smiles shyly at him. He needs to talk to her about all this. Soon. But not now. He's about to walk away, thinks a walk by the river might help clear his head, when he is stopped by a hand on his arm.

'Are you coming over for the sandwiches, Sergeant Gray?' Bridie Goldstone, Laura's grandmother, has appeared at his side. She is looking at him with the flashing eyes of someone eager for gossip.

'Ah, thanks, Bridie. But I think I'll just get myself home. It's been a tiring time—'

'Oh yes,' she says, 'Especially with your lady-friend being involved in it all. Awful business with that brother of hers . . .' Her sentence trails off. She looks disappointed. She can tell she's not going to get much out of him.

Davie smiles and turns away. It's best not to respond at all. Let her chat to her cronies about it all. He can't stop them. All he can do is avoid adding any fuel to their fire. He puts his hat back on, adjusts it at the sides. Smooths hair down behind his ears. He scans the crowd once more. They would pull together now, this community. They were strong. Resilient.

He'll just have to be the same.

No one knows about his guilt. No one knows about the part he played in it all. And that's the way it has to stay.

Secrets.

Everybody has one.

And just like old bones, sometimes they're best left buried.

Acknowledgements

As always, there are many people who help turn an idea into the finished book that it becomes. This time, I'd like to give the biggest thanks to my agent, Phil Patterson, for the never-ending help and encouragement. Huge thanks again to my fantastic editor, Karyn Millar, for the perfect insights that really made this book shine, and to Debs Warner for the copy-edit that made Graeme even creepier than he already was. To all at Marjacq and Black & White – thank you for everything you do.

A few people got to read an early draft of this: Steph Broadribb, Ava Marsh and Jenny Blackhurst. Thank you so much for your encouragement at the exact time that it was needed. Thanks also to James Law and Graeme Cameron, whose brainstorming brought Lego and Twitter into *my* Graeme's reign of terror and helped me see whose story I was trying to tell. Oh, and Graeme – thanks for letting me use your name to create the creepiest character I've ever written. You did give your consent, didn't you?

I am very lucky to be part of a great network of fellow authors, bloggers, readers and crime aficionados, both online and off – thank you all for making my first year as a published author life-changing and memorable.

To my family and friends, whose support is unwavering – thank you. I hope I've made you proud.

And finally, to JLOH, my tea-maker, my travelling companion and my partner in crime: One Love.